The Best Asian Short Stories

2022

The Best Asian Short Stories

2022

Editor
Professor Darryl Whetter

Series Editor
Zafar Anjum

Kitaab
Singapore

KITAAB

First published by Kitaab,
an imprint of Kitaab International Pte Ltd
10 Anson Road, #27-15, International Plaza,
Singapore 079903

Kitaab International
Singapore

ISBN: 978-981-18-2943-7

www.kitaabinternational.com

Contents

PROFESSOR DARRYL WHETTER

Chope: An Introduction

Should you try a general google search for a definition of *chope* instead of consulting an online Southeast Asian dictionary like SinglishDictionary.com, you will almost certainly, and rather fittingly, meet any number of restaurant reservation sites or apps, most in the island/city/country of Singapore. Restaurant reservations are not irrelevant here when a full third of these superb Asian stories involve food and eating.

To chope is to reserve something for yourself, such as a seat on a bus, or at a hawker centre, or even a book at the library. Singapore's busy, crowded hawker centres and the delicious food they serve were recently (and deservedly) inscribed by UNESCO on the Representative List of the Intangible Cultural Heritage of Humanity. The tables of these food courts, often open-air, usually have little packets of tissues or a compact umbrella left on top to mark that someone else has already reserved a particular seat. Artists and writers also need to reserve space, to leave their mark, in the busy, noisy public sphere. An anthology is also a kind of shared public meal, a collection of delicacies enjoyed with hungry strangers perched either side of you. Tuck in!

Like any proper introduction to an anthology of short fiction, this one is a celebration of, indeed a valentine to, the short story. One way we know we have read a great short story, as you will here again and again, is the recurrent, delicious mistake of feeling like we have actually just read a novel. I am not here committing that cardinal sin in fiction of pretending that short stories are 'just' mini novels or, as is too often the expectation in publishing, training ground for writing a novel. Short stories are dense and compact; novels are, by definition, loose and baggy. To read a short story in one sitting, as we are so often tempted to do, is to have the artistic equivalent of expanding a compressed computer file. So much life comes pouring out, jack-in-the-box or clown-car style, of these meticulously crafted sentences and scenes. One such computing tool for file compression is (or was) known as a "CODEC," an acronym for *compression-decompression*. These brave, talented, unforgeable writers from the Philippines, Afghanistan, India, Japan and Singapore have compressed so much life, so much hard-fought wisdom, battered grace, and sweet delight, into these seventeen moving stories in alluring voices.

Fittingly for any contemporary fiction anthology and especially for one devoted to a continent as large and diverse as Asia but also of only those Asian stories written in English—even listing the nationalities of our worldly, hyper-educated contributors is far from straightforward. One of the countless spot-on moments in David Nicholls's perfect novel *One Day* finds the recently graduated Emma Morley in a conversation with a new work acquaintance about what his "stroke" [or 'slash'] is: "Everyone who works here has a stroke. Waiter-stroke-artist, waiter-stroke-actor. Paddy the bartender claims to be a model, but frankly I'm doubtful." Peter Morgan, who closes our show, is a legal citizen of 2.5 countries, including Permanent Residency in Singapore. Sarah Soh has lived on three continents. Dawn Lo is in a lifelong elastic relationship with China, once again living in the Hong Kong of her birth after living for years in Canada and Singapore. Mia Aureus and Reginald Kent appear to like to pair new countries with new degrees, moving, for the former, from the Philippines to Singapore for a writing master's then to New Zealand for film school, while the latter is doubling-down on an addiction to Creative Writing programmes, following an MA at Singapore's Nanyang Technological Institute with an MFA in the States. Our two contributors from Japan, Suzanne Kamata and Simon Rowe, have lived there for decades. Even within the strong contingent of Singaporean writers—an inevitability given this anthology's focus on English-language Asian fiction and the acceleration of formal Creative Writing educations there—I am delighted to introduce Mohamed Shaker, a Malay-Singaporean writing of and from one of Singapore's founding cultures but one many lament as under-represented in dynamic, vibrant SingLit.

Speaking of hybridity, of strokes and slashes, our strong concentration of Singaporean writers also gives this anthology plenty of that other famous Singaporean dish: Singlish. Joanne Tan's remarkable story speaks for several here when it warns of social expectations that might make us "go crazy one." Reginald Kent's Singaporean characters warn each other that they "cannot expect to figure out so fast one," while Adeline Tan's haunting story includes the thrifty advice, "Still can use!" No collection of Asian writing would be complete without someone cooking, as Joanne Tan and Ken Lye's do, in the *agak-agak* style of measuring by guesstimating. A more sombre state of hybridity comes from our Indian contributors, most of whom were writing from Singapore while worrying about loved ones back in India here in the worst year of COVID.

With art holding its mirror up to nature, COVID is certainly a recurrent issue here in these stories of the moment, with titles like Anisha Ralhan's *Alone Together* and Kevin Wong's *We're in This Together*.

An anthology is such a beautiful way to come together, to gather and share. *Best Asian Short Stories 2022* also probably marks a lifetime high for me, my third book in three years. My 2020 climate-crisis novel *Our Sands,* from Penguin Random House, still feels like it hit Asian bookstore shelves just yesterday. My first anthology, Routledge's *Teaching Creative Writing in Asia* (2021), also brings together writers from India, the Philippines, Canada, Australia and the United States. Where I break new pedagogical ground with that first anthology on Creative Writing pedagogy in Asia, it is heartening to see that, thematically, the anthology in your hands is both timeless and current.

I believe it was last century that Salman Rushdie lamented that if he could sum his novels up in the twenty-second sound bites media expected of him he would write twenty-second sound bites, not novels of 100,000-words and more; all that was before the tyranny of the hashtag. Still, memory is its own kind of hashtag network. As I read the scores of submissions here, I would invariably recall stories by certain recurrent themes. Here, as always, are stories of love, death, displacement, transformation, desire, ambition, connection, and dysfunctional families (excuse the redundancy). Those same themes thrum through the work of the numerous brave and honest gay writers collected here, often from countries just now ceasing to perpetuate the English colonial law forbidding certain consensual same-sex acts. Just as this book was going to print, Singapore's government decided to, like India's did in 2018, take a major decriminalizing step towards letting love be love. These daring and caring stories reaffirm Percy Bysshe Shelley's two-hundred-year-old recognition that "poets are the unacknowledged legislators of the world."

Anisha Ralhan's *Alone Together* is a heart-warming story of warming hearts (and other body parts) that is an obvious show-opener as we collectively crawl out from two years sequestered in our apartments (and worries).

I could not be more proud than to include a story by Sahib Nazari, transplanted as he is from his native Afghanistan to Australia (via Pakistan). Far more than a story of his war-ravaged Afghanistan, his *Kochi* is a vibrant reminder of how fiction prefers life's moral grey areas, not black and white. The "fieldcraft" of Nazari's war-torn development workers balances keeping people alive with a version of Malcolm X's victory "by whatever means necessary." Whereas my Routledge anthology worries whether English-language fiction is universal or imperialist in its fixation on conflict and the transformed protagonist, Nazari shows that the social-emotional grammar of storytelling really is universal.

While other characters connect metaphorically, Simon Rowe's vibrant *Paris Match* finds two transplanted Japanese strangers in Paris, each looking to hit the romantic and professional restart button.

Short stories by and about the hard choices made by wives, mothers, daughters, sisters, and aunts recur in most miscellaneous anthologies of good fiction, including this one, although here we are blessed to have one written by a man, Singapore's Mohamed Shaker. His *Barren Sands* repeatedly won that quietest and most secret of literary prizes, an editor, me, getting up from my groaning desk to pause work and seek out my wife so I could read her some of Shaker's brilliant lines. Not once but twice, I had to stop *everything* I was doing to find my beloved and stun her with Shaker's arresting depiction of pregnancy:

> Pregnancy is a dam. You are the water. The dam holds you back and your water churns, ebbs, flows, crashes in on itself like waves on the shore and then new life breaks through the surface of your lake and emerges gasping, crying, sobbing, your water leaking out of its eyes.

I am so privileged to help midwife all these stories into print, especially for new writers like Mohamed Shaker.

As with other stories of the heart here, Sarah Soh's pitch-perfect *Pineapple Fengshui* reminds us that in love we are parliaments of emotion, not monarchies. Some decisions of the heart, Soh and others warn, maybe made by only a slim majority, with a disgruntled minority ready to sweep to future power. The voice in Sarah's fiction helps us feel a world, a character, and a soul through one crystalline word sewn against the next.

No one who reads Mia Aureus's *Home* will be surprised to learn that she divides her creative life between writing and film-making. While she also writes with a warm voice as palpable as it is audible, we are treated here to a movie unrolling in our minds. I would detail her story's allure more thoroughly, but—*spoiler-alert!*

In *The Shadow*, Prachi Topiwala-Agarwal continues the run of relationship stories that dominate this rich anthology. Prachi dares to map the peaks and valleys of a long-term romance as a couple chases career dreams, never equally, across three countries on three continents. As with so many of the romantic protagonists here, Topiwala-Agarwal's know that with love, and its shiny counterfeits, we might seek ruin as much as we seek release.

Joanne Tan's complex and multi-layered engagement with the expectations faced by women both permits and laments me saying that if we are going to have an anthology of Asian writing, it is fitting to have at least one story set in a kitchen with multiple generations of women cooking. Joanne's superb *Mei-Mei* also provides fiction's great "one-for-one deal" (to use the Singlish version of what is elsewhere called a "two for one" deal): we *see* a world through a voice we *hear* (and one we keep hearing long after we stop reading).

Although writing takes place in such profound, abyssal solitude, one of the playlist or mixed-tape joys of compiling an anthology is finding not just great stories but great stories that will wind up playing well together. While most of these stories concern love and/or death and/or displacement, two stories braid those themes (and more) into the legally curtailed lives of gay Singaporean men. Kevin Nicholas Wong's aptly named *We're in This Together* documents in fiction Singapore's annual gay pride event Pink Dot (a pun on Singapore's nickname as "the little red dot," a country not much bigger on some maps than the red dot used to denote it). Art is a much slower dating app, yet a SingLit Grindr message is waiting to fly between Wong's story and Reginald Kent's *Babi Pongteh*. Where Joanne Tan's kitchen story charts the horrors of a departing matriarch, Kent's soy-sauce elegy is for one already departed.

Romantic relationships wax and wane in the Wong and Kent stories but burst into first bloom with Suzanne Kamata's *What Lurks Beneath*. Both our Japanese meet-cute stories find characters coming together unexpectedly. With so many of these writers living, thinking and working in multiple languages, it is fitting to see Kamata's characters literally pass translations back and forth.

Vicky Chong's story *Transplanted Love* further explores the intersections, and oppositions, of romantic and/versus familial love. With all the languages spoken by these writers from seven-plus countries, does any language make the wise distinction and use different verbs for loving a family member versus being in romantic love?

Nash Colundalur's *The Mourners* shifts its grief from the biological family to the artistic version of Armistead Maupin's "logical family." Colundalur reminds us that artists also have their chosen families, their tribes. Here, too, a beautifully doomed meal finds its cast coming together and falling apart.

Jinendra Jain's *Impossible Innocence* knows acutely that stories love and need change. Like the country-hopping, career-chasing characters of Prachi Topiwala-Agarwal and Peter Morgan, Jain's bankers trade more than investments, finding that loyalty, too, has a different price when buying or selling.

Adeline Tan is a professional video editor who has appeared now in more than one edition of *Best Asian Short Stories*. When a video editor, that narrative professional, switches to fiction, we can feel the palpable delight Adeline takes in language. Her moving story may involve a literal last breath, but her art keeps breathing.

For Ken Lye's characters, transformation comes in a tiffin box. All losses in this superb anthology are not just death; Mr Lye is wise to recognise just how many people lost their jobs in this global pandemic. Here, too, the biological family meets the logical (but, fittingly, deliciously, with a little more butter).

The most apt and exciting phrases I could write about Peter Morgan's arresting story *First Draft: David in Singapore, Maureen in Wales*, phrases devoted to literature's most recurrent themes, would spoil this tender, affecting story. More indirectly, and to celebrate this story that, like so many here, fuses cultures, landscapes, and languages, I close by resurrecting an under-appreciated literary term. While many of us who keep a professional eye on word count and varying our vocabulary can replace the phrase "coming of age story" with the originally German *Bildungsroman*, a lesser known German literary term is *Künstlerroman*, for the story of someone becoming an artist.

My life has had few joys more profound than having watched many of these ferociously talented Asian writers becoming published writers and artists. I am so thrilled to collect and edit their stories and share them with you. *Ars longa, vita brevis*.

ANISHA RALHAN

Alone Together

Ira Sharma had been dancing for nearly two months in front of her laptop, since shortly after the Singapore government announced the closure of all offices and restaurants. Before that, she had tried meditating with an app but struggled to sit still through an entire session. *Imagine you're seated on the side of the road. Just watch your thoughts pass like cars.*

Ira's thought-cars came at her from all directions, fast and frenzied, unbidden—as though she'd been cast in an action movie. Her mind wandered from the diminishing supplies of milk and bread in the fridge—which would require another masked trip to the grocery store, to the grim Zoom discussions with her colleagues around the possibility of wage-cuts in the near future, to Hobbs—the rescued tabby whom Ira had gladly welcomed into her one-bedroom apartment a year and a half ago, shortly after she arrived from India. Ever since the Singaporean news came out about the cat in Hong Kong that had to be put down after contracting the virus, Ira worried more about Hobbs than herself.

The endless days of house arrest didn't seem so bad, thanks to the new work-from-home routine which allowed her to stay in bed till quarter past nine. Meetings weren't set up until eleven anyway. Her colleagues had homes to run, partners to argue with, dust to wipe, dishes to wash, kids to discipline. Ira didn't have to bother with dishes and dusting every day. Being single had its perks. She spent the mornings playing *Friends* in the background while preparing a quick and dirty meal for one. After lunch, she heard the marketing manager of L'Oréal sulk about the dwindling sales of a night cream that Ira was sure nobody needed. In the afternoons, which were astonishingly quiet—so quiet that she could hear the birds chirrup from her tiny Juliet balcony—she wrote feel-good emailers on her client's behalf to inform Singaporeans that all was not lost—their favourite eye cream was now available for fifty per cent less!

At night, however, she had trouble sleeping. Darkness had crept inside her mind, growing bigger and deeper like a cavity. Her head hurt thinking about the future she had smothered by refusing to move to San Francisco with Paul, even though he was the only guy with whom she could imagine having a future. After two years of dating, he had given her a hardback copy of *The Hitchhiker's Guide to the Galaxy* with a handwritten note that said: "42: The ultimate answer to the hopeless life I lived before I met you." They had met on the fourth of February. She loved his terrible puns, the unmitigated ease of his companionship. Yet, when he suddenly proposed during their holiday in a quaint town in the Himalayas, Ira had no choice but to refuse. She was only twenty-four then, with a job offer from Singapore's third-best ad agency.

Desperate to run away from her whizzing thought-cars, in bed Ira would scroll through Instagram and see her friends turn into chefs, yogis and artists overnight. It was there she had come across a sponsored post that said, "Sweat your worries away with Vinay's Cardio Jam." Over WhatsApp, Vinay Senthil told her to think of the online classes as dancing in a club but from the safety of your home. *You know, alone together*. Ira had been to a club once in Clarke

Quay; it was a disaster. The music was too loud. The drinks were overpriced. Every now and then somebody elbowed her in the boob. "It's like a cesspool of tequila mixed with armpit," she had said to her friend, Christine.

But dancing made her happy. She had spent her childhood kneeling before Britney Spears, Madonna and Michael Jackson at the altar of the MTV in her living room in New Delhi. Back then, at a wedding reception, she'd be among the first ones to toss away her heels and head to the dance floor. The text exchange with Vinay made her think, why had she stopped dancing?

*

Three days later, at quarter to seven in the evening, Ira swapped the printed nylon top she had worn all day for a half-sleeve V-neck t-shirt from Cotton On. She already had sweatpants on, the clothing equivalent of comfort food.

She moved her laptop from the rattan chair in the living to room to her monastically sparse bedroom. Somehow her efforts at personalising her apartment with framed posters of her favourite films, potted plants and colourful cushions had stopped at the living room itself. She hadn't brought a guy to her bedroom recently. There were no condoms buried in the bedside drawer.

She rolled up her hair into a top-knot bun and signed into her business account on Zoom. Joining a fitness class through her work account gave her a mild thrill. Like the time she commanded the office printer to spit out a hundred pages of a Murakami novella.

Upon joining the meeting, she was instructed by the app to turn on her camera. She decided not to. If the class was happening in an actual studio, she would have stood in a corner, somewhere at the back, where nobody would've noticed the lack of a gap between her thighs, the loose flesh that jiggled when she moved her arms, the thick cloud of disobedient curls coiled over her shoulders, the baby hair that jutted out from the corners of her hairline—making her head look like a giant rambutan. In India, she joked with her friends that she was a modest seven; seven and a half in a flattering outfit. But in Singapore—the land of the abs and clavicles, where the average women wore a size two, she placed herself at five.

While waiting for the class to start, Ira scanned the profile pictures of eight other participants. Her eyes darted towards the close-up of a tanned Indian man with slick hair, styled with a copious amount of gel. In the photo, he had that cocky half-smile of a Bollywood actor who's made it to the cover of GQ one too many times. "So, this is Vinay Senthil," she said out loud, as if introducing him to a friend at a house party. Just then, seemingly on cue, the hair model switched on his video. He was leaning into the camera, adjusting his laptop screen. From this angle, Ira could see half of a tattoo peeking out from beneath the sleeve of his round-neck blue tee. He was tall, lean and bearded; an attractive man, no doubt. His hair was pulled back with a multi-coloured cloth headband—the kind Ira had only seen on white backpackers in hostels in Thailand.

"Hey, guys, we're about to start in five. Make sure you're in a well-lit room, so I can see you nice and clear." He rolled his r's like Americans. A brown man with an American accent in Singapore—Ira had difficulty gauging where he was from. Was he Malayali? A Tamilian? Ira suddenly wished she knew more about South Indians. As he called out their names, five Singaporean women and a Caucasian woman blushed and waved from their well-lit rooms. Groupies!

She followed the groupies and turned on her camera. She told everyone she was there for a trial class.

The warm-up was short and quick. Ira rotated her hips, stretched her back, did some squats. When her hands didn't reach her toes, she looked up at the screen and realised she was the least flexible person in the class. Vinay, on the other hand, effortlessly touched the floor with his palms. Ira was sure his spine was made of playdough.

Vinay had chosen Sia's *Cheap Thrills* for today's class. "The song is all about enjoying life when you don't have money. I don't know about you, but I can surely relate." Ira giggled. She could feel her body relax.

Sia's peppy clarion call to night-club goers reminded Ira of her night-out with Christine a few months ago. It was playing at their usual bar on Cecil Street when Christine proposed to move the party to Zouk. "C'mon, it's Friday night," Christine had said, echoing the sentiment of the singer. Everyone was determined to get hammered at the newly renovated nightclub except for Ira and Neil, a friend of Christine's, who looked like the distant cousin of Henry Golding. He had been laughing at Ira's jokes all evening. When his shin grazed hers, neither of them flinched. They skipped Zouk to have one last drink at her place. He kissed her. She asked him to stay over. The gleaming gold band on his ring finger was impossible to miss but she was drunk, and her vibrator had been out of batteries.

"Focus, guys," Vinay said as the song rose to a crescendo. "Just watch and follow."

For the next forty-five minutes, Ira matched his steps. She shimmied her shoulders, stomped her feet, shuffled on her toes, glided across the floor. As the chorus came on, her moves grew bigger. "Come on, fire up your body," Vinay screamed on top of the music. "Give me all you've got."

Despite the strong air-conditioning, sweat trickled down her nape. Her face was on fire. Her heart drummed through her ribcage. She willed herself to keep going even though she felt like sinking into her queen bed. She thought of the brownies she had been ordering for dinner the past few weeks, as a form of reward, for just getting through the day. "Wasted day. Wasted life. Dessert, please," was her mantra these days.

Tonight, though, she would finally indulge in her dessert without feeling utterly horrible. The prospect of brownies kept her going till the end of the class. After, she was so tired that she dozed off. Only tonight did she fall asleep without opening the meditation app, without watching another documentary on Netflix, without looking up today's case count on *The Straits Times*.

Next day, Vinay posted a short clip of their work-out on his professional account called Dance_with_VS, which Ira watched over and over in between her Zoom calls and during her bathroom breaks. In a small rectangle, in row three, on her phone, Ira saw not herself but a twenty-eight-year-old woman leaping, lunging, looking fierce as a feline.

In the evening, Ira transferred 80 dollars to reserve herself a spot for the rest of the month.

"Glad, you're joining us," Vinay texted, with more emojis than she was used to.

Thereafter, week after week, on Tuesdays, Thursdays and Saturdays, Ira paced around the house high on the endorphins and cockiness that comes with regular exercise. While cooking, she hummed the tune she last danced to. She hummed in the shower and hummed while vacuuming. In the bathroom, after washing her hands once again, from fingertips to wrist, she lingered in front of the mirror a little longer, a smile slipping surreptitiously from her lips. Soon, she'd join the covetous League of Clavicles and Biceps.

The days she didn't have class, she'd spend hours looking at the videos posted by Vinay Senthil over the last two years. Jessica Chan from the advance class looks pretty even when she does the splits. She was there in most of the videos—shot in a red-walled studio. Ira didn't like the arrogant stretch of her spine, her pouty face that screamed *Look at me, I'm a Goddess in Lycra tights.*

Her envy receded only after she directed her gaze back at Vinay. There he was, in a burgundy beanie, drawing shapes in the air with his hips. Jelly in place of joints. Arms with full batteries. He reminded her of those inflatable sky dancers strategically placed outside a car wash.

Two days later, Ira had a dream in which she was dancing with the sky dancer in front of a giant mirror at a red-walled studio. In the dream, she wore a tank top and leg warmers on top of sheer leggings. In the dream, Vinay grabbed her waist and lifted her in the air, as if they starred in an MTV video. Then, slowly after he pulled her down, they kissed. Not one of those sloppy, too-much-tongue, too-much-saliva kisses, but a kiss that ignites every living cell in your body.

Ira woke up hugging her pillow. All-day, she had a dreamy look on her face, which Christine called her 'Disney princess face' on their Facetime call. The urge to know Vinay drove Ira to his Facebook profile. She learnt that he had a diploma in contemporary jazz and hip-hop from Peridance Centre—New York's top dance institute, according to Sir Google.

Other than the dance videos that Ira had watched over a dozen times, and the occasional Buzzfeed quizzes, which revealed that his spirit animal was lama and the city he was destined to live in was Berlin, he hadn't posted much on his wall. Most of his photo albums were private, barring the one captioned: *All The World's a Stage,* that Ira found impressive not because of the professionally-shot pictures of him performing at opulent-theatres in New York, Chicago, and Russia—well, those were beautiful, no doubt. But the title, the nod to the Bard, that was solid copywriting.

Vinay's bio said he was single. But what if he's gay? Nothing about his body language pointed to the fact that he could be into guys. In fact, in the videos she had seen so far, in which he never exposed his shoulders, never traded a t-shirt for a wife-beater, he exuded the suaveness of Channing Tatum from *Step Up*, even while performing to a Beyonce number. Overcome with the desperate desire to quell her doubt about his sexuality, Ira swiped through his profile pictures. No pride filter, no colourful prints, no special guy friend in any of his pictures. He appeared to be an ordinary guy outside the studio, who liked hiking, who drank Americano in hipster cafes, who frequented museums and jazz bars.

One Sunday afternoon, Ira sent Vinay a 40-second video of her dancing to Beyonce's "Single Ladies" that she had shot on her laptop. It was a routine she had learnt last evening. "Do you think I nailed it?" her fingers trembled as she typed.

Thirty minutes later, with her checking her phone throughout, Vinay replied, "Beautiful! The hips can be softer. But wow, great energy."

After typing and deleting and retyping, she finally wrote, "I didn't think I'd have so much fun. You make house arrest so much better."

"Aww! Glad to be of service. You live alone?"

Ira couldn't believe the guy she had fantasised about a few nights ago was prolonging the conversation.

"Yep, it's just us," she wrote under a close-up shot of her face next to Hobbs. The photo had already garnered over five hundred likes on Instagram.

"So cute!!!"

Winking-heart-eyes emojis, a gif screaming *adorable*. Okay, game-time.

She promptly replied, "Who?"

"No offense kitty, but I'd have to go with the lady in red."

Ira felt an instant connection with Vinay during the chat, supplemented with emojis and memes, that lasted all afternoon. He was mighty impressed by Ira's profession. "Omg, you're a writer, you must be so smart."

Ira had missed this kind of banter with a guy. The clever repartee exchanged like a ping pong ball was her favourite part of dating, the anticipation of his replies, the constant buzzing of the phone, the adrenaline flowing through the fingertips. Flirting via texts was so much better than flirting in real life, which made her feel as awkward and self-conscious as a pelican walking amongst a flock of flamingos.

During the next class, Ira had a stupid grin on her face, which she deftly recognised as the sign of an overpowering crush. To her joy, Vinay seemed different too. Effervescent, more smiley than usual. At the end of the class, he even made her dance solo to Britney's "Love 2 Love U." "I want all of you to imbibe Ira's sexy body language," he had said. Ira had never been called sexy before, not by a guy who looked like the next face of Garnier.

Over the next four weeks, during which they only left their homes to replenish the kitchen cabinets, they texted nearly non-stop. "Knock knock" was his way of initiating a conversation. He told her he cooked the best Bolognese spaghetti in all of Singapore—his dinner four out of seven nights a week. She said she was jealous that despite the carbs he managed to stay lean and taut, like raw spaghetti. He seemed determined to know more about her. "What book are you reading?" he asked. What brand was she currently working on?

They invented a game called Guess-What to fill the eerie, silent hours before bedtime.

"Guess, where I am from," he wrote.

"Singapore?"

"*Ya lah.* Born in Singapore but never felt at home here. My friends called me coconut. You know, brown on the outside, white on the inside."

Despite being born and brought up in India, Ira too had always felt like an outsider. According to her family, her choice of career was as unconventional as her need for independence. Had she stayed back at her parents' house in India, her father would have cornered a skittish Ira with a glass of whiskey in one hand and a fist full of banana chips, saying, "So, do you have someone in your life, or shall we start looking?"

Of course, it was too soon to say, but her conversations with Vinay had been so effortless up until this point that she could foresee dating him once the pandemic blew over. The thought caused a stirring in her stomach. She imagined what it would be like to breathe the same air as he did, hold hands on a romantic walk along the Marina Bay promenade. She couldn't wait to deepen the floaty intimacy she had shared with him over texts.

The Universe heard her loud and clear. On fifteen July, the Prime Minister announced the partial reopening of restaurants and bars. The following weekend, Christine called up Ira and said that she had booked a dinner reservation at their usual spot in Robertson Quay, "Can't wait for the gang to reunite."

"I'm actually hoping to see VS tonight." Vinay had yet to answer her text, in which she had asked what his plans were. Ira figured he might have scheduled a private lesson on Zoom at noon. But as the afternoon morphed into the evening, the cold-stone silence from Vinay became too much to bear.

Play it cool? Or listen to the hopeless romantic voice that said, *Chase him, don't give up.*

Finally, at seven-thirty, after Ira grudgingly emptied a bowl of cereal, her phone buzzed. "Craving some fish head curry, see you outside Sammy's in an hour?"

The fact that he just assumed she was free and still available to meet stunned her. Still she hopped into the shower, then emerged smelling like vanilla and lemongrass. The idea of dressing up after three long months cheered her up instantly. She chose a royal blue skater dress with a modest neckline—flirty but not quite slutty—and paired it with ballerina flats. Her face was mostly bare save for mascara and a tinted gloss.

*

Ira got out of the cab and glanced at the restaurants, gleaming like constellations in the dark and hilly Dempsey. In that minute, everything looked normal, as if the pandemic had occurred a decade ago. The alfresco bar next to Sammy's Curry was thriving with throngs of people, coiffed and in fitted clothes, guzzling colourful drinks topped with tiny umbrellas. Faces, free of masks, free of fear, smiled at her as if she was a guest at a party to which they had all been invited. Ira searched for her plus one on the paved street lined with trees. She had no difficulty spotting Vinay, whose face was partially covered by a surgical mask. She recognized his shoulder-length hair pulled back by a metallic hairband and waved self-consciously in his direction.

Seeing him in his workout joggers and a ratty tee, which clung to his sculpted chest, made her feel overdressed, that she had misread his text, assuming he had invited her for a date. But then he leaned forward to give her a big bear hug, not a casual side hug, and her whole body stiffened. His woody, spicy cologne was so strong and intoxicating that she could smell it even through her cloth mask.

The restaurant he had chosen was a slightly upmarket, roofed version of a hawker stall, replete with plastic chairs and steel cutlery. A striking contrast to the other, glittery eateries around them. It might not have been the most romantic place, but at least it wasn't crowded. The waiter who came to take the order spoke to Vinay in Tamil. Ira found it amusing how Vinay could speak in his native tongue without any traces of an American accent. The sudden switch of his tongue made her think of Hobbs, who would act imperial, full of restraint one moment, with his erect and guarded tail, then roll down on his back for a belly rub the very next. Perhaps, the trick with Vinay, too, was to not come across too eager in order for him to gravitate towards her. So she remained quiet, waiting for him to start a conversation.

"Alright, Ms Writer, here we are," he said as he took his mask off and poured chilled Tiger beer into two glasses.

"To the end of house arrest!" he announced, holding a frothy glass in the air.

Ira noticed his full mouth, a smile so wide and enchanting it reached his eyes. He folded his arms and complimented the legendary fish head curry they served here. He was surprised that Ira hadn't eaten here before.

"It's not even an island secret. Your lips will thank me after."

She asked him if he always knew that he wanted to be a dancer.

The way he stroked his stubble gave her the impression that he was going to say something profound about finding the discipline to pursue your passion. She was truly hoping to hear a story that would inspire her to quit wasting her time making rich corporations richer. Afterall, she was just another cog in the elaborate machine of capitalism—a cog with a penchant for catchy slogans.

But all she got was, "No, dancing is the only thing I am good at. And it allows me to travel abroad, meet new people. Like yourself, ha ha." He told her his dream was to open his own dance studio in Clarke Quay one day. "That's where the money is."

As she downed her first glass, Ira finally mustered the courage to ask, "So did you have a busy day? You practically disappeared."

"Aww, someone missed me," Vinay said with his signature smile.

"So," she asked, clenching her abs to keep the flutter from her voice, "why did you choose to spend your first lockdown-free night with me, not your friends?"

"Coz you're pretty and smart. Or should I say, pretty smart.

"See, what I did there?" he said in such a child-like manner Ira wondered if he was being deliberating corny—maybe to make things less awkward?

By the time the food arrived, Ira was convinced he looked older in person than he did in his pictures. His face had that weathered look of somebody who drank too much or slept too little. When he took off the hairband and stroked his hair, the ashy roots sprouting around the forehead were too striking for Ira to not notice. "How are you still single?"

"Who said I am?"

Ira's first instinct was to laugh it off but looking at his straight face, his puckered lips, she winced a little. The unavoidable sight of a fish with its eyeball hanging out of its socket in the middle of a goopy curry had already killed the little appetite she had, and now this.

"I am kidding. Just haven't found the right person yet. I guess I have always been a free spirit."

He told her he was used to being alone and that he had been depressed for a long time, especially after losing both his parents in a plane crash in Malaysia about six years ago. It's why he had relocated to Singapore. "To sort out finances."

For the first time that night Ira felt a genuine tenderness towards him. Had he told her this on a stroll outside, she would have stopped and pulled him into a hug. Nevertheless, she leaned forward to squeeze his hand.

"Sorry to interrupt but we are closing soon," the waiter said and slid a leathered cheque holder between them.

Ira instinctively reached for her wallet while Vinay scooped the leftovers from the dish in front of him.

"Thank you," said the waiter as he took the folded leather, which had only one card, hers. Ira had difficulty believing what just happened. Not only did he not pay for the dinner—which he ate most of, he didn't even have the decency to split the bill. A 'free' spirit indeed.

How rude! Christine would say, when Ira gives her a download of the night. *What kind of a guy doesn't pay for drinks?*

Then, as if he could read her mind, he finally said, "I'll buy us drinks.

"Sorry, let me rephrase. May I invite you for a nightcap at my place?"

At this point, Ira wasn't sure if she was comfortable going to a stranger's house, one who sounded way younger than he looked, whose casual attempts at flirting had been corny at best. But then, the thought of ending her first big night out in seven months at ten-thirty and going back to the same tiny apartment where she had been cooped up alone for more than half the year made her sad and disappointed. Besides, he was still better-looking than any guy she had been with before, and she did want to kiss him.

"Okay," she said. "But I'll leave before midnight."

"As you wish, Cinderella."

On the walk to where he had parked his motorcycle, they remained quiet. Her hand grazed his, and she felt a spark of electricity jolting through her fingers. She desperately wanted him to envelop her hand in his, but he didn't, as if signalling to her that they weren't going back to his place purely for physical reasons. She, too, concluded that she wouldn't have sex with him on the first date. Then again, she wasn't entirely sure if this even counted as a date.

*

He lived in a one-bedroom HDB flat on the outskirts of Clementi, which he had rented ever since he moved back to Singapore because it was too depressing for him to live alone in his childhood house. Just as they got off the bike, he announced, "The house isn't in the best-shape. You're entering a bachelor pad." She had found the warning endearing, because it's something she would say too before inviting friends into her house.

Once she stepped on the wooden floor, which creaked and had swollen in places, she realised he was not trying to be polite. The house looked uninhabitable, with magazines littered on the floor and dirty dishes lying on the open-kitchen slab. The living room-turned studio, which she had already glimpsed from the online classes, looked clinical and was stripped of any habitable furniture, barring a coffee table and the two bean bags pushed to the side under the shadow of a large cabinet. The patterned blue drape covering the main wall in front of which he danced was also familiar. In person, she couldn't help but notice its dusty and tattered corners. Imagining the kind of creatures which crawled underneath the faux-tapestry gave Ira the creeps. After he excused himself to put the beers in the refrigerator, Ira desperately looked for something for her eyes to hold on to. She noticed the half-folded lottery tickets with ink stains on the top shelf of the cabinet. Thankfully, she found something more interesting. A turntable next to a bunch of vinyl records.

"It was Dad's prized possession. I had to have it," Vinay said, dragging the bean bags to the centre of the room.

"Play something? I've never heard some of these before."

He chose Neil Young's *Greatest Hits*. At least, the guy had good taste in music.

Once she settled on the beanie with a beer, he insisted the ambience needed to improve.

Ambience? More like hygiene.

With great enthusiasm, he retrieved a standing lamp, presumably from his bedroom, and replaced the harsh, bright white light of an overhead light with the lamp's warm glow. In a second, the place transformed from being an assault on the senses to a cosy, minimalist bachelor pad. Ira wondered if he did this each time he brought girls home.

She took a large swig of her beer and said, "I bet I'm not the only student you've brought home."

"Umm, not true. I mean, I won't lie and say I haven't been hit on before. But it's a lot more complicated than you think. Mixing business with pleasure. If you know what I mean."

She recalled the text exchange, in which he told her he used to teach contemporary dance forms at Gold Fitness Centre. The Zoom class was a temporary, pandemic-only initiative.

"Getting involved with a student is frowned upon by the management. You know, why risk your reputation for a fling. Thank God we met online."

"A *fling?*"

He wouldn't be the first guy to want nothing more than a no-strings-attached relationship, or what the millennials called a 'Situationship'. There had been men before, older, younger, married, coupled up, or simply too scared to commit. Ira had started to want more. If the last few months of quarantine had taught her anything, it was the fact that she craved pillow talk more than steamy sex. She wanted pizza, Netflix and cuddles on the couch, friendly arguments over what to order for dinner, His and Her towels in the bathroom, a hand to slip hers into before those worrisome grocery runs.

As Ira looked up, she saw a thirty-something man-child in a ridiculously tight tee, a broke diva who thrived solely on looks, charisma, and quick and easy flings—swaying his hips in slow-motion to "Harvest Moon."

"Come, join me," he mouthed.

Come a little bit closer, Neil Young crooned.

Ira chugged the remainder of her beer, wiped her lips and stood up. She placed a hand on his shoulder and extended her right palm. He took it eagerly. She ensured the gap between them was wide enough to fit a tiny human. Each time he tried touching her neck with his lips, she took a step back and, instead, pushed his arms back so she could spin. He smiled blankly, looking like a conductor who has just been betrayed by his orchestra in a packed auditorium. Meanwhile, she kept on dancing, surrendering herself to the music and nothing else—determined to preserve this moment without a hint of remorse.

When the song ended, he lunged forward once again, to kiss her on the lips. She gave him her cheek.

"Listen, I had a great time, but I need to leave."

He looked at her like a child whose iPad had been snatched away.

"What's the hurry?"

"I need to feed Hobbs."

He stood there cluelessly with the same idiotic, unapologetic smile pasted on his face as when the waiter had come to collect the cheque book.

She sighed and looked at him for one last time.

"My cat, remember?"

Kochi

She was reason enough to turn a man against gods and vice versa. Peaceful white veil; rebellious red dress, worrisome wordless eyes, she entered the pathology supporting her petite mother who looked pale and weak like a brown skeleton in a black dress. She could barely walk. The doctor took the blood tests papers. Zyar, the senior lab assistant, told the girl to help her old mother on the old stretcher. The girl and her mother were Pashtun. They didn't understand Hazaragi like the doctor, Zyar, or me. Nor could we speak Pashtu. I asked the girl if she could speak Urdu.

The pathologist was a short, talkative, chubby man. His long nose, too big for his rotund face, hung right above his moustache, and made him look even shorter and chubbier. Whenever he smiled, he resembled someone whose mouth has been freshly fitted with a horseshoe. He wore the widest smile for a man, so talking was the secondary reason whenever he opened his mouth. He was quite conceited in his position and called himself *doctor* but, more importantly, he insisted everyone in the hospital did too. So we called him *doctor*, Zyar and me.

Zyar was a senior; I was a freshman. He was younger but taller and stronger than me and enjoyed throwing his weight and weightless wisdom around in the absence of the doctor. Hormones, height, and clumsiness—Zyar embodied them in abundance. His Hazara-Mongolide eyes, like two identical cuts from a sharp scalpel, disappeared from his face whenever he laughed. But he smiled seldom, often erupting like a volcano spitting ash and lava over minor issues. If it wasn't the doctor, the lab, his father or school work that pissed him off, petty objects like a pen, a syringe tube, or a wristwatch annoyed him to the point that he brutally smashed them under his feet. Even the placid, over-fed kitchen cat avoided him whenever they crossed paths.

The fluffy white cat belonged to Khala – the hospital cook. She was a fair but fierce lady in her late forties who always welcomed everyone with an open heart and never took anyone's bad behaviour. She worked hard, preparing and serving meals to over twenty staff members every single day. Khala and I instantly became friends because the lab and the kitchen's wooden doors stood facing one another, five feet apart. This otherwise odd layout was only ideal for spreading diseases in the already unhygienic hospital but this was Khala's domain, and she was one of the most fearless women I'd ever come to know.

"Don't they feed you at home? You look like a bag of bones," Khala asked me when Zyar introduced us on the first day during lunch break.

"No, they tied me up before meal times."

"Don't worry, my son. I'll tie you up, then feed you."

*

The lab was basically a small storage room merged with a small bathroom. A rectangular, single-panelled window offered a panoramic view of the hospital floor from the flight of stairs in the west to the main entrance in the east. Cemented with solid iron-bars from the outside, the window only allowed sunlight and misery through the dusty glass. In addition to the doctor's table paired with a squeaky wooden stool, centrally adjacent to the window, a small bench, a stretcher, and a decaying freezer occupied the storage end. There was a sink to wash and clean, hygiene supplies, and a tiny table to store equipment, across the bathroom at the end of the lab.

*

Mornings labouring in the lab then attending English language in the afternoons. Shortly after I started working as the lab assistant, the doctor made me a language mediator whenever Urdu was the only medium of communication between him and the patients. Zyar had to carry on as the blood, urine, and shit sampler that I was supposed to become. After this surprise, Zyar started resenting me. The other reason he always took the piss out of me was because neither of us made any money out of this job. We worked the lab for the wages of one skill-set, one meal a day, numerous potential deadly diseases. Khala told me that Zyar despised everything: the lab, the doctors, his homework, his father – the very reason he had ended up working in the lab before finishing high school. His father either knew, had foreseen, or simply feared for his son's future. Zyar only loved one thing: a power outage.

*

A power blackout was an everyday drama that paralysed the hospital like the rest of the city. Unlike everything else that never happened on time anywhere in Pakistan, the bastards didn't forget to kill the switch on the city for a single day. Like clockwork, almost every day, for hours and hours, the power was out. Zyar and the doctor prayed for blackouts; they didn't sabotage the doctor's fixed salary, and Zyar's zero income but no power meant no work. It was the perfect excuse for them to join the gossip circle in the male nurses' room. If by a chance, or a miracle, the centrifuge machines kept spinning the blood samples, it was a torturous day for them. On such occasions, the doctor and Zyar lost their tempers and bickered like an angry, tormented couple. I stayed inside with a book or more often caught up with Khala outside for chai and chat whenever the temperature in the lab touched the boiling point.

Khala had never married, nor did she have any family in Quetta city. The civil war swallowed up her father and two younger brothers, whereas her mother had succumbed to the posthumous pain of losing her three loved ones on the same day. War is a widow-making machine. Now in her forties, only the yellow gaps of her wrinkles glowed on her sunburnt face whenever she sat down in the sun with her cup of tea. But her still eyes told many more fables than her moving lips ever whispered.

"Are you in love with someone?" she asked me one day during a blackout.

"I haven't been blessed with the curse, yet." I blushed hearing the word *love* from an Afghan woman.

"Then you and I must pray that you're cursed soon enough."

"I've heard that love leaves holes in our hearts."

"It also scars our souls but we never pray not to fall in love."

Khala had fled Afghanistan before the Mujahidin-led coalition was overthrown by the Taliban that, later, turned her birthplace of Kabul into a city of grief and graves. However, unlike millions of other Afghans, war wasn't why she'd fled Afghanistan.

*

Between Zyar and myself, the doctor scolded Zyar the most. As a rebound, he directed all his negativity towards me to make up for the mistreatment he received from the doctor or his father. He crapped his pants whenever his father paid a visit but argued with the doctor like they were two sharp scalpels grinding against each other. The cold-war between Zyar's zany tactics and my passive-aggressive counter-attacks continued as soon as the doctor had gone for the day. Zyar was a strategic slacker who always fobbed a few jobs off onto me in the afternoon before his departure. But so did I. Instead of cleaning up, I'd leave the equipment unwashed, and join Khala outside to hear her stories knowing that Zyar had to wash and clean everything the following morning before the doctor's arrival.

*

The doctor's needle never missed a vein whenever he drew blood for a test. Even with infants and new-born babies, he'd stick a syringe in the veins around their tiny ankles with such precision that blood would instantly fill up the syringe. But on this day the doctor struggled to find a vein on the old Pashtun woman's arms. When he finally succeeded, he sighed as if he had just hiked to a summit. Then he told me to tell the girl to get a nurse to run an IV as her mother was way too weak and weary. I told the girl to collect the results after the lunch hour.

The lab couldn't preserve any donated blood in the freezer due to the persistent power blackouts. So the hospital depended on the local shoemakers and labourers to donate blood on the spot. Where they couldn't help out from their pockets, these donors gave from the heart – a selfless deed Zyar took advantage of selfishly. Whenever blood was needed, Zyar was the main man, having networked with around a dozen donors. But it all came with a cost.

Zyar fixed a price with the patient's family before approaching a donor who never found out about his end of the deal. In return, the donor received a refreshment pack of biscuits, juice, or a little cash if they asked for it. To top it up, Zyar always played the religion card: "You, my friend, and your good deeds have a place in heaven. God will bless you and your family in the hereafter." A bargain that paid off every single time. Zyar had found a loophole in the system, and over time, he'd become bloody brilliant in the blood-business. He kept a fine balance of demand and supply as there was always a willing victim who donated blood in the name of God, religion or a good deed. But on odd days, when Zyar couldn't find a donor, he'd become one.

The hospital was built on two separate ground levels: the eastern half, which included the X-Ray room, the water reserve, the kitchen and the lab, were all built on a foundation four feet lower than the freshly constructed western half – consisting of the doctors' consultation rooms, the nurses' room, the dentist, and the pharmacy. A gigantic steal door separated the old building from the new in the south, whereas a flight of stairs connected the ground-floor male ward to the second-storey female ward in the north. Adjacent to the stairs lay a tiny untidy garden resembling a junkyard.

The doctor, Zyar and I were busy with the business of the day when I heard the Pashtun girl's voice. She was standing at the lab door. Scrunched brows, the circle of her eyes like twin black-holes that could swallow up a cluster of cosmic hearts, and lips shy of a smile. She needed to borrow a pen. I kept a pen in my pocket like it was my pet. She thanked me. My heartbeats and her footsteps rose simultaneously as she walked back up the stairs.

When I entered the kitchen, Khala was sitting on the floor, a plate of lamb and potato soup in front of her, a piece of bread in hand.

"You fancy her, don't you?" She dunked pieces of naan in her soup.

"Your prayers have been heard. I've been cursed. Have I been cursed? Is this the curse?" I asked all those questions under a single breath.

She smiled. "No, my son, not yet, but this is one of the many symptoms."

I picked up a plate from the table, helped myself to some lamb and some soup, grabbed a piece of naan and said as I sat down beside her: "You must have been cursed several times."

"Life is too short to not to fall in love."

"How did you feel the first time?"

"Like a sharp blade cutting through young flesh."

Zyar returned to the lab after lunch. The doctor followed with a cup of tea in his hand. They set to work finishing the blood tests. The doctor was busy scribbling down some notes, lining them up on the table, when the power went down. He smiled, then said to Zyar, "This is all the test results for today. Make sure you hand over the results."

That was that and he was gone for the day.

Five minutes later, Zyar parroted the doctor's exact lines to me, only adding: "Ask each patient their names and the type of tests." And out he walked, his arms hanging off his shoulders, moving in all directions, like a puppet whose puppeteer has lost control over the strings.

*

Khala told me she had met the curse of her life in the carpet making shop in Kabul where she worked as a senior carpet-maker, training other children and managing the shop.

"He was a blacksmith," Khala said sipping her green tea. She was wearing a maroon dress with her standard khaki veil. "He walked from street to street, shop to shop with his toolbox on his back. He handmade, repaired, sharpened, and sold knives, scissors and all kinds of other tools. He was young, handsome, and to-die-for. I was a young and passionate woman who could kill for affection." Khala's sparkling brown eyes wandered in the blue skies as birds flew past overhead, chirping noisily.

"After a few visits, our friendship took off. Then, a month later, one freezing afternoon, having repaired some tools, the blacksmith presented me a handmade folding knife. Solemnly, he said, 'I pray that you never come across a bitter moment in your life, but should you ever need to use a knife, aim for the neck. It'll be lethal.' He smiled, holding the blade against the side of his neck. I remained silent. I fancied him but I hesitated to say yes. Still, I didn't want to say no. When he noticed my silence, his smile disappeared and his hand dropped. 'I was only joking. I'm a blacksmith. I can't gift you a gold ring or a carpet. Still, my neck is yours to kiss, with a knife or your lips.' He was a charmer. I played stubborn, told him that I couldn't fall in love with, or harm, anyone. 'Love and death are not much different,' he claimed. 'Both eventually catch up with us. But, love like death, will never come in just one form or by just one means.' He was a wise charmer. I chose love," Khala said with a sigh.

"From that day forward," she continued, "I carried his knife with me everywhere. During the sleepless nights, I kept playing with the handmade blade. I felt his iron hands every time I touched the razor-sharp edge." She picked up a sugar cube she had placed on a piece of tissue paper, tossed it in her mouth but sucked it slowly.

"My first kiss was on his neck. And so was my last one, but they sure felt different. The first one felt like love; the last one like the absence of love." Khala's white cat walked over to claim her spot next to her mistress.

I sipped my tea without taking my eyes off hers. Unlike her wrinkly sunburnt face, Khala's eyes still sparkled like a sixteen-year old's.

"A few months passed. My blacksmith and I broke down several boundaries and became like two blades of a scissors braced by a single nail. We sinned in secret, surpassing the sacred and the demonic social sanctions in that dark storeroom until one day I found him kissing Gulma in the same spot. Gulma was a new carpet-maker. She was young, innocent and shy like a lamb. I couldn't make much fuss about it as disclosing would have exposed me too. I stopped talking to my blacksmith, but he kept coming back to the shop. My blood boiled every time I saw him, yet I couldn't blame him for the betrayal. Nor could I stop him from coming to the shop. It was the shop owner's call. Besides, it wasn't about my job but my honour. I'd lose face and gain nothing but disgrace. I was helpless, and it was horrendously painful for a first love. First love always is. But I truly loved that sinful son of a bitch." Her voice was coarse as if she was crying on the inside. She placed her empty cup on the concrete kerb, petted the passed-out, purring cat, and refilled her cup from the kettle.

"If love is a curse, only karma can cure it. A few weeks later, I found Gulma weeping in the storeroom. At first, she refused to tell me anything. Until I threatened to visit her family, Gulma spilled. She said the blacksmith was not only a cheat but a married cheat. And that he was not serious with anyone. Gulma was unaware that I was going through the same hell, and that made me angry for both of us. I had lost my appetite and had struggled to sleep. I wanted to wipe out this curse. I wanted to sleep peacefully for once. Khala's face looked calm, but her eyes showed emotional unrest. She blinked a few times quickly to scatter the salty water forming around her eyelashes.

My heart was beating fast, my hands were hot but my cup of tea had gone cold. An army of amber ants had ambushed the sugar cubes. I put my cup down and shook the tissue paper to disperse the ants. The cat purred peacefully like it was sleeping in a paradise. Khala soaked her throat with a sip.

"On a cold Kabul afternoon, when everyone had finished work for the day, I summoned the blacksmith. I'd sent a young carpet maker earlier to pass my message to him. We sat down on the only bench in the store-room. I asked him how many girls he was fooling around with other than his wife, Gulma and me. He denied being married but nothing else. Said that he used marriage as an excuse to cut off flings. I didn't believe him. He was staring at the floor to say he was sorry, as if. But I had made up my mind over the many sleepless-hours of the cold snowy nights. So I stood up, put my hands in my pocket, and walked around the bench while unfolding his knife. Before he could take another breath, I swung my right arm and shoved his knife into his own neck, right under his chin. He was right. It proved lethal. He fell on the floor with a thud. Blood gushed from his neck like water from a burst pipe. That was my last kiss, and my last day in Afghanistan." Tear beads rolled from Khala's eyes and filled in the wrinkle gaps.

*

I cleaned up around the lab as required. I was busy tidying up the table top when:

"Would you be able to buy some juice and biscuits from the store for me please?" She produced a hundred Rupee note from her bag and held it in my direction.

"How's your mother doing?"

"She's still on the IV."

"Where did you learn to speak Urdu?" I took the money.

"At high school," she said, playing with a piece of tissue paper.

When I told her I liked her red dress, she blushed. Her restless eyes found the floor. As she looked up, a short immature smile curved around her lips. She paused to picture as if she'd just discovered smiling right then; as if she had always wanted to find out how it felt to smile, for once. I wished I had the power to freeze the moment but the moment had me frozen.

She thanked me again when she returned my pen. I stepped outside to watch her walk up the stairs. Before the last of the steps, she paused and turned to find me staring at her awkwardly. She smiled, then tossed the tissue paper in the direction of the messy garden, looked my way again as she disappeared behind the walls.

*

Normally, I avoided going to the general store as the young owner with spiky hair asked me questions about English language every single time I shopped there. *What are the most common modal auxiliaries? What is a phrasal verb?* He tried too hard but learned too little. I doubt he ever asked any questions in his foreign language class. I tried my best to avoid going to his shop, but that day I couldn't. I bought biscuits and juice. He handed me the bag and the change. But before he could open his mouth, I threw a question at him: "What's something you can wear, dressed or naked, and when you hug people, they'll feel but won't mind it?"

*

Lately, Zyar didn't bother calling a donor. As soon as he figured out a patient's blood group under the medieval microscope, and confirmed that it matched his, he supplied it. Often, twice a week. He didn't even need anyone to help him in the process. He'd grab an empty blood pack, sit on the stretcher, sponge his arm with a piece of antiseptic wipe, uncap the syringe and pierce his own vein to withdraw blood. Once the blood started bagging, he'd stick a piece of adhesive tape to keep the needle in place. Then he'd lie down. He was a perfect reflection of the society: sucking out his own blood and feeding on it; surviving but not thriving. But Zyar knew what he was doing and why; perhaps the society didn't. He'd found the perfect way to manipulate the system that manipulated him.

*

The Pashtun girl's eyes glistened in the autumn sun as she walked down the stairs. It was still humid but not hazy anymore. A breeze almost blew away her veil but she braced it just in time and tucked it beneath her brown bag. I handed her a sack of biscuits and juice. My heartbeat was bombarding me. As she took the change, she opened up her own bag. "You can drop it here," she said.

I got confused but didn't question. Instead, I hurriedly handed her the badly tortured coins, and walked away without saying anything. It happened fast, like in a dream. Before I knew, I was already back in the lab with my head in my hands.

*

Later, the Pashtun girl appeared holding her mother by the left arm and a female nurse was holding the old lady from under the right arm as they walked slowly down the stairs. They were leaving. She was leaving. The female nurse said goodbye, and they exited the gate.

I was paralysed. Khala kicked me in the heel. Go, my son, say goodbye, she said. I followed them outside and stopped at the store.

"The answer is perfume," I said to the shop owner, answering my own earlier question. As he processed his thoughts, I watched the mother and daughter get into a tuk-tuk. I asked the shopkeeper for the key to his pushbike. He was a slow learner but couldn't say no to his cost-free tutor.

"What's a determiner?" he asked instead.

At that moment I was determined to shove the Determiners and the entire English language into his mouth if he didn't reach into his side pocket.

I followed the three-wheeler for twenty minutes to the centre of the city. As the tuk-tuk passed Mizan Chowk, bearing on into the distance, I began to fall behind and feared losing them altogether. I focused on following the distinctive red cover – a portrait of a black and white flying eagle, wings spread in flight – and a quote: *Time is an unpredictable master.*

I kept tailing this tuk-tuk until Gowlamandi Chowk – the other side of the mountain, the Pashtun side of the mountain. At this point I pressed on the hand break, deciding to stop on a roadside, because I knew that if I kept going, chances were I might never return in one piece. What am I doing? And why? It's already too late. Catching my breath, I watched on as the painted eagle flew further away, shrinking from the sight, the red top of the tuk-tuk vanished in the dismal congestion of smoke-producing vehicles and their smoke-inhaling masters. In the background, above the sleeping silvery mountains, the sun was burning dismally in its own suffocating vapor.

When I scanned my surroundings thoroughly, all I found were men in turbans. Territorially, I was in the unauthorized part of the city. I didn't want to encounter any of these men at any cost, so before I attracted any unwanted attention, before they'd noticed my ethnically diverse features, and found me exotic enough to execute, I put my right foot on the pedal and pushed to turn the bike around. Then as swiftly as I could, I started pedalling away without creating any suspicions that I was escaping potential death. Once I gained speed, I didn't turn to look back. Time is an unpredictable master.

Back in the lab, tired, defeated and dehydrated, I sat down on the chair. All I could feel was an empty void and restlessness. The thought of never meeting the girl again was shaking me from within like an earthquake. I wished things had unfolded differently. I wished I lived in a society where, instead of ethnic and religious hatred, people shared love and compassion and cared for one another. I wished the future generations didn't have to feed on the fruit of the forbidden tree – the tree of hatred. The trees that our ancestors planted, feeding it the blood of the "other." I wished that the new blood stood up and wiped out the divided line instead of drawing new ones, uprooted the sickening trees and planted seeds of compassion that bore fruit of love.

I was a victim of the social circumstances, but even if I'd met that girl, what chance did we stand trying to find love in a society that thrived on hatred? The moment had slipped out of my hands, and all that remained within me was what's left after an earthquake.

"Would you like some green tea? It will eliminate your exhaustion," Khala called out.

"Can it eliminate my memory?"

"No, it will revitalise it," she replied, walking out of the kitchen with two cups of tea. "Come out of that cave and have a cup."

I walked out and picked up one of the cups she had placed on the curb next to the stairs.

"It's not wise to fall in love, is it?"

"It's always good to fall in love but it's much better to rise in love. Wisdom is in knowing that you can't stop falling in love." She sipped from her cup.

"Will I ever be able to heal the hole in my heart, or the scar in my soul?"

"Time will heal the holes, but the scar is everlasting."

"So, there's no cure for this curse?"

She went on to profess, "The cure is in the curse."

There was no sign of sorrow or sympathy on her sunburnt face. She stayed silent for a few seconds. Then a smile surfaced around her slim lips. "I'm so silly. I didn't get us any sugar cubes." She got up and walked to the kitchen.

I wondered if she did that on purpose or out of sheer humour. She returned holding some shiny sugar cubes on a piece of tissue paper. *The tissue paper.* I put my cup on the curb, stood up, and leaped over the four stairs into the garden. No one made a better use of the garden than Khala's cat that buries her dead there. The plants were plagued and sick like the hospital around them. No care, no love, no sunlight.

There it was, rolled up and resting in the mess of rain-stained newspaper, fruit peelings and empty juice packs. I leaned and picked it up the tissue paper. Out of curiosity, I started unfolding it. Then came the aftershock. As if someone pulled the earth from beneath my feet, my knees gave up and I dropped to the ground. When I returned to the present, the fat kitchen cat was staring at me while Khala was making up for the laughter she had missed out on during her youthful years.

The girl *was* a rebel. I was elusive of her rebellion; of the question she had asked me. A question she couldn't leave within; a question she couldn't leave without. I regretted not checking out the tissue paper when I first saw her throw it in the messy garden. Because, on the face of the wrinkled tissue paper she'd penned down her name and only message to me:

What's your name?

Kochi.

SIMON ROWE

Paris Match

Kenzo Sanjo emerged from Paris's Guy Moquet Métro station and stepped onto the rain-dampened pavement of Avenue Saint-Ouen with the worst migraine in his twenty-two years.

Somewhere beyond the grimy turn-of-century shop fronts which marched solemnly uphill towards Montmartre lay his destination—but where exactly? Clutching his rucksack, he set off up the avenue strewn with leaves the cold March wind had torn from the plane trees. A page of the *Paris Sports* blew against his legs. He kicked it away viciously and pulled his jacket collar tighter, his head pounding like a war drum.

At the next corner, he stepped onto the street but a horn blast made him quickly retreat. A taxi flew by, its driver scowling. No longer in south Osaka, Sanjo urged himself to be more careful.

Up ahead the cursive neon lettering of the Café Le Championnat burned in the soft, grey light of the afternoon. It stood on the corner of a side street, Rue Lemarck. Sanjo turned onto its rough cobblestones and climbed towards the Basilica of Sacré Coeur which rose grey and sombre against the sky. Could this be a street along which Hemingway, Fitzgerald, T.S. Eliot, or Gertrude Stein had trod? His foot flattened a dog turd.

"*Kuso-yarou!*"

He cursed himself, but mostly the Championnat's coffee drinkers who watched as he frantically wiped his sneaker against the curb.

He pressed on, his head wracked by thunderbolts, passing apartments with filthy glazed doors and numbers half-hidden in grime and graffiti. "Hell is the impossibility of reason," someone had scrawled on one.

A large, cold raindrop smashed against his forehead. Then another, until a violent deluge drove him beneath a sandstone archway. To his great relief, he found himself standing in the entrance of Number 26, and there, at the top of the tenant list, the name he had been searching for: "Enzo."

Inserting the key which his old high-school friend had mailed to him, he pushed on the door and entered. The lobby was dimly lit, redolent of wood polish, and opened onto a tiled courtyard. Fin-de-siècle apartments rose on four sides, and as rain cascaded down, Sanjo felt as if he was standing at the bottom of a giant well.

A birdcage elevator delivered him to the apartment on the top floor. It was exactly how Enzo had described: a small hallway, a kitchenette, bathroom, and one large lounge-bedroom with a cow skin spread over its wooden floorboards. The kitchen window looked onto the rooftops and chimney pots of the eighteenth arrondissement.

His gaze drifted downwards. On the floor below, in the apartment opposite, he glimpsed a woman standing in her small kitchen. She held a phone to her ear and her jaw worked quickly against it. She looked Asian—Japanese perhaps? He couldn't be sure. All at once, she slumped into a chair, tossed the phone onto the table, and held her head in her hands. She was crying. Sanjo lingered, unable to look away. Suddenly she looked up. Seeing him, she leaned to the window and pulled the curtain.

Sanjo shrugged; he had problems of his own, not least of which was his crushing headache. But the most pressing one, his missing luggage. He would call the Japan Airlines desk at Charles de Gaulle International Airport for an update at once. But when he reached into his jacket pocket, his hand came up empty. He tried his other pocket— nothing. A cold panic swept through him. He snatched up his rucksack and emptied it onto the floor, frantically sifting the contents.

He froze.

His gaze fixed dead ahead.

His mind reeled back to the Metro and its crush of people: the accordion player, the passengers of every creed and colour, the flurry of languages, and laughter … the two teenage girls with flushed faces and glassy eyes who'd fallen against him, apologetic, but somehow not … They had jumped aboard, then leaped off, prying the car doors open just before the train had departed the station.

Suri. Enzo had warned him about pickpockets.

Sanjo's frown deepened. His hand crept to his chest pocket. He plucked out the ten Euro note—change from his Metro ticket from Charles de Gaulle. In his hip pocket, he found another three Euros. He commenced an apartment-wide search, and after ten minutes had increased his net worth to twenty-eight Euros. The express train and Métro to the airport would cost 13.50. That left 14.50 to last him a week. What could he possibly do in Paris on two Euros a day!

He hurried to the kitchen and rummaged through Enzo's cupboards: spaghetti, salt, a jar of sugar cubes, a quarter bottle of olive oil, sachets of green tea, a half bag of coffee, and one brown banana. Inside the fridge: a carton of expired milk, half a wheel of brie, a rubbery carrot, and a jar of Dijon mustard. And what luck—a bottle of red wine!

In the utensil drawer he found a lighter and an unopened packet of Gitanes cigarettes. It had been a year since he'd smoked. Hadn't Hemingway lived off wine? Hadn't Orwell survived on kitchen scraps and foraged cigarette butts? Sanjo slumped into a chair and lit up. The irony was bitter-sweet; here he was, a postgraduate student from a prestigious Japanese university, house-sitting for a friend in the City of Light, researching a thesis on the writers of the 1930s "Lost Generation." The pulsing white pain in his head eased as the nicotine took effect.

He would have to find a public phone to call the Japanese consulate, cancel his credit card, and plead for assistance. Rain hammered against the kitchen window with greater intensity now. With only the clothes he stood in, it would keep him confined for the time being. Peering out through the streaked panes, an idea struck him—

The woman. *She* had a phone.

Of course he'd have to shower first; the eighteen-hour flight via Dubai had left his body soured and reeking of nervous sweat. Unable to decipher the settings on Enzo's washing machine, he leaped beneath the shower rosette and scrubbed first himself and then his clothes. To his relief, the tumble dryer worked at the press of a button. With time to kill, he wrapped himself in a towel and returned to the kitchen, intending to smoke another cigarette.

Kuso-yarou!

He leaped, howling, onto the chair and clutched his foot. Just below his big toe, a splinter of wood protruded. After a search of Enzo's bathroom cabinet yielded nothing, he limped back to the kitchen and his gaze fell to a carving knife—ten inches of tempered Swiss steel, tapered to a gleaming point.

The rain had stopped and sunlight now streamed into the kitchen. He climbed onto the kitchen table, held his foot to the light, and began coaxing the ten millimetre-long splinter with the tip of the knife. Slowly it moved outwards, until he held the slither of bloodied wood triumphantly between his thumb and forefinger. Sunlight caught the knife blade and sent a glimmer racing about the walls of the apartments outside. Glancing downward, his gaze hardened. There, at her window smoking a cigarette and looking at him, was the woman.

His first reaction was to leap from the table, but as he did so, the towel fell to the floor and a strange paralysis overcame him. He stood naked in the sunlight, the carving knife in his hand, staring down at her.

Her face, at first, was unreadable. Then, as if she'd been viewing nothing more than the miserable Montmartre sky, she butted out her cigarette and returned inside.

Sanjo groaned.

He snatched up the towel, threw down the knife, and hobbled back to the bathroom. Flushed with shame, he listened for police sirens, his headache threatening to

debilitate him completely. He wished he'd never come to
Paris. He wished that Enzo's grandmother hadn't choked
on a rice cake and died the week before. There would have
been no funeral, no reason for Enzo to return to Osaka, no
vacant apartment ... But could he really blame a rogue rice
cake for his lost luggage, for subway thieves, for dog shit,
inclement weather, and now this—a splinter in his foot? At
the very moment the tumble dryer stopped, an idea struck
him. He pulled on his warm, damp clothes, hopped into
the living room and took a marker pen and paper from the
desk drawer. He returned to the kitchen window.

A half-hour passed. Rain fell anew. Still no movement
showed itself in the apartment below. Sanjo felt his
confidence ebbing. He took the bottle of wine from the
fridge. Unlike Osaka convenience store wine, this one had a
cork; a stubborn cork, which he tugged at with Enzo's cheap
corkscrew until it had bent. Angrily, he hobbled back and
forth, grunting and wheezing, until the cork abruptly gave
way and his arm flailed into the air.

Kuso-yarou!

Attached to the corkscrew—half a cork.

He was raging mad. Mad at the world, at the gods,
and at the Frenchman who had invented the wine cork.
But most of all, he was mad with himself for coming to
Paris. He grabbed the carving knife, settled at the table and
began to dig out the remaining cork. Again, he felt someone
watching. He glanced down and his gaze met with the
woman's—she was smoking at the opened window again.

He set down the knife, picked up his message and held
it to the rain-streaked window. Her gaze lingered on the
paper a moment. She nodded twice.

Sanjo grinned. He snatched up the pen, scrawled on the reverse side, and pushed the paper against the pane. This time she didn't nod. Instead, she put the cigarette between her lips, closed the window, and disappeared back inside.

His heart sank. He slumped into the chair, snatched a chopstick from Enzo's utensil holder and rammed it savagely into the bottle neck. The contents spurted up, spraying his face. Even if he had cried, no one would have noticed his tears beneath the Bordeaux 2010 dripping from his cheeks. He wiped his face, filled a glass, and drank deeply.

The woman returned. She held at the window her own message—a question. Sanjo grinned. He nodded vigorously. He gestured for her to wait and hurriedly scribbled a reply.

She nodded, turned over her paper and wrote, *Where in Japan?*

Osaka, he replied.

What's with the machete?

Long story. Can we meet?

Why?

I need help.

She hesitated. *OK, but leave the blade.*

He grinned enthusiastically, then penned, *Where?*

Courtyard. Five minutes. Cigarettes?

He picked up Enzo's Gitanes and waved them hopefully.

She nodded, then was gone.

*

Sanjo waited nervously, watching rain drum on the courtyard tiles. The sound it made was like a wildly applauding crowd and it made his head hurt again. It hurt almost as much as the thought of her having seen him naked; a naked Japanese man holding a carving knife in Paris. Salvador Dali would have kissed him all over. His only hope was that she, also being Japanese, might put it down to the well-known trait of Kansai people to behave overly comedic when in trouble.

Ten minutes passed and he began to fret. Then a door swung open on the other side of the courtyard. She was shorter than she'd seemed from Enzo's kitchen, but this, he realised, was on account of her petiteness. She wore mauve denim jeans and a silver bomber jacket over a blue linen button-up shirt. Her sneakers were Vans high-tops, turquoise with a white stripe, and from her small ears hung silver hoops. She hadn't been wearing them earlier. She had also tied her hair into a ponytail, and though he couldn't be sure, it looked as if she had just applied makeup. He guessed she was in her late thirties, maybe younger—it was hard to tell because she was chewing gum.

"I'm sorry," he blurted.

"For what?" she said, shifting the gum to one side.

"For troubling you."

"You left the knife?"

He nodded and said, "Please let me explain …"

"Don't you want to know where I'm from?"

The question threw him and before he could answer, she said, "Kobe."

"Kobe city?"

She was working her gum now, watching him closely.

"I go to Kobe University," he said. "I'm a postgraduate student …"

"Nice. Did you bring the cigarettes?"

He fumbled the Gitanes from his pocket and handed them to her.

"Thanks," she said, slipping them inside her jacket. "So, what's your problem?"

"My phone's been stolen. My wallet, too …"

The sound of the rain on the tiles grew suddenly deafening.

"Let's go inside," she said.

He followed her across the courtyard and into a birdcage elevator whose confines forced them shoulder to shoulder. Watching the floors disappear below them, he could not help but breathe in her fragrance; it was zesty, something like citrus.

When they reached the landing, she opened a door into an apartment almost identical to his own, only neater, tidier, and decorated with art prints and paintings. She led him through to the kitchen.

"Drink?"

"Thank you."

She motioned to a chair at the kitchen table. "Wine, okay?"

He nodded gratefully, watching her pour two glasses. Then she sat down facing him and removed her gum. "Thanks for the cigarettes. I'm almost out."

"Thank you for helping me."

"I didn't say I was going to help you."

"But you …"

"Can you speak French?"

"No."

"What are you doing in Paris?"

"I'm house-sitting for a friend. I'm doing some research."

"What kind of research?"

"Have you heard of the Lost Generation?"

She lifted the wine to her lips and drank, watching him.

"T.S. Eliot," he said, to fill the silence, "F. Scott Fitzgerald, and Hemingway …"

"Hemingway!" Her outburst made him jump. "I *know* Hemingway. Everyone knows Hemingway."

"I want to write a paper about Hemingway and …"

"I have a problem," she said.

"A problem?"

"Let me tell you my problem first. Then you tell me yours." She slipped out the packet of Gitanes. "Smoke?"

He took a cigarette, accepting a light from her red leatherette Zippo, whose flame reminded him of a welder's torch. She then lit her own, leaned across in front of him to push open the window. In that brief instant he glimpsed the tattoo across her cleavage.

"What's wrong?" she said, sitting back in her seat.

"Nothing," he replied quickly.

She took a long draw on her cigarette and blew the smoke into the frigid air. "It's like this," she said. "I came here to meet Kenzo Takata."

"Kenzo, the fashion designer?"

"He's dead."

"What?"

"He died yesterday. The day I arrived in Paris."

"Kenzo is dead?"

"Choked on a macaroon." She took a quick and violent pull on her cigarette and Sanjo noted her glistening eyes. Her upper lip trembled and a tear rolled over her cheek and landed in her wine glass. "So what am I going to do now?"

Sanjo shifted uncomfortably. The last time he'd seen a woman cry was when Koko, their family dog, had died. His sister, still living at home, had been inconsolable for weeks.

"What am I going to do?" She sobbed unreservedly.

"If you don't mind me asking, why were you going to meet Kenzo?"

"I'm a journalist."

"For *Vogue Japan*?"

"For *Friday*."

"The soft-porn magazine?"

"It's a variety magazine. The interview was all arranged."

"That's *great*. I mean, that's terrible. I mean …"

"I don't speak French, I can't order food, Parisians are rude, the weather is shit. I planned to drive to Mont-Saint-Michel after the interview. I even hired a car." She lifted her glass and drank half her wine in three swallows.

"You have a car?"

"But I can't drive it."

"Why not?"

"I didn't know the French drive on the right-hand side of the road."

Sanjo felt strangely relieved—as if he was no longer alone in his troubles. He rested his cigarette on the ashtray edge. Through the window, he could see Enzo's apartment above them. He wondered if she had really seen him naked. He glanced back at her. "I've got no money. I've got no phone. I've got no clothes except what I'm wearing now, and I don't speak French—either."

A tittering rose in her throat, an odd sound, like a garden warbler, and it grew steadily into unrestrained laughter. She shook her head, unable to control herself. He stared back at her.

"Then we are totally fucked, aren't we?" she said, wiping her eyes.

"Could I use your phone to call the consulate?" he asked.

"Don't bother." She lifted the wine bottle and topped up their glasses.

"Why not?"

"Their hotline is busy with other Japanese who can't handle this city. I've already tried." She lit another cigarette. "They call it Paris Syndrome."

"But I don't have any syndrome. I just need to borrow some money."

"Go ahead then." She took the phone from her jacket and slid it across the table.

He pressed the buttons, waited, and listened to a recorded message advising him to wait or call back later.

"I've got money," she said.

He put the phone down and slid it back to her.

"Can you drive?" she asked.

"Yes."

"Good. I'll lend you money if you drive me to Mont-Saint-Michel."

"In Normandy?"

"It's only three hours one-way."

"Where's the car?"

"Outside."

"But how did you get it here if you can't drive?"

"The company delivered it yesterday."

"I should wait for my suitcase. The airline said they'd send it as soon as possible."

"Why don't you call and tell them to leave it with the concierge downstairs?"

"But …"

"If we leave early tomorrow, we'll be back before evening. You drive, I pay." She pushed the phone back towards him, then she rose from her seat. "Got to pee. Be right back."

He called the JAL service desk, and with no change in the status of his missing luggage, gave them his minor change in plan. Next, he cancelled his bank and credit card; he'd handle the rest back in Japan.

"So, it's settled then?" she said, returning with her wallet in hand.

"They'll issue a new credit card back in Osaka."

"No, I mean Mont-Saint-Michel?"

He'd forgotten. "A day trip?"

"Like I said, three hours each way. I'll even throw in lunch." She pulled out her wallet, peeled off two hundred Euros from the wad inside and placed them on the table. "This should tide you over. You *can* drive, right?"

"I'm from south Osaka. We have the worst drivers in Japan."

She frowned.

"What I mean is—if you can survive south Osaka and still have a gold driver's licence, you can drive anywhere."

"You said your wallet was stolen …"

"My passport and licence are together." From his pocket he pulled a red booklet with a chrysanthemum emblem on its cover, and slipped out the gold-striped licence. He handed it to her.

"Your name is Kenzo?"

"Everyone calls me 'San-chan'. What's wrong?"

"I came to Paris to meet Kenzo Takata. He dies the day I arrive, and instead, I end up drinking cheap wine with Kenzo Sanjo from south Osaka." Her laughter filled the small kitchen. For the second time that day, the surrealness of his situation struck him and a wry smile worked itself onto his lips. The wine, the fellow countrywoman—they were working their magic; his headache had gone.

"So, we have a deal?" she said.

He nodded. "But I didn't get *your* name."

"No, you didn't."

Her intense gaze caught him off guard. He glanced away.

"It's Koko," she smiled.

*

They met outside the apartment building a little after dawn. She wore a black leather jacket with a sheepskin collar, and beneath it a pink turtleneck sweater; her eyeliner was kohl-black, in the typical Kansai style, and she had on tight black jeans with ruby-red Doc Marten boots. He wore the same clothes as the day before, no longer damp.

That the rental car was a classic pink Citroen 2CV did not surprise him—it was her style—but even he had to admit the penis and testicles which someone had graffitied on the driver's door during the night made it a little too eye-catching.

"Motherfuckers!" she screamed up and down the empty street.

A short time later, hunched over the steering wheel, Sanjo guided the tiny car down Rue Lemarck, past Cafe le Championnat, and onto Avenue Saint-Ouen to join the rush-hour traffic heading west. He worked the gear stick like a one-armed bandit, one ear tuned to Koko's directions, which she read from her phone's GPS, the other on the honking horns of the frowning motorists which crowded in on him.

Presently, the Avenue des Champs-Élysées appeared, and at her request, he pulled into the flow of taxis, camions, and motorcycles moving slowly up the wide boulevard towards the Arc de Triomphe. She leaned across him, filling his nostrils with her citrus scent, as she peered at the ornate facades of the world's renowned fashion houses where tourists had already begun to queue in anticipation of opening hour.

"The most beautiful street in the world," she sighed.

"What's that?" Sanjo said, squinting into the distance.

"The Arc de Triomphe."

"No, I mean that sound."

A noise like popping champagne corks reached them over the traffic's hum. Ragged puffs of smoke billowed up ahead in the distance. A helicopter passed overhead. Unable to see past the small delivery truck in front of them, Sanjo wound down his window and pushed out his head. All at once, people were running towards him, wild-eyed and shouting. They wore yellow vests, and behind them came others, all of them fleeing from some kind of commotion. Sanjo sniffed the air. An odour like vinegar filled the car, tart and acidic. His eyes began to water. The yellow vests swarmed past in greater numbers, bringing the traffic to a standstill and setting off a cacophony of car and truck horns.

"What's going on?" said Sanjo, trying to sound calm. He shot a glance at Koko, surprised to see her finger-scrolling pages of Christian Dior's online store. She looked up. "Probably another demonstration."

"What demonstration?"

"The French hate paying taxes. They're always demonstrating."

Gendarmes in black body-armour rushed by them waving batons and shouting. Sanjo watched in horror as two burly police officers pinned a small, frail-looking protester to the Citroen's bonnet, double zip-tied his wrists, and bundled him off.

"Why don't we do this in Japan?" said Koko, her eyes unshifting from Dior's spring collection.

"You mean, protest?"

"Yeah. They keep raising our consumer tax, don't they?"

But Sanjo didn't hear; his attention was now on a towering gendarme directing traffic off the Champs-Élysées and into a side street. The Arc de Triomphe disappeared behind them in clouds of smoke and tear gas, and soon the sound of the melee faded. Sanjo breathed out; he loosened his grip on the steering wheel—but just a little.

Only when they were safely on the A13 motorway and heading away from Paris did he feel his soul make a tentative comeback. Slowly, an immense weight began to dislodge itself from his shoulders, and though every vehicle with more than thirty horsepower passed them with ease, he felt relief. No matter that truck drivers glanced down from their cabs and chuckled, or a busload of teenagers pointed and laughed, or a passing taxi driver grinned, all of them amused by the small pink Citroen with the dick-and-balls motif on its driver's door. Sanjo felt somewhat cheered; he even waved back at them.

As if noting the change in mood, Koko put a Gitane between her lips, lit it, and passed it to him.

"Thanks," he said.

"You know, Hemingway did a road trip just like this," she said, lighting one for herself.

"How did you know that?"

She pulled out of her bag a well-thumbed, tatty paperback and waved it in his face—a copy of Hemingway's *A Moveable Feast*, the Japanese-language version.

"You've read it?" he said incredulously.

"Last night."

"You mean, you read the whole story? Where did you ..."

"I found it in the bookshelf, and since you said you're into Hemingway, I thought I'd see what the big deal is. Y'know, give us something to talk about on our ownroad trip."

He glanced sideways. "What's a Japanese version of *A Moveable Feast* doing in your apartment?"

"It's not my apartment."

"Oh?"

"It's my *ex*-husband's."

They passed through the town of Neuilly-sur-Seine, then crossed the wide, grey torrent of its namesake, glancing to each side at the lazy swathe the river cut through the banlieues. They had to cross it twice more, at Rosny-sur-Seine and Tourville-la-Rivière, before the urban sprawl finally fell away and the rolling green pastures of Normandy opened out before them.

"Which part did you like the best?" he asked.

"Of the book? The part where they get lost on the way to Paris, and it rains, and Fitzgerald is drunk and thinks he's dying, but they're really just having an adventure!"

Sanjo smiled. She was right. It was the best part of the book. To escape the endless, and often pointless, drivel about staggering between bistros, bars and cafes, did break the monotony of the story. It took the reader on a trip.

Outside, the March sky threatened rain but neither of them minded; their conversation moved to Hanami, the coming cherry blossom viewing season in Osaka, and to Kobe, and the groovy old restaurants and bars which they knew and loved. They traded food recommendations and tried to guess the dish that the other would eat first on their return: Sanjo, a simple bowl of udon in bonito broth; Koko, a plate of deep-fried chicken with yuzu sauce.

Around mid-morning, they stopped for breakfast on the outskirts of Caen, and in a smoky bistro staffed by rotund waiters in tight-fitting waistcoats and wilted bowties, they talked about their own projects over *cafe au lait* and *pain au chocolat*. He asked her about her assignment. Sucking the chocolate off her fingers, she answered matter-of-factly, '*Shikata ga nai*—it can't be helped. Kenzo's dead. The editor wants me to write a travel story instead."

"About Paris?"

Her mouth was full, so he waited. "She wants a road trip story," she continued, "Like the one we're having right now. But I'll have to embellish it."

"You want to embellish almost getting killed in a riot on the Champs-Élysées?"

She drained her coffee and looked him in the eye. "You should be a writer."

*

Quaint towns of stone-built cottages clustered about a post office, boulangerie, and a bar-tabac, came and went in a light sea mist which had crept in from the Atlantic coast. As Koko scrolled her phone for points of interest along their route, Sanjo thought about what she'd said. He enjoyed writing, but until now had only produced academic reports—dry, heavy, annotated papers—which were little more than analyses of the opinions of other academics more knowledgeable on the "hidden meanings" in English and American literature than himself.

"Shouldn't we be on N814?" she said, as they passed a sign which read N518. Since Caen, the road had grown narrower, cars fewer, and now hedgerows divided them from the lush fields where dairy cows stood forlornly staring back through the fog. Her phone had lost its signal, but Sanjo pressed on blindly. They passed beneath an ancient aqueduct with its archways spanning a small river, then entered a village.

"*C'est la saison morte*," said the street sweeper they stopped to ask directions from. He eyed the graffiti curiously, then pointed the way out of town.

"What did he say?" asked Koko, as Sanjo gunned the engine. "I think he said Mont-Saint-Michel is this way."

They drove on, passing through sleepy hamlets with names like La Poterie, Les Poiriers, and La Porte, until they reached a fork in the road and Koko said, "Left."

"Are you sure?" he said.

"Trust me."

He said nothing, and veered onto the road whose sign pointed in the direction of a town named Villedieu-les-Poêles. He had no idea where they were, but her forthrightness was strangely reassuring. She lit them both a cigarette, and as she handed one to him, asked, "Got a girlfriend?"

"Did."

"You broke up?"

"We drifted apart."

She looked thoughtful, blew a tail of smoke through the gap in the window, and asked, "Was she nice?"

"Yes."

"But your interests didn't match?"

He gave an awkward chuckle, and for a fleeting instant, wanted to say something philosophical like "Isn't that always the way?" but just nodded and put the cigarette to his lips. She was watching him, compelling him to offer more, so he did. "She has a thing for Disneyland. She wanted to go to Tokyo every spring, summer and winter break, and in between, watch Disney movies every Saturday night. When I told her we should go skiing or snorkelling or do something outdoors, she got upset. She said I'd had a deprived childhood just because I didn't like Disney."

"Wouldn't a deprived childhood actually make you *love* Disney?"

"Exactly!"

She slumped back in her seat, smiling between puffs.

"What?" he said.

"My ex-husband was the same."

"He loved Disney?"

"No, he preferred fantasy to reality. He's a tattoo artist, a good one, but sooner or later you have to go out into the big, bad world and write your own story instead of creating someone else's for money all the time."

"Is the money good?"

"His clients are yakuza."

Sanjo's eyebrows betrayed his surprise, then he said quickly, "Did he do your tattoo?"

It was her turn to look surprised. "You mean this one?" she said, gripping the cigarette in her lips, then lifting her sweater with both hands. Sanjo caught sight of the long, lithe carp between her breasts, a luminous emerald-green creature writhing about the pink satin cups of her brassiere. He stared at it, transfixed. A horn blast split the air. His gaze swept back to the road, in time to glimpse a fast-approaching vehicle. He wrenched the Citroen's wheel and swerved onto the shoulder as the small camion flew by, its driver shouting within.

"I'm sorry," she said.

He brought the car back onto the road. "Me too."

*

Her phone signal returned as the town of Villedieu-les-Poêles appeared through a copse in a small valley. "You know the meaning of this town's name?" she said. "It means 'Town of the God of Frying Pans.'" So they stopped at a small supermarket on the main street and bought lunch supplies: Normandy brie, andouille sausage, baguettes, and a flagon of alcoholic cider—enough for a picnic lunch.

From Villedieu-les-Poêles, they rejoined N184, and under clearing skies motored on towards the Atlantic coast.

"So," she said, after a while.

"So?"

"So, do you have enough to write your thingamajig?"

"My thesis?" He laughed. "No, but I have a new perspective." He held the wheel of the tiny Citroen steady, feeling the madness and mayhem of the past forty-eight hours dissolve and an epiphany take their place. What she had called "Paris Syndrome"was really just a matter of perspective. If you couldn't handle reality, then you were better off staying at home.

They turned onto a long straight road which led across a causeway. Sunlight streamed through a fissure in the clouds and it cast Mont-Saint-Michel, the ancient island monastery now rising in the distance, in an almost divine glow.

"So ..." she said, her gaze fixed on the majesty before them. "Do you want to meet in Kobe? I mean, I'd be happy to read what you've written, kind of like, how do you say, *peer review*?

He glanced at her and grinned. "Kenzo will be very happy to meet you and answer your questions."

MOHAMED SHAKER

Barren Sands

My niece Anisa's wedding is this weekend. This whole weekend. Today, Friday afternoon until almost midnight, the entire family has come to set up the decorations and tables and help cook the food. Saturday is the *nikah*, the Islamic solemnization; Sunday is the reception, with the bride and groom sitting, *bersanding*, together on the dais. The wedding doesn't end until late Sunday afternoon, very near sundown, when the last guest leaves, the last tables are folded, the last of the food is spooned into plastic bags and Tupperware and given out to whichever relatives have hung around to see the wedding to its end.

This evening is warm and stuffy and warmer and stuffier under the glare of the fluorescent lights we've strung up to keep the void deck brightly lit. It's still early and the sun hasn't even set. The friends and relatives who have to work through the weekend and won't make it for the actual wedding will start to stream in slowly. Anisa's father, my late sister's husband, is getting the drinks ready on the side, stirring rose syrup and condensed milk together in a large plastic basin to make *bandung* while my grown children and their cousins help bring paper cups and bowls down from his flat upstairs. We're doing tonight and tomorrow at his house, the bride's side, and then Sunday will be at the groom's. There's too little work and too many hands, so the relatives with nothing to do idle about, hanging around tables and chairs or stepping out from underneath the void deck to smoke without risking a fine. My husband and some of my brothers and cousins form a small circle, cigarettes held in their fingers, talking loudly about tomorrow's arrangements. The kids too young to smoke will eventually saunter off to a nearby playground to do just that. They'll think they've outsmarted us, and we'll let them think that. The youngest kids are running around on the dais, the *pelamin*, with their mothers turning their heads away from their conversations every few minutes to make sure no one's broken anything.

*

The shadow of my late sister's absence stretches long and dark over this wedding but I'm the only one who sees it. Maryam should be here. It's her daughter's wedding, after all. Her only daughter. She lived just long enough to have two children, neither of whom was old enough at the time of her passing to remember her. Like us, they're only a year apart, but unlike us, they're getting married in reverse. Younger sister first, older brother second. I got married more than half a decade before Maryam, started having kids before she had even met her husband-to-be.

It's selfish but I wish Maryam's children looked more like her. They don't resemble her in the slightest. Maryam was all round: a chubby, moon-shaped face even in adulthood, a flat pear of a nose sitting right in the middle, a padded jawline smooth as a pebble plucked from a riverbank, its surface eroded by the water's relentless surge above it. Maybe if she had had more children, one of them would have ended up looking like her. Her kids are all their father. Hard, rough lines chiselled into a square shaped face; narrow noses perpendicular to a pair of eyebrows so straight, they look drawn on. The only one at this wedding who looks like her is me. Maryam would have liked to have had more kids.

I know this because when we were pregnant, the only time we were pregnant at the same time, me with Zakaria, my fifth and last, and she with Anisa, her second and last, she told me that she wanted to have more kids than me.

"All I have to do after this one is pop out one more and then have triplets and then I'll have you beat! Easy!"

We laughed when she said things like this. Pregnancy is not easy on any woman, no matter what people say, and does not get easier with successive children. It becomes regular. We normalise it. We act like it's nothing for me to have had five kids in eight years. A full year would not even pass and there I was, my womb filling to bursting until I burst, my period stoppered. But Maryam bled. She bled a lot, through both pregnancies, all the while insisting that she was fine when I knew she wasn't. She couldn't be. Pregnancy is a dam. You are the water. The dam holds you back and your water churns, ebbs, flows, crashes in on itself like waves on the shore and then new life breaks through the surface of your lake and emerges gasping, crying, sobbing, your water leaking out of its eyes. When she was pregnant with Aman, her firstborn, it was as though she had a nine-month long fever. She was never well. I had my share of feet so swollen I wanted to drive a nail into my soles to release the water, breasts so sore I wanted nothing more than for my born children to latch on and empty me, a stomach that coiled and contorted and rejected anything that I tried to put in it. But no pain, no agony, no sickness I had could compare to Maryam's. She had everything: nausea, heartburn, bleeding, headaches, fatigue, bloating, cramping. She would be constipated for days and then the diarrhoea would come, dark and bloody, clumps of tar amidst the sewage that poured out of her. Her body would heat up and flush a sunburned red and then cool off, her skin bleached and clammy like a dish rag that wasn't dried properly. As though she were a kettle that her unborn child was playing with, putting her on and then taking her off the stove, watching her boil over and simmer down again and again.

It was still very early on in her first pregnancy when she started experiencing these symptoms. Enough time, in other, less polite terms, to end the pregnancy before the child started kicking, impatient to be let out. Enough time before second thoughts could worm their way into her mind, and she might actually start thinking that it was worth it to suffer to let this baby, drowned in her as it was, breathe. Of course, this is what happened. I don't know exactly how we would have gone about terminating the pregnancy. At that point, we lived separately and away from our mother, who still lived in the old flat in Marine Parade, the one we moved to when we were forced off Pulau Brani when we were young girls. Though the *kampung* no longer existed in its wooden houses and zinc roofs, the network of people who once lived together persisted, a web of rafts connected by thin rope stretching further and further apart as time moved forward and the memory of the village and the island retreated into the distant past. My mother would know how to find someone. Or she would know how to find someone who did, someone who could brew a special tea or recommend a combination of herbs. No questions asked, no payment expected. *Dulu satu kampong*, my mother would say, by way of explanation. Before, we were one village.

The living are the living, the dead are the dead, and the unborn are neither. Blasphemous as I may sound, many of my people, Muslims, Malays, women, what have you, would agree with me, but only when they're sure no one else can hear them. If the choice is between raising your unwed daughter's child, your grandchild, as though they were your own or eliminating the pregnancy altogether, I know what many women would choose. People only see the women who chose to keep the pregnancy. They only see the women who pretended that their grandchildren were children of distant relatives or neighbours. They don't see the daughters forced to carry children that they don't want. They don't see the unwanted children, lied to by everyone, told that their grandmother is their mother, that their mother is their sister. They don't see Maryam in agony, the blood pouring out of her like a geyser as she delivered her firstborn child into the world. They don't see that the next one killed her.

*

I want to go home but everyone is still sitting down and besides, we have to be here when the other guests arrive. The preparations are basically done. The sun has just set, and the sky is a gentle blue fading to black. I don't dare look away and my heart breaks to blink my eyes because I want to see the colours change. I want to see the last yellow in the sky blend into the blue that darkens into black that lightens into grey once all the streetlights and corridor lights turn on. From my chair at the edge of the void deck, within sight and smell of the cigarette-choked *longkang*, I can see the sky blacken and ashen like a wilting flower from above the trees and behind the blocks that jut into the garden of the heavens like weeds.

A sudden need to jump into the Kallang River, hidden and dwindled behind our HDB estate, possesses me. Something sits on my shoulder and tells me that I should jump in and let the river, slowly slithering its way towards the open ocean, just take me away. Of course, the rivers don't really flow on their own. They've been hacked at, moved around, warped, stretched thin and bent. On hot, dry days, when only gravity and the irresistible pull of the moon drag them out, they flow at a snail's pace. When it rains, the canals that they've been shoved and barricaded into resemble the rivers they must have once been, charging like fish caught in a net, leaping for the freedom of unrestricted waters.

Nobody is allowed to jump in, of course. Not anymore. Singapore's rivers are for other, higher purposes, like collecting five dollars a head to bring people from one end to another. No ships set sail from them, on them, anymore. Old creaky, leaky things that brought us from the mainland of Singapore island to Pulau Brani, Sentosa's smaller, now unheard-of sister, tucked to her side. Of course, you can't go to Brani now. Not anymore. The navy took over and everyone was kicked off. I would say they flattened our houses or demolished them or that they knocked them over, but I really have no idea because I don't know what it looks like anymore.

The Coast Guard and the Port took over after. When my son Zakaria enlisted for N.S., he was sent there after his basic training. That was the first time I felt envy towards one of my kids. It shook me. I didn't like it. I felt it crawl its way up my body, burn my throat and flood my mouth with its bile. I retched and heaved but it didn't come out no matter how much I contorted my oesophagus to try and force it out. It made a home for itself in my mouth and mingled with my saliva and I taste it now more than ever.

But how could I not envy him? I wanted to ask- did you know? Did you know where you went? What land you were on? What water you crossed? Did you know that we once lived there and that we visited after they brought us to the mainland but before they bulldozed the house I was born in and built a navy base on top of it? Did you know that you were the first to set foot there after so many years? Did you ever walk through your base or whatever it is and think— maybe this is where my mother lived? Maybe if he ripped up the floor, he might still find the foundations of our houses, buried just beneath. He would have been possessed, like me, with the desire to do so. Because he is my flesh and my blood and my water and my salt and my ocean that I poured into him when I birthed him. He would have known where he was standing. He must have smelled the salt wafting through the air, so salty that he would have licked his lips, unbidden, in the middle of the day to taste it. He must have looked up at the full moon hanging like a clam shell in the ocean of the sky and seen stars that are no longer visible in our night sky, but he saw them because has my eyes. I gave him my eyes. He must have walked out of the toilet in the base one day and suddenly he was there, in my childhood home, barefoot like I was, every splinter in the wood tickling his feet. He could look out my window and see the sea beyond. And he might have cried when he blinked and my eyes closed and his opened and he was back there in that Coast Guard base, the dust of my home somewhere beneath his feet.

*

I made a pact with God before I realised that He doesn't deal in such petty mortal affairs. I told God that if He let Maryam live through her first pregnancy, I would sell my gold and sacrifice a sheep for every child she had. I had exactly two gold bangles at the time, and I'd give up both if she lived. I would find other ways to pay if I had to. If I couldn't find

a sheep, I would find a chicken and slit its throat myself.
I'd done it before; I wasn't scared. I would let her have as
many kids as she wanted. I would let her be the mother
and wife she wanted to be. Her whole first pregnancy, I
begged her. Let this be your first and last. It's okay to have
only one. You don't have to have as many as me. Why do
you want to, anyways? She would laugh and laugh and just
say I didn't understand. I already had the kids, after all. It's
okay to die, she said. It's okay to die because a mother that
dies in childbirth goes straight to heaven. But your kids,
Maryam, your kids will live here on earth, in hell, without
you. I know you didn't mean that in the way you said it. You
didn't want to die. Who wants that? No one who wants to
bring life into this world wants death to follow it. No one
who loves the life in them like you did wants to scar that
new life with the taint of death. But we were both wrong,
Maryam. You thought you could bargain your way through
your suffering. If you suffered, you thought, and you did,
you suffered, you were in agony, you nearly died and then
you did, you thought that suffering would pay the price and
you would be rewarded with children, as many children as
you were willing to suffer for. And I thought I could help
you. I could bargain like you. I could go into debt, pawn
my bracelets until I had no more. I was ready, I thought,
to steal my husband's rings, the earrings we had bought for
our daughters when they first pierced their ears, anything,
to pay for your life. If you made it through this one, God
would let you make it through all the rest. When Aman,
your firstborn, came into this world, we believed we were
right. You had suffered and I sold off my first bangle and
arranged with one of our mother's friends to have someone
in Batam do the slaughtering, and here he was, your son,
safe and sound. We had cracked the code. You would be
able to have as many children as you wanted.

When we became pregnant at the same time, it was further confirmation that we were on the right path. This pregnancy was even harder on you. On top of everything else, you were probably diabetic. We didn't know it back then but when our mother developed diabetes years after you passed, I realised you, too, were diabetic at the time. Your ripe cheeks withered and wrinkled. The weight that enveloped your body fell off and I saw the shape of your hips, angular, sharp, two hooks on either side of you, for the first time. You peed constantly and were always thirsty; you lost weight but ate more than I had ever seen.

When someone dies, everyone analyses their last actions, the last things they were seen doing, and they always reach the same conclusion: the one who died knew they were going to go. You wanted to eat all that you could, drink every last drop of whatever was put in front of you, because you knew, somewhere in your heart, that you were not long for this world. Every time you played with your child, something every mother does, was reinterpreted as you desperately squeezing out a few more precious minutes with the child you would soon leave behind. Every time you laughed, it was because you knew that it would be your last time to be happy, every tear you shed because you knew you would be gone soon, every nap you took in the beam of sunlight that fell onto your armchair in the afternoon because you wanted a last taste of this world. Nonsense. None of them knew you like I did, Maryam. You did not know you were going to die. I didn't. No one did. Death surprised us because we didn't realise it was possible for us to be wrong. God is not the man at the *pasar* vegetable stall. You can't sweet-talk him into throwing an extra bundle of kangkong into your groceries. You can't reason with him about things as human as money, as gold, as suffering. Your suffering was preordained. It was not a bargaining chip. It was a warning. We went ahead anyway, and you paid the price with your life, and I didn't sell any more of my gold. I say that we went ahead even though it was your decision because I bore witness to your suffering and let you suffer anyway. I didn't protect you from yourself, from the both of us.

You died minutes after childbirth. I don't think you got the chance to hold your daughter and I doubt they would have let you. You were not supposed to die. Whatever bargains we had tried to make with God, we had made a decade before with the Singapore government. When they forced us off our islands and out of our villages and shoved us into housing blocks higher than any hill I had ever seen, they told us this would be better. We would have toilets inside our homes, running water in our taps, electricity to power our lights. We would have buses and trains and cars and planes. We would go to work at factories. Our kids would go to school. We would never go without food or water. In return, we would forget that we belonged to the sea and the land and the air. We would reject them or be punished. We would no longer pick the overripe mangoes that thudded onto the ground when their juices became too heavy for the tree branches to hold. We would no longer go out to the beach with our strainers and sift through the shore at low tide to forage for clams and mussels. We would forget the names of all the different herbs and vegetables that grew wild in our forests and our swamps and settle for those that could easily be found at air-conditioned grocery stores. Our whole way of life, our homes, would all be buried beneath the asphalt. Our kids would never see the world of their grandparents. The shores that our ancestors landed on when they travelled freely throughout this archipelago but decided to dock in Singapore would be swallowed under sand and brick and condominiums. The hills would be levelled. The forests would be cleared. The swamps would be drained. The stars would disappear. In return, we would never die. Oh, of course we would die one day, preferably when our age slid into the three digits, but we would have a long, full life to enjoy before that. But death followed us into our new housing blocks. People jumped to their deaths from the twelfth, thirteenth, fourteenth, fifteenth (the number kept going up) levels and died with a splat on the ground. The cars grinded human bodies into paste beneath their wheels. The trains opened their giant snake jaws and swallowed the people who threw themselves in front of the great beasts whole. The factory machines ate people's limbs and left them to bleed out on the floor in front of everyone on shift while an ambulance came too late. Police hunted our brothers and fathers and sons and they disappeared behind the walls of the great fortress at Changi, emerging only as shells of who they had been before they were taken, if we ever saw them again. Death mutated. It persisted. People still died. It didn't matter where.

But your type of death was supposed to be eradicated. No more women were supposed to die in childbirth of all things. Women were supposed to be happy and healthy and provide for their families and take care of their households and hold down a job and still get home in time to make their husbands dinner. Women were not only supposed to survive childbirth; we were supposed to survive many childbirths. Singapore needed the manpower. We were the factories. Bonuses were given out for your third, fourth, fifth kid. The more, the more. We were supposed to have more kids than we could afford and then we would be blamed for what we could not provide. But we were not supposed to die. We were needed. You were needed. You are needed. Your kids needed you. I did my best, especially with Anisa, but they needed you. She's getting married and you're not here. Your absence is a presence that will sit on the *pelamin* with them tomorrow when they are officially, Islamically married. When the *tok kadi* reads his prayers and gives his marriage sermon, when your daughter, her husband, her father, their witnesses, all sign the marriage certificate that will be passed between them, you will be there. You will be there on Sunday, at the reception, in between the guests and the dancers and the drummers and the *silat* practitioners. I say you'll be there, but of course, you won't. You can't.

*

I'm sure I've seen the sun set before but, in this moment, I can't remember a single time. When the kids were young, my husband and I would bring them to East Coast Park with all their cousins on those rare times when the stars aligned and everyone's off-days landed on the same day. We'd arrive when the sun was still blazing overhead and find shelter underneath the shade of a tree, sharing our food with the ants and flies that were impossible to keep away. By nightfall, the flies were replaced with mosquitoes and the soothing sound of the waves crashing endlessly on the shore was interrupted periodically by someone slapping at their own skin. The kids spent the whole day in the ocean, emerging wrinkled like old fruit with sand stuck to their feet and lower legs. They ran in and out of the water, chasing the foam that covered the sand in a thin blanket. The older kids would walk out into the water until they were on their tiptoes and then cut through the waves and tread water somewhere near the horizon. They all knew how to swim, or at least how to float, so we didn't worry. Maybe we should have. Sometimes they played this ridiculous game where they held onto a stray tree branch that came over from some nearby island or a bit of flotsam ejected from an unknown vessel and just let the waves spin them around.

Beef *satay* skewers and marinated chicken sizzled over the small charcoal fire my husband built in one of the pits that lined the beach. We often heard the rats fighting over leftover bones and the fatty bits of *satay* that clung to the skewers in the rubbish bins nearby, squeaking and shrieking and knocking one another loudly against the sides of the rusty metal bins. Sharifah Aini and Sudirman scratched out of a small portable radio one of my brothers would bring and we'd sing along when we knew the words and ad lib when we didn't. The kids were too young to remember their uncles, my brothers, some of whom were still single, and their father sneaking off to the hawker centre to drink beers under the pretence of buying soft drinks for the young ones. It annoyed us, my sisters-in-law and me, but we never said anything. They eventually stopped and we just chalked it up to the long adolescence that men refuse to emerge from and never spoke of it again.

If I ever looked to the right, to the west, to see the sun setting, I don't remember doing so now. All I remember is the horizon chunked into pieces by the barges and huge container ships in the distance. I remember that if I stood where the water met the sand and felt the salty air sing through my nostrils and the wet sand burrow its way in between my toes, I could no longer see Brani or Semakau or any of the other small islands that clustered around Singapore's southern shoreline like eggs under a mother hen. I remember running my hand through the sand and the sea and coming up with fistfuls of empty sand and empty shells, devoid of the mussels and cockles that the ocean once spat onto our shores for our dinner. I remember seeing our kids in the distance. It could bring me to my knees now, thinking about our kids. They couldn't see what I saw. They couldn't see our islands barricaded and hidden behind these ugly barges, our horizon broken apart and shattered. They didn't know that the sand was barren.

*

This always happens. I blink and I miss something. The sun has set. The horizon swallowed the red in the distance, leaving only the black night sky. Guests are starting to come and help themselves to the *tulang merah* we cooked earlier, the bone steak whose thick red juices coat their hands and run down their arms. Anisa and her fiancé get up from their table and make their way around slowly, greeting their guests with hugs and wide smiles for their friends and gentle kisses on the hands of their older relatives. Even her hair isn't like yours, Maryam. Yours was short and wavy, a perm you never had to pay for; hers cascades down her back and drapes across her shoulders like a waterfall. When she looks over at me and smiles, I want to blink and see you in her place. I want to close my eyes and open them and see you, walking around like you did on your wedding day, smiling on your husband's arm. I will my eyes to see you, but they don't because you're not here. Only as big a fool as me would continue to try to bargain, would keep testing God after He has tested me time and again in this life. I would give anything for you to be here, though I don't have anything more to give. I cannot pay as you paid. You are gone, Maryam, and all my suffering can't bring you back.

SARAH SOH

Pineapple Fengshui

"You are so … *Singaporean*."

A vendor said this to Hwee Chin after she pushed for an earlier delivery date.

A foreigner. What would *he* know about being Singaporean? She was born here, had lived all twenty-five years of her life here. What else would she be other than "so…*Singaporean*"?

Still, Hwee Chin felt faintly ridiculous as she lifted the pineapple out of the massive shopping bag laden with all the accoutrements necessary for today's door-opening ceremony. Teng, her fiancé, stood shoulder-to-shoulder with her in the HDB flat's dark, airless doorway, rereading the instructions left by the fengshui master in his ten-page report. The small two-bedroom flat would be their first home away from their parents', but, more importantly, the biggest financial commitment they had ever made in their lives. They were going to fengshui the fuck out of this place.

The huge pineapple, its hide bumpy and rugged, felt substantial in her arms, like a fruity baby dinosaur. Its fragrance, though, was delicate—she knew she would smell it on herself for the rest of the day. It wasn't her favourite food, but three months on keto—no sugar, no grain, no fruit, and oh my god so much meat—would make anyone daydream about sinking her teeth into a hunk and letting the tart, sweet juice fill her mouth. Her teeth ached.

Still, the diet was worth it. She would look skinny for next week's pre-wedding photoshoot. The photos would be used on invites, the wedding website, be blown up and displayed in the reception areas on their big day, to be admired by hundreds of guests. She had already earmarked a wall in the flat where the best portrait would hang for many years to come. Yes, the sacrifice was worth it, even with the bad breath, the constipation, and the savage urge to snatch ice cream cones from passing children because the little idiots were letting the sweet nectar *drip* and go to waste!

According to the fengshui report, the auspicious window was 9 a.m. to 11 a.m. Their phones showed 8:59. Hwee Chin took a few selfies of her and Teng waiting at the door. The photos came out too gloomy—her last Instagram post received only twelve likes, she needed a winner—so she moved into better light, refreshed her makeup, and asked Teng to take pictures of her holding the pineapple, running through her repertoire of expressions and poses until she felt she had enough options. Teng did not complain but pointed out the time when the clock hit quarter past.

Almost immediately, they ran into their first problem. The instructions said to "roll a pineapple from the front door into the middle of the living room." How exactly did one roll a pineapple? Many of their friends were getting married and moving into new flats with fengshui ceremonies, but no one had specifically discussed pineapple-rolling techniques. Should they swing and release, as with a bowling ball, hurling good fortune into their new home with speed and vigour? Or should they guide the pineapple with their hands, escorting it and all the wealth it promised with the deference that such an all-important blessing deserved? They conferred and settled on deference; the more respectful option was safer.

The pineapple, though it was the largest, fattest, and most bounteous-looking specimen they could find, was not long enough to fit all four of their hands when laid on its side. Teng solved the problem by spinning the fruit around so that she would have the smoother end while he suffered the prickly leaves. Squatting side by side, they coordinated their hands, turning the fruit reverently but firmly on the floor towards its destination. As per the instructions, they shouted "*Huat ah!*"—Prosper! —all the while, Teng with gusto, Hwee Chin a little self-consciously. She was grateful he made up for her shyness. Already, the heat of the apartment was making sweat bead on his tanned forehead, lightly pitted by teenage acne, but Teng was grinning. Not for the first time she congratulated herself. *This man will make a good husband.* She considered their two-year age gap a healthy one; everyone knew that boys took longer to mature than girls—this way, they were even.

When they reached the middle of the living room, they gave the pineapple a final press, fixing its luck in their home, and straightened up. There was a lot more to do.

First, they opened all the windows and doors to let the *qi* in. Then, Hwee Chin retrieved the Tupperware box that held a mixture they would scatter into every nook and cranny of the flat: salt and tea leaves to cast out evil spirits, green beans for fertility, rice for abundance. *Mmm…chicken rice*, Hwee Chin thought, running her fingers through the grains.

There were still the red packets with coins, to be placed in the four corners of the flat. Then more fruit—apples, oranges, pomegranates, melon, peaches—each tasked with a different blessing, to be arrayed on a platter on the living room floor next to the exhausted pineapple, its crown of leaves now crumpled and worse for wear.

Hwee Chin adjusted the composition of the fruit, which smelled delicious—*skinny*, the diet was worth it 'cos she was *so skinny* right now—and angled them to better catch the light. She took a few pictures, careful to crop out the ugly floor tiles. She would edit them for a post later. *You can't tell how small the flat is from the photo, can you?* Maybe they should have waited until their careers were more established and they could afford a bigger—no, no, no, no…she reminded herself it was smart to buy a flat now, while their salaries were below the income thresholds for government grants. They got a fat sum for being first-time buyers of HDB flats, and another for living near her parents. She cradled the combined figure in her mind, comforted by its heft. What did it matter this flat was dinky? Their careers would take off. They would move to a bigger flat, near good schools, then a condo. They would acquire a maid and a car at some point. Yes, they were smart to take advantage of the system while they could.

Her phone chimed two high-pitched notes, a custom tone Hwee Chin had set so she would know immediately the message was from Sandra.

"Is that your boss again?" Teng's voice was as irritated as it got. He bent down to replace an apple that had rolled off the platter. "Just because she's a single workaholic who doesn't have anyone to hang out with on the weekend…"

Sandra wasn't her boss; she was her boss's boss, maybe even her boss's boss's boss, if you counted her deputy. Sandra had been leaning on Hwee Chin ever since her deputy went on maternity leave. Maternity was only sixteen weeks, and the deputy might be back in the office before that—Hwee Chin had a limited window to shine.

"Just let me answer this." She hurried to compose a reply that sounded cheerful and competent, comprehensive, but also not longwinded. She deleted her first try and rewrote it, all the while aware that Sandra was waiting.

"Does she still have the hair?"

"Shhh…I'm concentrating."

It was true that Sandra had hair that you couldn't help noticing. It hung down to her waist and was left completely untreated, with the odd grey shooting through. This was especially striking on a tall, forty-something-year-old woman with powerful shoulders, who wore no makeup, and dressed like fashion was a required subject she studied just enough to pass.

Teng was now doing a credible impression of Sandra swinging her hair off her shoulders.

"Oh, stop it, Teng!" It was uncanny how Teng caught the way Sandra always rocked side to side, pendulating all that hair before swinging it behind her.

Hwee Chin couldn't help laughing a little, but only a little. She had the instinctual pity coupled people reserved for single ones, boss's boss or not. If she thought that Teng seemed a little harsher on her female boss than his own male ones, she didn't dwell on it.

She sent her carefully calibrated message, held her breath for follow-up questions but was soon dismissed with an "ok thx." Hwee Chin turned her attention back to preparing for the beginning of the rest of her life. She poked inside the big shopping bag. "We almost forgot to plant the beans."

"No, *you* nearly forgot to plant the beans. I have my list right here."

They pressed green beans into damp cotton wool in a shallow takeout container and placed them next to the fruit platter—sprouting the beans would turbo-charge their fertility. *Just two*, Hwee Chin thought, *better for the finances*. The flat would be shut and left alone for three days, during which time the fruit, the rice, and the beans (all the food Hwee Chin wasn't allowed to ingest) would work their fengshui magic and give them the best possible start to their married life. After that, the builders would come in on another auspicious date and hour, hack away the dated five-year-old fittings, and install their dream home in the "Japandi" style—the product of the felicitous marriage between Japanese minimalism and Scandinavian functionality.

Hwee Chin took a few photos of the beans sleeping in their cotton wool and plastic incubator—people were more likely to comment on posts related to babies. She checked the time; the ceremony took longer than she had budgeted. "I should go."

Teng folded up the now empty shopping bag in his usual methodical manner and tucked it into the backpack he had bought from a small, independent U.S. based company after weeks of research. He glanced up at her, a novel thought dawning in his eyes. "Maybe I'll come with you to your reflexologist. He must be good, since you go so much."

Hwee Chin started. "Oh … erm, it hurts like hell … you … you wouldn't like it." Hwee Chin had converted sceptics to traditional Chinese foot reflexology—her dad was now a believer—but Teng wouldn't be one of them, she knew. "He trained in Taiwan in the sixties ... he's really old-school. The first time I went, he made me cry. Mr Pang says if it doesn't hurt, it doesn't work." Hwee Chin described Mr Pang's narrow shopfront in Clementi, tucked between a Chinese medicine hall and a hair salon, where faded acupuncture charts covered the walls, and the arms of all three leatherette chairs were ripped in the exact same spot by customers gripping on them in pain during the sessions.

Teng considered a corner of the living room where they had been a little too enthusiastic with the rice and frowned, like she knew he would. Teng favoured clean and modern things, like air-conditioned multi-storied mega malls, preferably new, preferably in town. "If it's so painful, why do you keep going?"

"I ..." How to explain to someone like Teng? "When Mr Pang massages my feet," Hwee Chin demonstrated by making a loose fist and raking her knuckles firmly down the length of an imaginary foot supported by her other hand. "It really, really hurts ... but also ... also you can't think about anything else? You can't think about your project deadline, your to-do list, or why your last post only got ten likes, and whether everyone thinks you're a loser. You can only focus on the pain, wait for it to come, hope that it will stop."

Hwee Chin shifted her weight, pointed and flexed one foot, as if feeling Mr Pang's knuckles already. "Nobody thinks about their feet, right? During reflex, you *feel* everything— every tendon, every ligament, every muscle. He digs his nail into this bit between your toes," she pinched the webbed skin between her fingers, "it hurts like a *bitch*. But you're also thinking, *oh, I didn't know that was there*, like, you're rediscovering your body. And after it's all over, you feel *amazing*, like a brand-new person ... so light," Hwee Chin raised herself on tiptoes, her arms drifting upwards. "And also, that you've *earned* the lightness because you *suffered* for it." Still floating, she glanced over at Teng; his face was completely blank. *Shit.* She came back to earth and put her arms down. "I, er ... I always sleep very well after a session," she finished lamely.

"Okay, if it helps you sleep. You need good sleep to be productive." Teng nodded, face polite.

As they were leaving, Hwee Chin took one last picture of the living room to capture all the things that would soon be gone: the knee height crayon drawings on the walls, the prison bar-like window grilles, the busy floor tiles that somebody had thought beautiful, now defaced with rice and fruit. This was the "Before" picture, to be posted side-by-side with the "After" of their stylishly remodelled flat in a triumphant reveal. She expected to feel anticipation but was instead hit with a queasiness low in her stomach. No time to dwell, she had an appointment to keep.

*

"You're Singaporean?" John, the man she met on a BDSM forum, asked. It wasn't his real name; they had agreed on fake names: they both had lives—and people—to protect.

"Yes." The café was in a mall that was always quiet despite its central location. *Bad fengshui*, Hwee Chin thought.

"The kink community here is so small. It's been hard to find a new sub since I moved back."

Ten minutes ago, meeting him in person for the first time, Hwee Chin had been a little disappointed. He looked like one of those soft banking types walking around Raffles Place MRT, with his glasses and slight pudginess. Now, as he showed her his collection of "impact play" implements on his iPad, she saw he had beautiful hands—long-fingered and elegant, but capable-looking.

"Now, have you thought of a safe word?" John pushed up his glasses with his long fingers. "It should be easy to remember, but not something you're likely to use during play."

"Yes," Hwee Chin caught a whiff of the delicate, fruity scent again. "Pineapple. My safe word is pineapple." Her mind shuttered through the frames of her life in rapid succession: her diet, the wedding, the flat, Teng, Sandra, work. There was a picture of her holding the pineapple as if she was about to drop it. It was a little goofy—which would get more attention—but her face and body still looked good. She would post that one.

Home

"You know I 'heart' you, right?" Joey said, softly kissing Anna on her coral pink lips. He smoothed her long, black hair and caressed her face. He was about to kiss her again when a passenger announcement alert echoed across Changi Airport Terminal 1. The walls of the massive interior were panelled with sleek steel that shone under fluorescent lights. Check-in for Philippine Airlines bound for Manila would be closing in ten minutes, yet the queues at the counters were still long. Filipinos coming home for the summer had their carts loaded with bags and *balikbayan* boxes filled with an assortment of merchandise for their families. Joey only had a backpack and he checked if he had put his passport and boarding pass inside. His flight would leave at quarter past midnight. "I'll see you on Sunday, babe."

"Come back soon or I might heart someone else," Anna teased. She was still wearing her white tank top with the Boulevard logo on the left breast, paired with black skinny jeans. Anna was slim and taller than the average Filipina. She had changed into her ballet flats so she was just about an inch shorter than Joey. She slipped her arms around his waist and tiptoed to kiss him. Joey tasted strawberry on her lips and smelled cigarettes and beer on her skin.

"You shouldn't kiss me like that or I won't be able to leave at all," Joey said, running his fingers through his neatly cut obsidian hair streaked with silver.

"Yay for me," Anna said, winking.

"Okay, I need to go." Joey had not been home for a year and he did not want to miss his flight.

"Wait. Let's take a selfie." Anna took out her iPhone and she took a picture of them grinning, puckering, and giving a peace sign in front of Changi's famous bronze kinetic rain. The tawny light cast a glow above Anna's head like a halo. But Joey felt the two of them were far from saintly. Some people looked at them as they walked past. Could they tell?

"Hey, don't post that on Facebook. Or Instagram."

"I know." Anna changed her wallpaper to the photo of Joey sticking a peace sign on top of her head like devil's horns. "There. You can go now."

Joey laughed and handed her two ten-dollar bills. "It's late. Take a cab."

"Thank you, sugar daddy."

Joey winced. "What did I say about being called sugar daddy?"

"It makes you feel old."

But feeling old was the least of his concerns. He looked around to see if he knew anyone in the crowd. So far, no one. Joey gave his girlfriend one last hug and a smack on the lips.

"Don't forget me..." Anna whispered. "Please."

"I'll be back. It's just for one weekend."

*

Joey blinked as his vision adjusted to the bright halls of Ninoy Aquino International Airport. Sitting for three hours on the plane gave him a crick in the neck and pins and needles in his right leg, not to mention a mix of excitement and dread at the pit of his stomach. He breezed through Customs and walked out the exit doors. Cars picking up friends and relatives honked, while a huddle of people waited behind metal gates. It was only about four in the morning, but the air clung to his skin like cellophane. As he walked up to Bay 11 he watched a driver help a short lady push a massive box of a flat TV into the back of a van. Joey thought she probably had also stuffed her suitcase with branded clothes and accessories, not to mention packets of imported chocolates for her family and neighbours. They would worship her. Joey only got his ma a simple Swarovski necklace and his pa a Glenmorangie whisky bottle from duty free. A car beeped and he looked up. A familiar red Nissan Sentra stopped in front of him and a six-year-old girl in pyjamas climbed out and ran to hug his waist.

"Papa!"

"Hey, Clare Bear!" Joey embraced his daughter and sniffed the innocent smell of Johnson's baby powder. She had grown so fast. Last he saw her, she still had round cheeks that looked like the hot morning buns sold at the bakery across from their house. Now, her face was more oval, like her mama's. In fact, she was looking more like her mother: willowy, rice paper-skinned, brown-haired. The only features she got from Joey were her eyes, shaped like little avocadoes, and a scooped nose. "Where's your mama?"

"Here." His wife, Cecilia, slightly limped over. "Welcome home, honey," she said as she gave Joey a peck on the cheek. "We have to move fast. Can't really park here."

As Joey sat in front, Cecilia ushered Clare to the backseat and strapped her in. He checked his phone and saw Anna's message: "Miss you already." Kissing emoji.

"Everything okay?" Cecilia asked, as she started the car.

Joey jammed the phone back into his pocket. "Yup."

"How are you adjusting to your new job?"

"Not too bad. This one's more stable. Higher pay. Better benefits."

"Thanks for doing this."

"We just need to make some sacrifices. Have we paid our car insurance?"

"Not yet."

Joey squeezed his eyes.

"Your daughter is proud of you."

Joey peeked at Clare through the rear view mirror and remembered his presents. "Oh, I got you girls something."

His daughter bounced in her seat and clapped. "What is it?"

He gave Cecilia a lavender blouse and handed Clare a slender pink box. "Oh. Barbie."

"Don't you like dolls?"

Clare shrugged. She took the Barbie out and tugged at her corn-yellow hair. "I guess I can stick her head on Ironman."

"What?"

"Tito Andrew gave me masher toys. I can swap Captain America's and Ironman's heads. Or their arms. Or legs. Look!" She showed Joey a toy figure she had brought along. It was an abomination. He doubted even the X-Men would invite it to their club.

"You shouldn't ask your uncle for expensive toys."

"But he's rich."

"She didn't ask, honey. You know Andrew. He likes giving things." Cecilia stopped when the light turned red at the intersection of NAIA Road and Domestic Road.

"Mama said it's okay to take what he gives."

"Isn't your Barbie pretty? Don't girls in your class play with dolls?"

"I want to be a superhero." She rolled one sleeve up and showed Joey her thin pipe of an arm.

Joey looked at his wife who just shrugged, eyes on the road. "How's your knee?" he asked.

"Might take a year to heal. Diana has taken over my PE classes."

Joey sighed. The salary increase he got only evened out Cecilia's pay cut. He envied his older sister, Mary, who just had to doll herself up and flash a fake smile at her husband's charity events. "Mary offered to lend us money for Clare's fees."

"That could free up some of our budget for car insurance."

"But let's leave that as a last resort. Don't want to borrow from her too often."

"She loves Clare. So does Andrew."

"Sometimes, it feels like Clare is their child more than ours."

"Maybe I can find work in Singapore too?"

"Living expenses are too high. And if Clare studied there, school fees would kill us. Let's bear with this a bit longer. A few more years of saving, we can put up a business and things will be better."

"Okay."

Nocturnal street lamps had gone to sleep by the time they hit Magallanes Avenue. Cecilia turned on the radio and the DJ chirped, "Good morning, Pilipinas!" He sounded like he'd already had three cups of coffee. Joey turned it off. The smooth and steady hum of the engine felt more relaxing than the migraine-inducing radio jabber. Not much had changed in Manila since Joey visited a year ago. Flattened plastic bags and crushed food containers stuck to the curb like spat-out gum. Unwashed children lay asleep under makeshift shelters in the alleys.

"Why don't you grab some sleep," Cecilia said, rubbing his shoulder.

Joey smiled and closed his eyes. "Good to be home," he whispered.

*

Gold ribbon draped the open, square clubhouse at BF Homes Subdivision in Quezon City. Mary had everything arranged from the yellow balloons down to the champagne winking in guests' glasses. The balloons bobbed underneath spinning ceiling fans as Beatles' songs blasted on the speakers, transporting Joey's parents back to their wedding day fifty years ago. The old couple danced at the centre, their hands locked around each other's hips and fingers intertwined like vines bound for eternity.

Joey watched his pa, who looked quite charming in his beige *barong*, whisper something to his ma, making her laugh and glow in her lemon floral dress. Behind them hung a banner screaming in gold letters: Happy Wedding Anniversary Angelo and Tanya! Printed below were their youthful faces, posing before the altar, with the Lord nailed to the crucifix as witness to the vows they made.

Joey took a photo of them and sent it to Anna. "Now you know where I get my charm," he texted, smiling.

"Where's your foto?" she texted back with a pouting emoji.

Joey looked around and saw his wife helping Clare go up and down the blue Little Tykes slide. He quickly took a selfie for Anna, who replied with a picture of herself sending a smooch. "Hanging out with Elsa today," she texted again. "Going shopping! #fungirls"

"Which one looks nicer?" She sent him pictures of herself in a cute peach midi dress and in a sexy white halter-necked dress. Too sexy. He could not have other guys looking at his girl in that.

"Peach."

Amp feedback pierced Joey's ears and he winced. The song had ended and the audience applauded as his parents kissed and bowed. Joey's pa took his ma's wrinkled hand and led her back to her seat at the table in the front row.

"Mic test," his sister said, as she walked to the front, tapping and blowing on the microphone.

Joey clicked his phone shut and put it in his pocket just as Cecilia sat next to him and put Clare on her lap.

"Hi everyone. I just want to say a few words," Mary continued. "Lao Tzu said, 'Being deeply loved by someone gives you strength, while loving someone deeply gives you courage.' Ma and pa gave each other strength and courage, allowing them to withstand the tests that rock the foundations of marriage. It is rare to see marriages endure these days. But my parents are proof that they can. Love is tricky. It can come as your truest friend with roses or a *false friend with a knife at your heart.* I am glad my parents found genuine friends in one another. A toast to Ma and Pa!"

Joey felt Cecilia reach for his hand and squeeze it. She smiled at him, while he gulped his champagne. Friends and relatives cheered as his parents kissed. Joey also kissed Cecilia on the lips and asked for the anniversary gifts she had put in a paper bag.

"Happy Anniversary, Ma," Joey said, tapping his mother on the shoulder and handing her the small wrapped box with the Swarovski necklace.

"Oh, Joey!" his ma said, eagerly unwrapping the gift and thanking him.

"Wanted to give you something special."

"When are you going to invite me to Singapore?"

"Soon, Ma. Don't have space yet."

To his pa he handed the Glenmorangie. They patted each other's back and locked eyes for a second. His father turned away first, and Joey wondered how long he had kept Jenny a secret, even *how* he managed to keep her a secret. He did not see his pa's former research assistant among the guests. He figured no one really suspected something went on between the two back then since they spent so much time holed up in their little office analysing survey data. Joey would never have suspected had he not accidentally picked up the phone one evening when he was thirteen and heard them talking.

Joey had wanted to call his best friend to ask him if he wanted to play basketball. So, he took the wireless phone from the living room and ran back to his room.

"Can't right now, Jenny."

It was his pa whispering on the phone in his mini study.

"Tell her we need to meet Ka Tony for the fishing rights research."

The crackling sounds of chicken being fried in deep oil rose from the kitchen and he heard his ma shout if pa wanted egg and tomato salad for dinner too.

"Yes, please," he answered, before whispering back on the phone. "It's Sunday, Jenny. Family day."

"I can light up some scented candles. Give you a little more … incentive?"

"Does that come with a massage too?"

"If you want."

Joey could hear his father breathing heavily.

"Give me half an hour." Raising his voice, his pa said, "What happened, Ka Tony? Yes? Okay. Meet me in my office in thirty minutes." He lowered his voice again. "Happy?"

"We'll see who's happy later. See you soon." Jenny giggled and there was a click.

Joey listened to his pa shout from his study that he had an urgent meeting to go to and would have to skip dinner. "Can you save the salad for me?" he said. Tanya asked what time he would be home, but his father's voice got drowned by the sound of the front door slamming and the car engine snarling as it left the driveway.

His pa did not return until past midnight. The summer rain had ceased pelting needles against Joey's window when he heard footsteps in the hallway. He pretended to come out of his room to go to the bathroom.

"Hey, Joey."

"Ma put your salad in the ref."

"Thanks."

"How's Ka Tony?"

"He's good." His father stood in the dim glow of the light bulbs left on at the porch and in the backyard. The narrow hallway stretched behind his tall figure and opened into a spacious living room filled with the hunkering shadows of bookshelves. Joey could only see half of his father's silhouette, as if someone blotted out parts of him with a black crayon.

"Was Jenny there too?" Joey bit his tongue. He should not have said anything. He should have just stayed in his room and pretended he never heard anything.

"Did you hear me talking to Jenny?"

Crickets played a grating staccato music in the weed-ridden lot for sale next door. They were always louder and happier after a nice cool shower. Joey ran back inside his room and his father followed.

"What did you hear?" His pa took a chair from the study desk and sat across him from the bed.

Joey stayed silent. His father sighed and his rain jacket rustled as he bent forward and rested his elbows on his knees. He clasped his hands and looked at Joey. Light bounced off a small bald patch on his head.

"Son, I love your ma. Don't you ever doubt that. But, sometimes, someone comes along, and, you love that person too. And you risk certain things in life to feel that. Do you understand?"

Joey shook his head.

"I know it's not quite right. I don't know. I'm confused myself. But we can't hurt your ma. Or your sister. You're becoming a man now, and men don't tell on each other. So let this be our special secret." He gave Joey a soft jab on the shoulder. "So, what do you think Ma wants for Mother's Day? We can take her to that new restaurant at SM Megamall. What do you say? Would you want to try that after church?"

Joey nodded. His pa ruffled his hair and bid him good night.

*

Relatives swarmed the dance floor after Mary's speech. Joey's parents felt too old for the fast beats and went around talking to other elderly guests. Cecilia asked Joey if he wanted to dance but he refused. "Too tired," he said. So, she and Clare left him brushing icing off his chocolate cake. His daughter hopped and danced with her new Barbie, while a cousin salsaed with Cecilia. She tried to grind her hips but she looked constipated, making Joey laugh. He loved his wife. But what would he do without Anna? They got together a year ago when he moved to the same flat she was renting with a gay Filipino couple in Bishan. That was how they started. Housemates. Friends. Two people far from their families sharing the same cravings for rice, *pork adobo*, *tinola*, *crispy pata*, and *halo-halo*. They spent their first few days eating at the cramped-up food courts in Lucky Plaza. Joey felt grateful for Anna. She made life in Singapore bearable, if not less lonely. She was the one who held his hand the night he came home wanting to quit his job. He'd had an altercation with a client at the start-up who complained to his boss that Joey could not understand English and went as far as questioning the company's hiring qualifications. "Just apologise. If they find you too assertive, they might revoke your work pass," Anna advised. Joey also called Cecilia that evening but he could not reach her. When he finally spoke to her the next day, she said her phone had signal problems because of the typhoon. So Joey clung to Anna. By the time he told her he was married and had a daughter, it was too late.

Joey was about to send Anna a message when he saw his sister zig-zagging towards him.

"What did you think of my speech?" she asked. Mary had a thick layer of concealer cracking around her eyes, revealing dark rims. She seemed to have not slept for weeks and Joey wondered how stressful charity events could be.

"I didn't know you read Lao Tzu."

"Oh. I just googled that. Just type love quotes and you get plenty of these stupid quotes. Makes you look smarter than you actually are."

"You're smart, Mary."

"Ha! Try being a housewife. You get dull. And fat. Like Tita Letty over there. She looks like a sausage in that tight dress. Do you think I'm fat?"

Mary looked like a clothes hanger swallowed by her gold Armani dress that slightly bulged on the hips. "No. I think you need to eat more." Joey took the champagne glass his sister was holding and placed it on the table. "And drink less."

She was trying to reach for the glass when her husband came up behind her and massaged her shoulders. "Party's almost over. You can relax now."

Mary looked up at him and smiled. "Leaving soon, love?"

"Got a patient appointment at three. I'll see you at home." Andrew quickly kissed her cheek and left.

"So, how are you and Cecilia coping with long-distance?" Mary asked Joey, but her eyes were fixed on her husband's back as he exited the hall.

"Been rough—"

"I think that bastard is cheating on me," Mary blurted as soon as Andrew was out of sight. She scooted her chair closer to Joey. "I made sure he heard my speech. That motherfucker." Her breath reeked of wine and champagne.

"How do you know?"

"He often comes home late. Even takes appointments on Sundays."

"C'mon. He could really just be helping patients. Andrew is such a kind guy. Offering us free therapy for Cecilia's knee."

"Fine. But how do you explain the pearl earrings?"

"What pearl earrings?"

"I saw a box of pearl earrings in his drawer last month. I thought he would give them to me as a birthday present. I got so excited and pretended I didn't see them at all. Practiced my surprise face. My birthday came. You know what I got? A fucking toaster."

"Didn't you need a new toaster?"

"That's not the point. Who got the pearl earrings? Why would he give something like that if the person isn't special? Am I too wrinkled now for pearl earrings?" She took out her phone and showed him a photo of two teardrop pearls with gold clasps, radiantly white, lying on a black velvet box.

"He could've given them to his mother?"

"Then why hide it from me?"

"I don't know. Maybe because you'd compare gifts? You do that, Mary. You always resent it if someone gets a bigger or more expensive gift than you."

"Well then I'm going to check with his mother. And if she didn't get any earrings, it's Andrew I'll toast." Mary downed what was left of her drink. "When are you flying back?"

"Tomorrow evening."

"You just got here."

"I know. But I can't be off work."

"Poor Cecilia. At least she has Clare." Mary touched her tummy.

"You and Andrew have stopped trying?"

"I'm forty, Joey. And all Andrew does is work and sleep when he gets home. That asshole. After everything I've done for him. Sacrificing my career as a stewardess. He goes around stabbing me in the back."

Joey asked for a caterer to give him champagne and hoped Mary did not notice his hand shake as he brought the glass up to his lips. A new pop song had started playing and he smiled to see his wife twirling their daughter as if no one was watching them. It was refreshing to see Cecilia laugh. She always moved about with a checklist of things she needed to do. And she was doing it all on her own. No time for frivolities such as shopping for silly summer dresses like Anna. Oh, Anna. He remembered he wanted to send her a message. He looked at his sister who seemed lost in her thoughts and pulled out his phone from his pocket. His girlfriend had texted him twenty minutes ago. "You like?" she asked after sending a photo of some lacy black lingerie.

"I thought you're shopping for dresses?"

"Yeah. But I saw this. Thought we could celebrate when you get home?" Winking emoji.

A chuckle escaped his throat.

"What's funny?" Mary asked.

"Nothing. Just Clare over there. Hopping with her Barbie. By the way, have you seen that weird toy she keeps playing with?"

"Yeah. I love those mashers. I'd swap Andrew's face with Tom Cruise's anytime. They're brilliant."

"Really? I think it's terrifying."

*

Later that night, Joey slipped in and out of a dream where he was making love to Anna, except her face kept morphing into Cecilia's. He woke up with a jolt. What time was it? His iPhone by the bedside table flashed 6:03. Cecilia slept next to him. The flushed tinge of sunrise reflected on her face and made her look celestial. Joey moved closer and caressed her belly. He missed his wife. His hand moved up her chest and he ached to touch every inch of her. Cecilia stirred and Joey cupped her small breasts and started kissing her neck. But she turned away from him, murmuring she was too tired. Joey sighed and rolled over. The blanket stretched over them like a rubber band pulled to its limit.

The next time Joey woke, the other side of the bed was empty. Two white pillows were stacked next to his head and he stared at the neatly pressed blue shirt and brown trousers hanging on the cabinet handle. A neighbour's rooster crowed and a tricycle rattled past their house. Joey rubbed his eyes and the smell of coffee pulled him up from the bed. His feet searched for rubber slippers on the cracked linoleum floor. The women across the street buying hot *pandesal* from the bakery cackled and he wondered what they were gossiping about at such an early hour. He reached for his phone and saw Clare had left him a stick figure drawing of himself under a sign that said, "Wanted: Papa." Next to him were the twiggy versions of superhero Clare and her mama standing inside a house with a billowing chimney. Joey dove back into the bed. Maybe if he slept again, time would stand still and he would not have to leave. But he was hungry. He heard the firecracker sound of pork sizzling in oil and forced himself to get up.

"Papa's awake!" Clare sat at the dining table and had Barbie punching the Captain America masher.

Joey kissed her on the head and slid towards his wife, who cracked an egg into a pan. He slipped his arms around her waist and buried his face in her neck. She smelled of the spicy pepper and browned garlic scent of fried *pork adobo* that filled the kitchen. She smelled of home.

"Hey, hun, I was thinking. Maybe I can call in sick tomorrow."

"Don't be silly. You can't throw away your ticket."

"But won't it be worth it for one more day with you?"

Cecilia stayed silent.

"I just wish I didn't have to go. I miss you. And Clare."

"And we miss you. But like you said. We have to make sacrifices. We can always chat on Viber. I know you're busy, but please don't say you'll call when you won't. Because she waits for you." Cecilia looked at Clare and instructed her to get ready for breakfast.

"I'm sorry. I'll get better at this long-distance thing." Joey lifted Clare up to reach the sink, and they washed their hands.

After Cecilia had laid the food on the table, the three sat and bowed their heads to pray.

"Are you dropping me off at Lola's place today, mama?" Clare drank her Milo.

"No. Papa's here. We make time for him today."

"You spend Sundays at your grandma's house?" Joey asked.

"Yeah, because mama has errands."

"What kind of errands?"

"Groceries. I do grocery shopping on Sundays. But we did the shopping last Friday, didn't we, Clare? Because papa is home this weekend."

"Mama got me Koko Crunch."

"Great. So, what's the plan today?" Joey said.

"There's mass at eleven, then maybe we can have lunch at Shakey's near the church?"

"Yay!" Clare clapped and her elbow almost knocked the Milo cup off the table.

"So finish fast and shower, Clare Bear."

"Will you help me, papa?"

"Sure."

After breakfast, Joey showered and dressed, then helped his daughter pick her Sunday attire. They both agreed that the yellow frock looked best. He asked Clare to raise her arms so she could slip into her dress and he tickled her armpits. Clare curled on the bed laughing and squealing. Joey then clawed at her tummy like a T-Rex and Clare fought back saying she was a raptor.

"Raptors don't squeak. They roar!" Joey said and tickled Clare some more.

When they both got tired of wrestling they lay down on the bed, side by side, staring at the ceiling. Joey felt his phone vibrate in his pocket and he sat up. Anna had texted, "Can't wait to see you tonight!" He typed, "Me too," but deleted it. He looked at his giggling daughter tumbling on the bed and thought of what to say to Anna.

Clare jumped on his back and tried to strangle him. "Who's Anna?" she asked.

Shit. Joey had forgotten their daughter could read now. "Just my friend," he said, hulking and getting ready to lunge at Clare again. But another text stopped him. "So, should I wear the thing tonight?"

"Give me a minute, Clare Bear."

"Why? Tell her we're playing!"

Joey turned his back on his daughter, thinking of what to say to Anna.

"This is why I like Tito Andrew. He has time to play with me." Clare slid down the bed and walked out of the room.

"Papa's not busy anymore!"

The shrill sound of Mickey Mouse singing the hotdog song blared from the living room. Joey remembered his daughter's drawing and swore. "We need to talk," he texted Anna. The app showed Anna was typing, but she stopped. She typed again and stopped. He closed his eyes. When he opened them, Anna had finally decided what to say.

"I had a feeling this would happen."

"I'm sorry," was all he could write back, to which Anna did not reply any more. Joey wondered if he could afford to move out of the flat in Bishan and find his own space. Renting a room with an elderly couple might not be so bad. Maybe it would even be cheaper and allow him to come home more frequently. He rose from the bed and went to the living room where Clare sat on the couch mesmerised by Mickey Mouse's miska muska chant. He asked her to turn it off because they were leaving and his daughter did so without speaking to him. He watched her stomp out the door and sit on the porch steps.

"Hun? We have to go if we want to get seats at the church."

"Be right there." Cecilia came out of the bedroom wearing a short-sleeved mid-length denim dress, exposing her thin white legs.

Joey noticed she was limping more. "What happened?"

"I banged my knee in the shower."

He took her hand and led her out the door. She smiled at him just as sunlight struck her face and gave her that same celestial glow as when sunrise had found her still sleeping.

Cecilia was a superhero. Raising their beautiful daughter alone, taking care of their home. He kissed his wife on the cheek. As Joey helped her down the porch step, a wind blew and tossed Cecilia's hair. He reached out to fix it for her, tucking soft strands behind her ears. Pearls. His wife was wearing pearl earrings. Lovely little teardrops dangling from her perfect ears.

PRACHI TOPIWALA-AGARWAL

The Shadow

My hands tremble as I part the window curtain, just enough to see the visitors' parking lot opposite our second-floor apartment. He is standing there looking straight at me, the lights from the Marina Bay Sands' laser show dancing up and down him. He blows a kiss at me. I spring back, let go of the curtain and run out of my bedroom. How did he notice such a slight movement?

For the last two days wherever I have looked, wherever I have gone, the tall, bald, man has been there. I saw him in the condo gym this morning, at the supermarket yesterday and at the restaurant in Dempsey when I was having lunch with my friends the day before. Who is he? It has to be someone from our condo. How else could he get into our gym? But I have never seen that blue-eyed, moustached man before. Maybe he is visiting someone here.

I need to talk to Ajay. The clock on the living room wall shows half past nine, half past one in the afternoon in London. Maybe Ajay's conference has broken for lunch and I can call him. Or not. What if he has a lunch meeting? Should I message him instead? And say what? Someone is stalking me. That sounds ridiculous even to me. I look at my reflection in the ornamental mirror on the wall behind the dining table. Way into my forties, and always slightly overweight, I look as always, like just plain, simple Smita. No one has ever chased after me, even in my teens.

I walk to the kitchen to get a glass of cold water, rotating my phone in my hand, debating if I should call Ajay. The phone rings just as I step into the dark kitchen. I drop it in surprise, try to catch it midway through its fall, but lose. When I pick it up, I can see my husband's name faintly through web-like cracks.

"Hello?" Half-expecting Ajay'svoice to be broken too.

"Hey, Smita."

"Ajay? Ajay, I was just thinking of calling you."

"Ya, I came out to get lunch. What are you doing? Riya and Vivek in bed?"

"Yes—"

"Oh, I should have called a bit earlier. I can't believe I haven't spoken to them since I left."

"Ya."

"Hold on for a second." Then a softer, "Hi, could you warm the sandwich please. It's to go. Thanks." Then he's back. "Were they asking about me?"

"Huh?"

"The kids? Were they asking about me? Did you tell them I am coming back next Friday?"

"Ya… ya, I told them."

"Why do they make packets of chips so difficult to open?"

"Hmm."

"What is wrong with you? Why aren't you talking properly?"

"I am. Ajay, I was going to call you. I am getting very nervous."

"Why, what happened? Kids are alright?"

"Yes, yes, they are fine. *I* am scared Ajay."

"*Arre*, why?"

"There is … a man here. In the parking lot. He has been following me for two days. Wherever I go I see—"

"What? What nonsense. Who would follow you?" He was munching loudly now.

"I don't know who he is. But he is here. Right now. Under our bedroom window. He is looking at me."

"How is he looking at you? You are standing at the window? How can someone come into the condo?"

Pssshhhht. Did he really open a soda can? How is he holding the sandwich and a bag of chips and now the soda while talking to me on a phone?

"I am not in the bedroom now. I saw him earlier."

"Is Prerna's daughter home from university?"

"Huh? Are you even listening to me?"

"Yes, I mean isn't their window just above ours?"

"Ajay, I am not stupid. I know he is following me. He was at the Cold Storage yesterday. And day before at Prerna's birthday lunch, he was at the table next to ours. He even raised his glass in toast when I looked at him."

There is a sigh from the other side.

"You don't believe me, do you? That is why I didn't tell you all this while. Who would follow your boring, fat, old wife, isn't it?"

"I didn't say that, Smita. Why are you shouting?"

I clench my fists to lower my volume. "No you didn't say that, but I still have to convince you."

"I believe you. But why would someone do that? Look, why don't you call the security office. They will check. Such things don't happen in Singapore."

"If you don't believe me, then why will the management office?"

Another sigh, "What do you want me to do? Come back early?"

"I didn't say that. I don't know what to do." I fiddle with the tassels of the cushion on the living room sofa. In front of me on the shiny grey rectangle of the television I can see the black silhouettes of my head and the slow swirling fan.

"Why don't you call Prerna over? Or go to her place?"

"What will I tell her? This stranger is following me, so I want to pile it on you? Anyway, she is busy. Her daughter's friends are over."

"Ok, this is not going forward. I have a meeting in ten minutes. Listen, think about what you want to do or want me to do and tell me tomorrow. But for now just go to bed. Lock the door properly and sleep. No one can come into the apartment."

"I always lock the door at night."

"Ok. Good night. Love you."

"Ya."

I sit staring at the split lights on the phone's face. Then they go black on me too and I stand up to get ready for bed.

In front of the bathroom mirror, I run my hand over my double chin, pinching the flesh and cursing myself for never remembering to do the face exercise I learnt in yoga. I look up and open my mouth, flexing my lower jaw, opening and closing my mouth, slowly, stretching the loose flesh, coaxing it to shrink.

I double-check the locked front door, stop outside my room for a minute before turning away. Riya's bed is queen sized, so it would do for tonight. I slip under the covers, and rest my head next to my twelve-year-old daughter's. That's when the doorbell rings. I jump out of bed and rush to the door. I wait behind the closed door cursing the landlord for not letting us drill a peephole through his fancy, over-styled, wooden door and Ajay for always giving in to all his stupid demands. The bell rings again. This time multiple shrill *dinggg-dongggs*. I step closer to the door, trying to gauge who is on the other side. As though if I strain my ears hard enough, I would know if it is the man from under the window.

"Who is it?" I croak after it rings for the third time, afraid that the noise would wake up my sleeping children.

"Hey, Smita. It's me, Prerna. Are you awake?"

I close my eyes and exhale loudly at the sound of my neighbour and best friend. I hadn't realised I was holding my breath. "Ye...yes give me a second, wait." I shout as I fumble with the lock and the latch above it.

"Sorry, did I wake you up?"

"No...no. I was just getting into bed."

"Oh ok. We're out of ice. These twenty-year-olds can drink and how. Can put you and me to shame." Prerna winks.

I notice the icebox she is holding out and nod as I take it from her and walk towards the kitchen. She follows me in. I stumble on the raised threshold of the kitchen, drop the metal icebox and cringe at the clanging as it hits the floor. If the doorbell hasn't woken up my children, this certainly would.

Prerna tells me about the party her daughter is having at home for her friends since she is here from university, how the youngsters are drinking and the noise they are making as I fill the ice bucket.

I wipe the dew that has precipitated on the shinning, steel handle of the box as I give it back to her. It slips out of my hand and lands with another loud crash. There is broken ice all over the kitchen floor.

"Are you alright, Smita?"

"I am ... I am fine." I squat to pick up the fallen ice.

She sits beside me and looks me in the eye, her brow creased.

"You don't look fine to me. Is everything ok? Is Ajay ok?"

"Prerna, if I tell you something, will you laugh at me?" I avoid her eye, focusing on picking up the ice before it melts and I have a pond in the kitchen.

"Of course not, tell me?"

"Someone has been following me since yesterday morning."

"Someone as in *some man*?" she asks.

I nod.

"Seriously?"

I steal a quick glance at her to see if she is mocking me. "I thought I was over-reacting for a while. But I have seen him so many times now. And he is always staring at me … in a strange way."

"How does he look?"

"I don't know. I haven't been staring back."

"*Arre*, tell me what you saw."

"Umm … he's tall. Taller than Ajay, maybe six feet. Bald. Maybe in his early thirties."

"Thirties?"

I ignore the disbelief in her voice and go on. "He has blue eyes and a moustache. In the morning he was wearing gym clothes. Right now it was too dark, I couldn't make out what he was wearing."

"Right now? You saw him right now? Where?"

"A little while ago. He was under my bedroom window." I point to the room with my eyes.

"Really, in the condo? He's still there?"

"I don't know. I didn't go back. I am going to sleep with Riya." I throw the fallen ice cubes into the sink.

"Come, let's go and see him." She drags me towards the room.

I stop at the door of my bedroom and point at the window. Prerna walks in and pulls the curtains apart.

"There is no one here, Smita," she says.

"Really?" I cover the fifteen feet to the window in four, quick strides and stand next to her. There is no one there. "Maybe he left," I mumble.

"Maybe you were mistaken," she says a bit too quickly. "Let's go get that ice." She pats my arm with a smile that makes my face burn. I look at the empty car park again before I follow her out. I should have checked before I told her.

"Are you sure you don't want to come back for a drink?" she asks me at the door.

"No, I'm okay. Thanks."

"Listen, don't worry. No one is following you. It's just your imagination. Chill."

I keep my eyes down and nod as I shut the door. Skinny bitch.

*

"Bye-bye, Sweethearts." I wave to Riya and Vivek in our condo's circular driveway as they get onto the school bus.

It's not very warm yet, I debate if should go for my usual walk, or go back home. I slept fitfully the previous night; maybe I should walk in the evening.

At the entrance to the lift lobby I see him again. I can feel my heart beating in my throat, my mouth. He is at least six feet tall. I slow down. He is certainly not over thirty-five. I suck my stomach in. He is in his gym clothes, again. If I enter the lobby now, I will have to get into the lift with him. Alone. He is looking at the numbers lighting up next to the door of the lift. He hasn't seen me.

I turn around abruptly and exit the building's main entrance. If I just walk around the condo for a bit and come back, he will have gone by then. Again I am tempted to call Ajay, but it's midnight in London. Anyway, he would laugh it off. No one would be that interested in you, he had said. Although he wasn't always this insensitive. Twenty years ago, at our wedding, he was a different man.

When I first met him as a prospective bride for arranged marriage, in a coffee house in the buzzing college street in Kolkata, he was so attentive to my immature babbling. He listened with interest to my stories about my Arts college classes, about my friends who were also steadily lining up in front of other such prospective grooms, about my favourite Indian movies and actors. How he had praised my juvenile attempts at painting when he came home for the first time later that week.

So when I saw our wedding invitation card printed less than six months after we had first met, I was thrilled to read "Smita Chatterjee weds Ajay Mukherjee" printed in red on golden paper. Now, when I think about the letters he wrote to me from Harvard, the oh-so-expensive weekly calls during that year between the engagement and wedding, I find it hard to imagine it was the same Ajay and the same me. Maybe he was a different man then, but I was a different woman too.

Back at the entrance of the lobby, I discreetly peep through the glass doors to check if my stalker is still there. The cleaner and his cart block my view. I take a step closer and there it is, the shadow, that is certainly him. I go out again. One more round, even slower this time.

"I am being chased by a shadow." I laugh as I say it aloud and then look around to make sure no one has heard me. My husband and my best friend think I am crazy; I don't want the condo gossip-wine focused on me talking to myself and laughing.

Was someone really chasing me? I don't remember the last time someone new even noticed me. My husband has shown no interest in me in years. Sex has become rare and routine if ever. I am a shadow myself, the dark stain behind my dashing, Harvard-educated, Investment Banker husband, heading Asia-Pacific operations for Bank of America. How I had swelled with pride at our wedding when everyone remarked at how handsome he was; how I burned in shame when everyone said how young and fit he still looked at forty-seven, at a recent bank party. The eyes I lowered in shame had nothing else to look at but my stubborn ten extra kilos. I could practically feel the obstinate greys sprouting out just a week after I'd coloured my hair.

An uncertain, stumbling shadow of the girl I once was, who dreamed of becoming a painter, who wanted to travel the world, who jumped in excitement when her fiancé landed a job in Bank of America in New York. NYU, with its renowned art school felt within my grasp. My dreams had ballooned into what I hadn't ever imagined possible in the first twenty-three years of my life in India. In my overprotective house, where to step out after sunset I needed to convince my brother to accompany me; in my walled world where I wouldn't dare to stop and eat my favourite *puchkas* on the street in Kolkata if my mother wasn't with me. My father hadn't allowed me to study anywhere else but in the local girls' school and college. Fate had arranged my marriage to the sunny-faced Ajay who would deliver me straight into the lap of the best college I knew.

But reality hit as soon as I moved to New York. Ajay was starting as a trainee with a very low stipend in a *very* expensive city. I had to work full-time in those initial years, bussing tables and working cash registers so his shoes wouldn't look cheap in front of his colleagues. My pay cheques, his belts. University could wait for a couple of years, he assured me. Once he paid his dues to the firm as a trainee, worked fourteen-hour days, showed them his worth, a jet-setting career would be his, ours. And then I wouldn't need to work. I could study or take a break, could finally, really paint. But the years slipped by and before I knew it, Vivek was on his way into our world. I packed away my painting dreams and set out knitting booties for the coming baby, while Ajay leapt, as he had promised, from Vice President to Assistant Director to Managing Director. The landscape changed from snow and the Statue of Liberty to grey rain and Big Ben, and then to sweltering heat and sun and the Marina Bay Sands. The quicksand of keeping a home sucked me in, deeper and deeper.

*

I am back in the lobby and look out for the shadow. There is no sign of "that man". I increase my pace, press the button for the lift and wait impatiently as it makes its slow descent. If that pesky Nirmala from the tenth floor holds it for too long, I will complain to the management office this time.

The lift doors start closing as I press for the second floor. Just then a hand pushes through and makes the doors jerk back. He enters the lift with a smile that sends goose bumps all the way up my legs and down my back.

He has deep blue eyes that hold my gaze as he steps in. I wish Prerna was here and could see that I wasn't hallucinating.

He follows me out of the lift and leans lazily against the wall as I unlock my door, still not taking his eyes off me. I look behind him at the empty hallway, as I hold the door open.

On the way to the bedroom I pass a framed picture of Ajay and me taken at our wedding. I pause for a second at the smiling young faces, eyes sparkling with dreams. I turn it face down as I lead the shadow in.

JOANNE TAN

Mei-Mei

The calendar on the fridge says it's Saturday, twenty-sixth of May. Below the date, *Keong's birthday* is written in a pinched scrawl that must be mine. Next to the calendar, a list of items and names are written in the same handwriting on a small square of paper pinned to the fridge with an *I Love NY* magnet still wrapped in its original plastic packaging — *Saturday: Mee Sua, 2 packets. Sun Brand. Rachel - abalone, cake.*

I've never needed to take notes and write lists of things I had to do. Notes are for those who are not organised and always ill-prepared, like that Janet who brought twenty paper-plates when she knew there were thirty of us attending the women's meeting committee potluck. I had given her my best disapproving look as I picked the bits of tissue paper off the sticky skin of the *soon kueh* I was eating. Who eats *soon kueh* with tissue paper? *Nobody*, unless you have an incompetent cheapskate for a co-chairperson.

My mind has always been like a computer — so quick, so sharp, seeing everything and forgetting nothing. Doctor's appointments, every single test, exam or tournament my children participated in, what that two-faced Linda said about the *bee-hoon* I made for the block party two years ago — *everything*.

Until last Sunday.

I was standing outside Tien Tien Confectionary, the one next to the wet market where I always get the soft bread that Keong likes, and I couldn't remember why I was there. I buy bread only on Mondays. And I wasn't sure if it was Monday. It didn't occur to me to check my phone because I've never needed to.

"What can an iPhone do that I cannot?" I had said as Jon pointed out all the little pictures and their functions on the new iPhone X my children had bought for my birthday in June. "And anyway, why are you wasting money? My old one still can use."

Jon, my youngest and always so good with computer stuff, just sighed and said, "Ma." He continued to demonstrate how the camera takes better photos than my old Samsung phone. Rachel chimed in and said I can take photos of her boys and show the photos and the phone to my mahjong *kakis* next week when we play at Bee Hwa's house. Poor Bee Hwa has one grand-daughter and her only son said no more, close shop already.

Aiya, what to do, I had told her as she glared at her row of mahjong tiles as if it was her daughter-in-law's shuttered womb, you cannot force young people nowadays, let them make their own choices.

I smiled as I watched Jon point the camera at Rachel's two boys sitting across the table eating mango cake. My handsome *sun zi*. I wished they looked more like Rachel, but I guess it's *some* of their father's *angmoh* blood that makes them so good-looking with their curly hair and big brown eyes. The rest is Rachel – their bright smiles and the *ling jing* look in their eyes that people can tell they're not just handsome, but also very smart.

"… and look, Ma," Jon said as he swiped his finger across the screen of the phone, "Press this, then you can share the event with us."

"Why do I have to share like this? I can just call you and tell you. Why? You don't want me to call you?"

He had nothing to say to that but I let him continue the demonstration anyway.

Last week, my phone went "ping" while I was lining the kitchen shelves with new paper. I would never admit it to Jon or any of my children, but I would have forgotten about Keong's birthday dinner if my phone hadn't reminded me. I took a piece of paper, wrote down the list of things to do and buy for the occasion, and pinned it to the fridge.

It's Saturday, twenty-sixth of May, and I am making *mee sua* and some of my other signature dishes for Keong. My husband. Who never wants to go out to eat, not even on his birthday, but he would for our children's birthdays – Pizza Hut and the Swensen's at the airport. Ping, Rachel and Jon loved such occasions. We splurged and let them order a soft drink and any dessert they wanted.

On the door of the fridge, the calendar with its picture of a red and gold sunset stands out among the faded recipes torn out from *Women's Weekly* and business cards for the plumber, electrician and Ah Teck, the gas-supply uncle. I know all these numbers by heart, but my family doesn't. Touch wood, just in case I'm not around anymore. A Proverbs-31 woman plans for the worst but prays for the best.

The verse of the month printed over the sunset tells me not to be anxious and that God's peace will guard my heart.

Don't *kan cheong*, I had murmured to myself earlier this morning as I held a tablespoon of soy sauce over the pot. I couldn't remember how much soy sauce I already added to a broth I had made hundreds of times before. My hand shook and I put the spoon down. Don't panic. Just taste and see.

That's what I tell my daughters when I am teaching them to cook. Just taste and see. They were always annoyed that I don't have written recipes or exact measurements for ingredients to give to them.

"What is *a little bit*? What is *just go by feeling*?" Rachel had said when I was trying to teach her to make the meat filling for *ngoh hiang* two weeks ago. She was frowning as she slowly tapped the contents of a bottle of five-spice into a bowl filled with chopped pork shoulder, chestnuts and prawns.

"Just taste and see."

"This is raw meat."

"*Aiya*, when you make enough times, you will know."

Maybe I should start writing my recipes down. There are so many more dishes I haven't taught them. Like this *tau yew bak* I'm also making for Keong's birthday. Poor Keong. No more pork belly braised in my secret soy sauce broth after we got the results from his last health check-up. But for his birthday, we can close one eye to his cholesterol levels.

As I slice the *tau pok*, the familiar rhythm of my knife on the chopping board and the neat triangles of fried bean curd stacked in a pile comfort me. The whole seasoning thing earlier was just a memory slip. I have so much to do and too many things to think about. Take it easy, Fen, Keong always tells me. Ha, if I took it easy like him, nothing would get done. The lightbulb in the kitchen toilet has to be changed. Jon's had that cough for two weeks already. The herbs and bird's nest I have to send to Ping. This Ping, she would again miss her father's—.

"Ma, where's the sieve?"

I turn and there's a slim, fair-skinned woman in front of the stove. Steam from the simmering pots behind her blurs the outline of her body.

"Ma," she says again. A quick shake of my head and I see her. She is tall with slender legs in a pair of white shorts. Her skin is smooth and clear, glowing even without any make-up. I am not a vain woman, but I am proud that after three kids, I can still fit into my wedding *qi pao* and the stallholders at the wet market call me *Ah Jie*, not *Aunty*. The way she stands, hands on hips, mirrors the way I stand when we are in a hurry to leave for church and Keong needs to use the toilet again or can't find his car keys. The way she presses her lips together and tilts her head as she waits for my response is mine too. But her eyes; where mine are smaller, narrowing further when I detect deceit or mulishness in my children, hers are large and expressive. They fill with sympathetic tears as she takes your feverish hand and murmurs soft words of comfort, and dance as they catch yours in a shared private joke. *Shan-Shan*.

She cocks her head slightly, brows furrowed. Her mouth opens to speak.

No, not Shan-Shan. Rachel. This is Rachel. My younger daughter. Mei-Mei. And that's what I quickly say as I brush past her to open the cupboard next to her. "It's here *lah*, Mei-Mei. It's always here."

Rachel takes the sieve from me. The frown on her face is gone but her eyes stay on me as she tears and separates the leafy stalks of *chye sim*. Her hands are fine-boned, beautifully pale, the red on her fingertips and the diamond on her left hand catching the light with every flick and twist.

I am proud. This is how my mother taught me and this is how I've taught my daughters. Rachel still knows her way around the kitchen even though there are hired hands to do this work for her now in her own home. It's Ping I worry about. I hope my oldest still remembers how to parboil pork bones for double-boiled soups and soak vermicelli long enough before stir-frying, and that she has not replaced these recipes and lessons with starchy cheap Chinese takeout or greasy American fast food.

"What are you thinking about?"

"Nothing," I sigh.

Rachel just smiles as she picks up another bunch of *chye sim*. Waiting.

"Have you spoken to your *jie* lately?" I finally say.

"Last night. She —"

"Mummy! Nate doesn't want to take turns!" A boy with messy brown hair runs into the kitchen. He is about five years-old and a Pokémon trainer according to his juice-stained t-shirt. Rachel brushes a strand of hair from his damp forehead. Eyes like the glossy brown-sugared brew of *tang shui*, fringed with thick dark-brown lashes, stare back at her.

"Didn't you have your turn already, Alex? It's his Nintendo, right?" Rachel says in Chinese. She only speaks to her children in Chinese, going as far as ignoring them if they speak to her in English. Jon had laughed at her, saying her *kantang* Mandarin will probably do more harm than good to her children. Rachel pinched her brother and said, "Idiot. Better than nothing. I have to do this or they're going to struggle in school next time. *And* I would like to remind you that my *kantang* Mandarin got me into N.U.S. Law."

I had wanted to laugh at the irony – how much she used to cry and complain before her weekly Chinese tuition lessons as a child. "I'm not Chinese, I'm English!" six-year-old Rachel had shouted, stamping her foot when I tried to drag her into the tutor's flat.

Instead, I asked, "What about English? That's important too."

"Ben will take care of it."

Ben is always out of town on business trips. Faraway, exotic places like Monaco and Belize. Helping rich people hide their money, Rachel had said with a laugh when I asked her what Ben did and why couldn't he go on normal business trips to Hong Kong or Kuala Lumpur like other husbands.

"Well, I'm not complaining. I always get something nice when he comes back. He can get you something too if you like."

Thirty-seven years and I still can't tell if this daughter of mine is being serious or what was that word I learnt recently from *Reader's Digest*? Flaky? No. *Facetious*. Yes, Rachel was always facetious in the worst moments.

I continued to press her. When Ben is in Singapore, he barely gets home early enough from work to see his sons. How to practise their English? And how do you spend enough time with your husband? Rachel just scowled and I decided to hold my tongue because Rachel, unlike Ping, is made of the same fire as I am.

Or used to be.

The children think I'm a tyrant, always pushing them to excel and never letting them settle for slipshod work. Especially this Rachel. So smart, so gifted but the minute I turn my back, this girl would take any shortcut she could find. How she would fight me – every page on her Maths assessment book, every piece of vegetable on her dinner plate, every minute of piano practice.

My fiery tiger mother, Rachel had said to Ben when he heard for the first time that she had been quite the accomplished pianist as a young girl. They had been dating for almost a year before she finally decided to bring her British boyfriend home to meet us. According to her, I had been the reason behind the ten years of suffering she endured, running through scales over and over again while other children played outside, and missing birthday parties on weekends to perform at recitals. She claimed I was also the reason why she quit when she was sixteen.

I just smiled at Ben and held out the platter of chicken curry to him. He placed his hand over his stomach to decline, "I've had too much al–" but his bespectacled brown eyes met my narrowed ones. He took two more helpings.

My children think it is fire, always burning and furious at their backs, not allowing them to slip up or fall short.

But the truth is, the fire went out the night Shan-Shan died. What remains is steel — the kind forged in the crucible of mistakes and failures. Steel, not for blazing a trail, but for staying the course with unbending will to ensure the past will not repeat itself.

My girls will have to know so they, especially Ping, will not make the same mistakes as I. But how do I tell them that their ma had been selfish and failed her sister, her only *Mei-Mei*, and how it was too late when –

"Por-Por…"

I shake my head and keep my trembling hands under the kitchen table.

"Por-Por, can I have a Yakult?" Those big brown eyes are now fixed on me, peering over the edge of the kitchen table.

Rachel frowns. "Alex, *jiang hua yu.*"

"But I'm asking Por-Por and I speak in English to Por-Por." He glibly replies to his mother in Chinese and turns his attention back to me. I'm reaching for the handle of the refrigerator door even before he utters sweetly, "Please, Por-Por?"

Before he runs out of the kitchen with his bottle of grape-flavoured Yakult, he turns and says with a dimpled grin, "*Xie xie,* Por-Por."

I smile and then laugh out loud when I catch the disgruntled expression on Rachel's face.

"This boy," Rachel sighs. "And you," she continues sternly.

It's karma, I want to say. The number of times she had ruined her appetite at Sunday night dinners with Keong's family by sneaking sweets from her uncle. Oh, and that pink and yellow *masak* tea-set she had pestered me to buy every time we passed the provision store downstairs. She returned home one evening from a stroll with her *ah kong*, swinging a red plastic bag with the tea-set inside. The grin on my father-in-law's face disappeared quickly when he saw my narrowed eyes and pursed lips. "She asked me to buy one."

Rachel walks over to the sink in front of the wide kitchen windows. As she reaches for a plate from the dish rack, she pauses when she sees the bowl of fish-balls next to it. She quickly pops one fish-ball into her mouth then giggles when she catches my eye. Hand over mouth, she mumbles, "One only *lah*, Ma."

A hand, cold and strong, grabs my heart. And tightens. I cannot breathe. She's standing by the window, sneaking bites of the *you tiao* Ma made as a rare treat for us. Her mouth is full of the hot bread, eyes dancing above her small pale hand. *Shh, don't tell Ma, one piece only.*

Then the kitchen windows are wide open, an overturned stool, Ma on the floor crying her name over and over –

I startle at the soft hand on my arm and a sweet, flowery scent pulls me out of the daze. Rachel's perfume. She's worn this fragrance since she was in university. I pull my arm away. "I'm okay *lah*. Just a bit of headache. I'll take Panadol later."

Forty-eight years and still the image of that grey dawn in my mother's kitchen is as real as this Saturday afternoon in my kitchen with my daughter. *Rachel*. Not Shan-Shan.

Forty-eight years has also taught me how to shut the memory and guilt away. I swallow hard and as calmly as I can, I ask, "So, what did you talk to Ping about?"

"Not much. She had a class so she had to go. There's no space on the stove. I need to blanch the *chye sim*."

"The *tau yew bak* is done. Put it next to the kettle. Make sure you use the cork thing. She doesn't even want to talk to you? Why?"

Rachel lifts the claypot off the stove with a pair of oven-mittens.

"Rachel, the cork. The pot is very hot. If you place it directly on the —"

"I know, Ma. I heard you." A flash of irritation crosses her face as she sets the pot back on the stove and pulls out a round corkboard from the drawer below the stove.

"So, why doesn't she want to talk to you?"

Rachel's voice is muffled as she bends over the drawer again. "Can I use this pot? *Aiya*, Ma, she's just really busy. Some new project."

"Not that one. Use the smaller one. The one with the red handle. What project?"

"Science?" Rachel lifts her hands and laughs.

If it wasn't for the way Rachel could laughingly soothe any tension and nod sympathetically to the laments of both sides, my oldest daughter and I would probably have stopped talking to each other a long time ago. But now, I'm irritated. It's so hard to hold on to a train of thought lately, and this ha-ha-ha attitude of hers doesn't help.

"Relax, Ma. Jie is fine. She's just busy, and when she's busy, you know her…"

But I don't know her. I thought I did; my firstborn, my oldest daughter who never had to be told twice to help out with the housework, and who declared after reading a book about Marie Curie when she was eight-years-old that she was going to be a scientist.

I thought I knew her because she was me.

Like Ping, I was an excellent student. My form teacher in junior college said I would definitely do well enough in my A-Levels to get into a university and encouraged me to try for a scholarship to Nan Da. Like Ping, I also had a younger sister who thought the world of me, and a mother who had big expectations of me.

But unlike Ping, disappointing them did not cost her everything.

I watch Rachel dip the sieve of vegetables over and over again into the pot of boiling water. She is saying something, something about a holiday she wants to take with Ben next month, but the mellow rhythm of her chatter is just background noise to another voice I hear.

There should be two daughters, not one.

They were the first words Ma had uttered after we returned from the columbarium and I was standing at the stove, reheating some soup.

There should be two sisters, not one.

Rachel fishes out the last of the vegetables from the pot and turns the fire off. There is a plate of wantons I had fried earlier sitting next to the stove. She reaches for a piece and her lips curve into a smile of pleasure as she chews. No more of that sullen, dark anger she had carried with her the first year after Ping left for America, but it's been almost twenty years. Maybe she's forgotten the feeling of abandonment. And resentment. That we had given everything to Ping's education and left little for hers.

She tells friends she's proud of her big sister. When I hear her say that, I search for traces of bitterness, the guilt churning in me like a bad stomach-ache, but there is none. That's the way Rachel has always been – quick to anger but also quick to love and forgive. Rachel's generosity and adoration of her *jie-jie* makes me even more upset at Ping.

Don't get me wrong. I am proud and have always been proud of Ping's accomplishments – every *ting xie* and spelling test, and every report card with its column of A's. When I attended their school's annual awards ceremony where Ping would sweep the Science and Mathematics prizes, teachers and parents would come up to me and say, "You're Deborah Koh's mother!" My heart would swell to the point where it felt like it was hurting, but I am not *haolian* like Keong's sister, Judy, whose children's achievements did not warrant the kind of bragging she did. Second prize in some National Day art competition and one mention in the Marine Parade GRC newsletter. Very good—Danielle, sure can get into Harvard.

I don't have to fish for compliments like Judy. People tell me all the time I must be so proud, my daughter the scientist, writing big important papers and speaking at conferences. When Ping won the scholarship to go to America for university, I was proud but also scared. It's okay, I told myself, you've raised her well, she will come back and she will remember her family, her roots – *yin shui shi yuan*. But after MIT, she said Stanford has a place for her and Stanford is where she's been ever since. I should have known better. This oldest daughter of mine has never done anything in a half-past-six way. Now she's *Dr Deborah Koh Hwee Peng*, one of the youngest associate professors in the Stanford Bioengineering department.

When people tell me what a brilliant daughter I have, I smile and say nothing so they think, "This Fen, always so modest and humble." Smiling to acknowledge my daughter's achievements hides the disappointment that has sat in my heart since she decided to make San Francisco her home. And the disappointment grows every time we celebrate a birthday or eat reunion dinner and her chair at the dining table is empty.

Like tonight. Her father will be sixty-eight. Keong's eyesight has not failed him on his dawn route driving the first passengers in his taxi and he still swims twenty laps every Saturday morning at the neighbourhood public pool. He still has a full head of hair, but there are more greys in it now. Last week, he tried to fix the hinge on our bedroom door, but he had difficulty holding the screwdriver tight enough to turn the tiny screws. He had to wait till Jon came home to help him.

Jon is a good boy. My mother-in-law had crowed with such joy when she heard she was finally going to have a grandson. For a moment, I forgot my anxieties about raising a boy. Then a cold fear crept into my heart. What did I know about raising a good man? With Ping and Rachel, there was no question I would make good women and good daughters out of them because I am both. But a son.

One thing I had been sure though, my daughters would be worth as much as my son. They would have their place and they would not be forgotten or overlooked. Why should they? Girls are pillars of the family — pillars of the family they are born into and pillars of the family they raise. Sons carry the family name into another family they will build without you. In my mother's last days, I was the one who sweated over the hot stove to make fish congee and loquat soup. I was the one who fed each spoonful through my mother's thin cracked lips and rubbed *feng you* into her aching joints.

However, I was not the one who led the funeral procession holding Ma's portrait. Nor did I cry and wail so loudly that all the relatives were impressed by my filiality. No, my brothers did all those so my daughters and I were free to fold stacks of powdery, gold-stamped papers into ingots for Ma to spend in the afterlife, and clean up after the groups of mourners.

I look over at Rachel, who sits at the kitchen table, frowning at her phone. "Why? What happened?"

"Ben might be late to dinner. He has a couple more things to do in the office."

"Office? It's Saturday! And his father-in-law's birthday," I add for good measure. Rachel doesn't look up from her phone as her fingers tap on the screen. "Rachel."

"Ma, I'm dealing with this," she says without looking up.

What kind of man goes into work on a Saturday and then says he has to stay late? A man up to no good, that kind of man. I frown as I look down at the green plastic chopping board in my hand. What was I going to do with this? Rachel has already done the vegetables. The mushrooms? No, those have already gone into the stew.

"He has to finish some work before his trip next week," Rachel says. Her words are hurried. The faster she speaks, the less she has to explain. "His boss thinks highly of him, so he keeps adding these projects. He has to go to Switzerland next week because of this big client."

Isn't this the second time this month he has to go to Switzerland? The last time he went, he travelled with that blonde Australian lady from his department who wears too much lipstick. I remember her because she drank so much at their Christmas party last year at their place, Ben's friends had to carry her out to the taxi. Monica. Even her name suggests she's up to no good. When Rachel and I were replenishing the fruit platter in the kitchen, I pointed out that Monica's breasts were spilling out of her red dress, and how she would brush them against the arm of the guy she was talking to, Ben included. Rachel just laughed, cupped her own breasts and said, "Don't worry, Ben's only interested in these." My daughter is too confident for her own good.

"Remember Aunty Indra's daughter," I tapped Rachel on the back of her hand. She pulled her hand away quickly as if my touch had stung and flicked her hair over her shoulder.

"*Tch*, don't think so much, Ma," she said with a light laugh. "Will go crazy one."

Yah, like Shanthi who didn't think so much about her husband's frequent business trips and then what happened? Five years into their marriage, Shanthi found out he had a second family in Mumbai. You really never know with these men. The richer they are, the less they need you.

I know these *ah sia kias*. Their houses in Bukit Timah on streets named after British royalty, the chauffeur-driven cars that would come to pick them up after school and the way they would grin and leer at Shan-Shan as she handed them their bowl of noodles and change. I made her swap duties with our youngest brother. Let Ah-Di collect money and serve the noodles while she stayed in the back to wash the dishes. Still, that didn't stop those *hao se* boys and their crazy hormones from talking to her when she went to use the toilet behind the school canteen.

Something bites into my hand. I look down and see it, white and clenched around the edge of the chopping board. I set the board down on the table and reach for a knife. I look around for the scallions and see none. I just washed them, right? They're supposed in be in the blue basket next to the sink. Did Ah-Di move them? Or Shan-Shan? Where's Shan-Shan? Did she go out to use the toilet again? I need to find her, need to stop her from looking for those boys.

I swing around, hands flailing, clutching at air.

"Ma! What are you doing?" A hand grabs my shoulder. I brush the hand away and take a deep breath. Something savoury is cooking, peppery with hints of star anise and cloves.

Tau yew bak. It is Saturday, twenty-sixth of May and it's Keong's birthday. I walk over to the claypot sitting on the counter next to the stove. I'm making *tau yew bak* for Keong's birthday. Rachel and her family, and Jon and his new girlfriend are coming to dinner. Ping is not coming. She's in America. Dinner is at six o'clock. The stew needs to simmer for at least an hour and a half. Why isn't it on the stove?

It isn't the loud shatter of the claypot as it hits the floor that pulls me out of the fog. It's the searing white-hot pain that courses through my hands and legs. Dark broth and pieces of meat, mushrooms and garlic are splattered all over the kitchen floor. I stumble forward and someone cries, "Don't move!" Broken ceramic pieces crunch under my feet. Another flash of pain ripples through me. I am being carried and helped onto a chair. That same voice says "Oh my god, oh my god!" over and over again as a damp cloth is patted gently all over my limbs. There's a child crying, "*Por-Por, Por-Por.*"

A cool, soft hand brushes the hair off my forehead and a pair of eyes, bright with tears, searches my face anxiously. I reach out, ignoring the throbbing pain in my arms, and press my hands to her soft, pale cheeks. I close my eyes. Rachel, not Shan-Shan.

KEVIN NICHOLAS WONG

We're in This Together

FOR DUANE

I tell them we should have brought umbrellas, peering out of the taxi on the way over. One must always be prepared for the worst-case scenario – being gay, things almost never go your way here, unless you're blessed with a symmetrical porcelain face, plated cheekbones, and a high metabolism (or make up for it with a jacked-up body).Pins of rainwater fall daintily against the windowpane, preceding a kind of weather that necessitates curling up in bed with the latest Oprah Book Club selection, or cuddling with a pencil limbed man you just met on Grindr, or, if you're lucky, both.

My friends all laugh and click their tongues, their sassy Morse code. I look over at the taxi uncle, wanting to apologise. His old, soppy face is clenched, his eyes tiny globes dipped in black oil, tilting upwards on a fixed, intolerant axis. He had that same fine-tuned look as we made our grand entrance, the scene playing out like those cartoons depicting an infinite number of clowns trying to fit into a toy car, exaggerated in our gestures and voices, muffling the Faye Wong song playing on the radio before he loudly asked where we were going.

One of them scolds, *This Gabriel, such a worrywart, so uptight, must loosen you up good.* The others roar like hyenas hungry for meat; our friendship was built on similar hunting grounds, always chasing the next high, that lush, tropical 'Insta-worthy' life. We would spend weekends by the rooftop pool at Pat's upscale apartment in town, basking in the sun in our skimpy trunks getting that rich, rich tan; or having brunch at a new swanky café decorated with pastel walls and potted plants birthing origami leaves, where you paid fifteen dollars for avocado toast. Of course, these adventures had to be captured on our phones, posing for the thousands of followers we had on Instagram. Their virtual hearts had meaning, like we had accomplished some awe-inspiring feat, even if it was hard to pinpoint exactly what that was.

Fingers from behind drum buoyantly on my shoulder. Together with the tiptoes of soft rain from outside, the vibrations amplify the anticipation of what's to come. *You know how they say it never rains on National Day?* Pat whispers. *Pink Dot's the same, but with a slight difference.* In our folklore, Section 377A of the Penal Code has been the legendary monster to vanquish, criminalizing sex between men still to this day, and each year, twenty-thousand people huddle in a circle at Hong Lim Park calling for our freedom to love. But it is unlikely that we will see change in our lifetime; to me, visibility without action is only to our detriment, prey exposing our position to a predator.

Because this is my first time attending Pink Dot (after 10 long years since its inception, horrible me!), my friends help to paint a picture. Moody grey skies always colour the park at first, hovering menacingly like the security guards deployed around the perimeter for what is meant to be a celebration, not something to be feared (but as "fear mongering" gays, we are driven to love it; we live for drama and theatrics). *Not to worry*, they say, the clouds will soon sail past, dirty rags in the sky drifting away like a watchful eye from above, a stern warning that we mustn't overstep our boundaries.

You have this one day, but beyond that, there will be storms and rain.

They can't see me from the back, but I catch myself in the side mirror sulking, my smudged reflection garbled and incomplete. I am wondering how I ever got here, agreeing to this excursion out into the world, exposed, wearing pink for everyone to see. I can't even bear to look at the taxi uncle again, his sour-grout frown sprinkled with ash. Inside, we can take him, the folds of his belly playing peek-a-boo with the overlytight buttoned shirt he has on, it's four against one. But outside, we are the minority.

We alight the vehicle, almost dancing, oblivious to the snide glances of harsh faces that linger outside the park, as Singaporeans do when they see a crowd. People regard us the way we look at migrant construction workers and maids who flood the blanched, time-frozen halls of Lucky Plaza on weekends – as if a vacuum is lodged in our throats, pulling the half-bitten crescents of our eyebrows and the edges of our thin mouths downwards into a pained, sick expression. But we could choose not to be judged this way, we could easily assimilate with the straight working man's crowd, correcting our gait to walk in short, controlled steps, in attires of inoffensive white, black, and blue; and sometimes I still think it might be better – to stay in line.

I stand there in my stolidness, lurching behind the rest trying to hide like a shy, awkward child who chews on his fingernails. Thirty-four, considered over-the-hill by most freewheeling homosexuals, and I still hadn't grown up, unsure of myself as ever, needing someone to hold onto.

For a time, Leonard was that someone, an unusual young man riddled with contradictions. He was only twenty-two, and yet his Spotify playlist was a jukebox of songs from the age of vinyl, his favourite artist Aretha Franklin. Once on the way back from watching a movie, I accidentally stepped on an unfortunate snail lying prone on the pavement; Leonard's face turned into babyish marshmallow as he bent down to observe the crushed animal, its shell spread open like a rose. *It doesn't have a home anymore, all gone*, he said guilelessly. That same sweet voice had turned impish that same evening as we made love to one another in the shadowy dwells of a gay bathhouse, blended within the walls of Clarke Quay like skin-coloured bandages, daring me to fuck him harder. His body was fibreglass whenever I had my arms around him, strong and able; underneath his clothes was a man, yet he chose to cover it up with crystals, frills, and fur. Those contradictions made life more interesting, like opening a door to find another one right behind it.

We were loitering outside the local Hard Rock Cafe the first time we met, after the last song was played. Situated in the heart of Orchard Road, the rock-and-roll restaurant would turn into a dance floor on weekends after ten, where gay disco nights were held every month. Green and purple lights would encircle the room like a flock of migrating birds and cool mist showered down from fog machines attached to the ceiling, creating a miniature aurora borealis just for us.

What caught my attention was Leonard's unusual lack of hair. There were no noticeable grains of stubble on his slick golden skin, which seemed to sparkle under the surrounding lamplight; even his eyebrows were missing. And yet he didn't look strange or funny without them. Perhaps it was the way he moved, tipping his head slightly upwards, the gentle sway of his hips, looking forward, never breaking his line of sight. In fact, he looked settled within himself, like those missing parts we tend to associate with being normal were parts of his machine, fully operational.

I couldn't help but look over as he settled a few feet away from me, his boisterous laughter sending little earthquakes down my gut. Under the cloak of evening, Leonard shone brightly, wearing a cropped flannel shirt that barely covered his knightly chest and fishnets dusted in tinsel; he was a comet blasting through the universe, too quick for the rest of us to catch up. I wanted to get to know him, but the words didn't follow. What came was an unspoken prayer, invisible, like a quiet unassuming breeze, never wanting to generate more wind than required.

What are you staring at?

Nothing.

Don't "nothing" me, I know you.

Have we met?

I'm the one that kissed you earlier, silly boy.

It was only then I noticed the faint streaks of makeup on his face. I had only been a casual spectator when drag queens performed at the club between DJ sets, like a foreign episode of *RuPaul's Drag Race,* where we'd fawn over a bottle of wine through an impenetrable glass screen. But earlier that evening, I found myself in the front row of the drunk whistling audience, pulled into the spotlight by what I later realised was a female-presenting Leonard. We were standing on a so-called stage, a flimsy raised platform just wide enough to take five good steps across each way. It wasn't that our drag queens weren't talented, they just didn't have the space to do their numbers. But Leonard didn't need it. He was rooted firmly in one spot, cocooned in a floor length beaded gown, mouthing (no, *embodying*) the words to a slowed down version of Cher's "The Shoop Shoop Song," only leaning forward to kiss me at the end of it. I felt the cold shiver under my skin as he shoved me back into the audience with one hand and ripped the bottom of his dress with the other to reveal a leotard, dancing seamlessly to the next up-tempo number. Only in this black square, smaller than the ballroom we were watching from, could those queens exist, filling up the void with as much colour and glitter as possible; outside, they were vampires, allergic to the light.

A club, a stage, a park – we had to be sequestered in order to survive. *Beyond these four walls, who were we? Or better yet, who were we allowed to be?* I often wondered.

Dragging his feet against the cruddy asphalt, he stepped even closer, our eyes meeting, bodies edging like the folded cheeks of a hearty peach. The crimson glow from the Hard Rock Cafe sign traced the outline of him, accentuating a devilish aura that he always possessed.

Do you want to fool around?

I'm not into that sort of thing, sorry.

Okay Mister, how about supper?

His face was stone, unflinching. He shifted his hand onto his hip, one arm akimbo, as if he had planned it, a stage direction to push the narrative forward because I didn't have the nerve. Looking back, his spark, the trepidation between comfort and risk, like each time you board a plane, is something I miss.

*

We arrive at Hong Lim Park at a respectable hour, fourish in the afternoon. Calling it a park is an act of self-aggrandisement, akin to calling a matchstick a bonfire. It is simply an empty field plopped randomly in the middle of Chinatown, a sole patch of burnt green amongst the sterile office buildings with windows the colour of dark water. There is a circular stage built in the front, perfect for an outdoor concert but never so used (the police would be overwhelmed by the influx of complaints). Instead, the space is used for peaceful rallies, the only place in Singapore where they're legal.

Applause fizzles like a frying pan without enough oil. The host on stage, a heavyset man with pepperish hair and poorly made angel wings on his back already shedding feathers, yells into the loudhailer he is holding; he sounds like he's just stubbed his toe. *Come on everyone, you can be louder than that!* The crowd squeezes out an unenthusiastic angry cheer, as if we are in a classroom greeting a teacher we must tolerate. A signpost outside the park reads "Speaker's Corner," and that's exactly what it is: a corner, a sliver of a wedge, a whisper that will be competing with and instantaneously lost to the noise of the traffic outside, even if we raise our voices.

Oh my gosh, can they faster or not? I'm melting here! Marcus cries out, holding one of those handheld folding fans trying to cool himself. The hand fan is as wide as a plate, unnecessarily ostentatious with lacklustre wind power. His bee-like nasal voice downplays his masculinity; he is Super Mario on steroids, complete with the moustache.

We get it, you're hot. There's no need to show off, Pat says with a condescending drawl that gives away his age. He is the oldest amongst us but doesn't look it, with a wrinkle-free face thanks to the rewinding wonders of Botox (being friends with a dermatologist has its perks, although Pat tells me I still have a good two years before considering a visit).

Shut it, Marcus. You're the one practically wearing half a shirt, I hiss.

Say people, say yourself, you whore!

We laugh like school kids who share a giddy, secret language. The queers around us are staring; it happens. There's always a certain *je ne sais quoi* whenever the group gets together, the way heads turn minutely like hands of a clock, eyes lingering for a tad too long, different from the regular passer-by – the look of shock, jealousy, and admiration all at the same time. Though none of us are willing to admit it, we *are* showing off, boasting our bronzed chiselled bodies carved out from hours at the gym, wearing shirts we would never admit might be straitjackets. The gays here search for the sharp curve of muscle before anything else. I always thought that if I could get those six-pack abs, finally climbing the raised ladder that they resemble, that I would be greeted with some triumphant reward. But now that I've reached the figurative peak, the view is pretty much the same, and I have no one to share it with, besides my so-called friends, perpetually looking somewhere else.

The clouds are withering beards in the distance, far away now. The sun has grown tired, shrinking into a pale beige dot, seeking shelter behind the glass towers surrounding the area, though the heat is still inescapable. You can detect the brimming sizzle in the air if you look hard enough. The stereotypical dance music is loud but obnoxious. No one around us is dancing. We're all just limp, sweaty figures, waiting to be let in.

Waiting, we're always waiting, in this perpetual state of queueing, rarely taking the time to relish a moment, even when it calls out to us so effervescently. Something like the pure expression of love can pass you by in an instant, just as how people always say when conversation runs thin: *Can you believe how fast the year has gone by?*

I was reminded of such a passing when the inkling of love slipped through my inexperienced hands, when the possibility of a future together, of day-to-day domestic mundanity, seemed within reach. Leonard and I had booked a 'stay-cation' to celebrate our three-month anniversary, the only time we could be alone. Before this, we settled for afternoon meals and casual strolls along the veined routes of Neil Road and Duxton Hill lined with antiquated shophouses converted into an alternate shuffle between shoddy Korean barbecue joints and intentionally darkened bars, a safe haven for the queers.

When will we ever have a place like this? Leonard sang longingly. It was one of those modern service apartments that came furnished with everything one needs for a home – including a stainless-steel fridge amidst a decent sized kitchen, and even a washer and dryer stacked atop each other beside it, all of which communicated an unsettling but exciting permanence, like the prickly feeling of falling off your bed even though you're nowhere near the edge.

Once I reach thirty-five, I guess, I said. *You too, that's the rule for us, you know. Since we can't get married here.*

That's HDB, government owned. Different. We can't spend our lives waiting for things to be handed to us. And have you seen the new showroom models lately? Civil servants really have no taste.

His body was facing the glass bay windows which overlooked the Marina Bay waterfront, his expression sanguine, looking past the crystalline skyline and into the distant blue yonder, his eyes gleaming like fresh water from a spring; I had a feeling he wasn't just talking about the apartment.

Maybe one day, in the blank, cloudless future he was trying to picture, there would be a place for us, just maybe.

We spent most of our time huddling in bed after sex, watching videos from my laptop, exchanging our lives, telling our stories through other people, the role models who shaped us, for in them, we could find ourselves; there wasn't anyone like us then. Our favourite Madonna concert was *Who's That Girl*, not *Blond Ambition*, with the iconic conical bra (the only difference was I had watched them on laser disc, while he, the millennial, stumbled across clips on YouTube).

I always wanted to be the boy dancing next to her during the opening number; he wanted to be Madonna.

Why?

Well, who wants to be the backup dancer? Wouldn't you rather be the star?

Beyond the confines of the apartment, there were excursions to get groceries to test out hip Bon Appetit recipes and making the necessary trips to the indoor gym. While I did the usual dumbbell routine, Leonard had to be different. After finishing my last set, I found him sitting by the empty corner in a most peculiar position, his legs split wide open forming an almost parallel line to the floor, a wishbone on the cusp of breaking apart. His chest was touching the ground, his head floating just above, looking like a turtle coming out of its shell.

My gaze shifted to his feet, which were incongruously sparkling. He had on red bedazzled heels, like the ruby slippers from *The Wizard of Oz*, but a grown-up version, if Dorothy had grown up to become a stripper still stuck in Kansas; the spiked acrylic ends of the heels could easily puncture a tire. I imagined the insides of my cheeks to be like them, resplendent, shining brightly behind a dull layer of nude. We were trains running in opposite directions – one headed to Pasir Ris, the other to Joo Koon – extreme ends of the island that made our worlds seem separate, two things that shouldn't go together, but did. In those three days, without the rest of the world watching, anything seemed possible.

*

Over here lads!

Sandy waves from the other side of the barricade, an albino giraffe amongst the less endowed animals in this zoo. Himself, Luca, and Robert had arrived early to establish the base (we called them the *ang moh* contingent, dividing our clique between East and West), and ours by extension, slipping a tarp mat underneath the metal gates to save us a seat inside the already crowded park. This separation is even more pronounced now; they haven't been able to enter ever since the new rule. Gantries had to be set up, identification was now needed to enter.

They start handing over bottles of wine and gin with tonic pre-mixed in Dasani bottles masquerading as water, their hands reaching over the barriers as if they weren't there. One of the *ang mohs* starts to sing, and the other two steadfastly join him without missing a beat, their deep burly voices amalgamating into one bellowing foghorn.

Will you join in our crusade?

Who will be strong and stand with me?

Somewhere beyond the barricade, is there a world you long to see?

The rest of us just observe while pouring each other a drink, cheering as they conclude the short number with a resounding baritone. Perhaps they didn't know it, but I did. *Les Misérables*, the musical; but why didn't I sing along? I figured it was a cultural thing. Westerners, they are like sliced white bread, soft and supple, while we are the hardened brown toast; Singaporeans do not know how to put on a show. We are the awkward audience members pulled up onto the stage by the entertainers, not knowing what to do after being thrust into the spotlight, with our effete limbs trembling.

We don't even know how to pull off a Pride event.

Brighton Pride on the other hand is a cynosure of sheer positivity; I was there a year ago on a solo trip across England. The event warrants such prestige, it is important enough for the entire main street to be closed off for the marching parade. Open-top buses saunter down the road –

one carrying an all-male gay chorus decked in tuxedo jackets and skin-tight shorts singing *I'm Coming Out*; the next filled with half naked fellows (and the occasional lady) blowing kisses at you. People would stop to watch the dizzying formation go by, queers were everywhere you looked, teeming. If not standing on the sidewalk, throngs of lively supporters would be on bus shelters and rooftops, their legs dangling from wooden scaffoldings of an Italianate building under renovation, waving their hands at you like a coloured pinwheel spinning continuously.

A man actually came up to me on this busy street and complimented the Spice Girls T-shirt I had on that day. He had a funnel-shaped nose and friendly blue eyes, his relaxed open frame welcoming the air that passed easily between us. I remember his hand on my shoulder the entire time we were talking, like we had known each other for years. You couldn't help but to absorb it, accept this love – yes, it *was* love – and say a meagre little thank you.

Brighton was a moving kaleidoscope, pieced together like a pattern of a butterfly's wing zoomed in, the shifting shades of colour from clothes to skin. But back home, we are somehow blinded by something in the Singaporean air – some phantom malleable force that builds invisible walls around us, while pressing mercilessly down on our bodies, disrupting our optic nerves; looking at the same subject, all we see is a nasty flying bug.

It happened one malaise of an afternoon, one where sweat beaded on your skin before even stepping out of the house, a burning premonition that bad things would happen. We agreed to meet at Saveur, after having not seen or spoken to each other in a week. An array of discarded street signs plastered the main wall of the cafe, filament bulbs hung on wires from the ceiling which gave a yellowish manila shade to the room, like we were being transported back to a different time and place. It was where Leonard and I had our first date, and in many ways, seemed like it. We were careful and methodical with short bursts of pleasantries, not wanting to offend one another as we tangoed through our orders with the waiter.

Leonard kept dragging his fork against the plate while waiting for our food, his lips scrunched up in a knot, his whole body stiff, as though prepared to turn and check if anyone was behind him. The past few months had already been an escalation. Leonard had started to become restless. He had been kicked out of his parents' home after they found pictures of him online in drag; he had stopped taking off his makeup before meeting me for suppers; he even had volunteered to write articles for various LGBT organisations, with lambasting headlines bordering on sedition: *'We're Here, We're Queer: The Continual Erasure of Gay Culture in Singapore. Who Is to Blame?'* He was undergoing a metamorphosis, shedding the feathered coat that could once concomitantly sting and make me feel protected; now he was an effigy of stone, not the Leonard I once knew.

What do you see in those boys? They're nothing but 'body', no brains.

He couldn't help glaring at the ignition of messages on my phone which lit up like a distress signal, all from the group text chain I recently formed with Pat and Marcus. In some way, I too had come into my own, connecting with other similarly built men on Instagram who didn't take themselves too seriously. I didn't have to prove myself around them. I was enough.

You're being mean.

I'm only speaking the truth. They're what's wrong with society today.

Not everything has to be a crusade. You just seem angry all the time now. What's happened to you, Leonard?

Finally, he placed his fork delicately onto the linen covered table, clasping his hands together and drawing them towards his chin at an old man's pace, the emptiness between us giving way like a sinkhole on a quiet ordinary street.

One day, very soon, you'll leave me, he said. *Because you're afraid. Someday that fear will be too much for you.*

His pronunciation of words loosened. An accent had begun to form, the expressive, uncensored mix that revealed his Malay and Filipino heritage. I suddenly had the image of Imelda Marcos in my head, having recently watched a documentary about her. Everything about the woman was for show, her puffer-fish face caked with makeup, in a structured dress with arched sleeves fitted like armour, shielding her from persecution after decades of pilfering from the Philippine people. Something the former First Lady said in the film stuck with me, so coolly, without any hesitation to the cameras, unaware how fractured and tired she looked: *Perception is real, and the truth is not.*

I wasn't living my truth then, nor have I ever; I haven't learnt how to. But wasn't it more exhausting having to keep proving who you really were?

I won't. Even in those two simple words, my voice had skidded and slipped into a childlike tune.

Then why are you so afraid?

I am not. I just don't want that kind of attention.

You forget that I'm here. We're in this together. Right?

He tried to clasp my hand then, but I shook his grip off like an annoying housefly, like something that shouldn't be there. Initially I felt that tinge of guilt, painfully slipping down my gut like swallowing thick cod liver oil. I told him I was sorry, but the words were translucent; I wasn't sorry. Leonard dipped his head sheepishly, with his steely eyes constantly aimed at me, unwavering, just like Imelda's, their minds long made up on who was right and who was wrong.

We were two trains again at opposing sides of the station, counting down in that momentary dreadful stillness, before finally setting off on our own.

*

From a distance, I spot them, a group of drag queens coming towards us. They look so different in the daytime, like spotting mouse deer in the depleting Singaporean wild. They flap about delicately in figure-hugging gowns, brushing and consuming the grass beneath them. Their doll faces, thick and intricately drawn on, bear weighty grimaces as they float through the crowd, waddling in six-inch heels hidden behind the peplum tails that fan out at the bottom, tolerating the pain and the heat.

A gruff voice echoes by my ear, like a stranger creeping from behind harbouring evil intentions. There are two of them, a man and a woman in their early twenties. The man has an insignificant flat face which bears an unbothered bovine expression; while the woman, with dead raisin eyes hidden behind her straw-coloured fringe, is just tall enough for her head to rest neatly on the nook of his shoulder. But both boast a certain callousness, dragging their feet on flip flops whilst leaning back slightly as though cushions are pressed behind them. Hell, their shirts aren't even pink, just hints of it on a badly printed logo, probably plucking something they already had in their closets.

The man elbows the woman using the near empty bottle of beer he is holding. She jumps as if being awakened from sleep. *Ha! See those chao ah guas. They do better makeup than you leh.* His insult slaps me across the face, my cheeks burning with nostalgia: the meek little boy that once was, with virginal white socks hiked up to his knees being called that derogatory term in primary school, along with the other usual suspects *'sissy'* and *'faggot'* in between classes. The woman laughs on command, cackling, like the Wicked Witch of the West who thinks she has it all figured out, looking down upon us feeble monkeys who were less than. If only grown-up Dorothy with the stripper heels could show them.

I call out to the two nuisances, but they don't hear me, bobbing off into the distance, becoming lost amid the other faceless people walking about the park. They will walk out unscathed, unchanged in their opinions about us, back into their straight, uncomplicated lives. A swirl of darkness grows into a fiery knuckle duster in my chest, breaking down a wall I had built against the naysayers – on the other side stands Leonard and the drag queens fighting to be themselves. A droplet of rain grazes my arm, then another on my forehead, then nothing. I look up. The blazing sun has reappeared, its crown top peeking out from the passing rain cloud that spreads out thinly like a moustache. The pearly light desaturates the pink from the already solemn crowd; like a dissipating Asian flush from my own cheeks, all of this will be gone tomorrow, as if something to be cleansed from.

The drag queens saunter off in the other direction, their arms linked together in a chain, forging a bond that is innately familial. In a sea of thousands, I suddenly feel so alone. I search for Leonard's face amongst the group, hoping he is there. I want to tell him I'm sorry, that I did not have the courage to speak out, stand up, and pick a side. But they're too far away now, and I still can't seem to find the words.

SUZANNE KAMATA

What Lurks Beneath

What Sophie had been most looking forward to about this summer was Chester. She was a dog person—or, more accurately, an animal person—and she had already decided that one day she would work with them. She had never had a pet herself—well, except for a goldfish adopted from an expatriate family that had moved back to Australia. Her mom liked to travel, and her dad, a pro golfer, was always on tour. But one day, she would have a cat and a dog, and maybe a guinea pig. She'd been hoping to volunteer at Heart Tokushima, the animal rescue centre run by a Canadian woman and her husband, or maybe at the sea turtle museum down south in Hiwasa, but then there had been the pandemic, and Uncle Ted had died, and they'd had to come to South Carolina, so those plans had been postponed.

As soon as her mom had parked the rental car in front of her aunt's beach house, Sophie put her hearing aid back in one ear and hooked the speech processor of her cochlear implant over the other. She affixed the dutiful magnet to the side of her head and covered it with her hair. Now the world was noisy again. She climbed out of the car and inhaled the salty breeze coming off the Atlantic, which was just meters—no, *yards*—away. To her delight, she was immediately greeted by Chester. His tail wagged furiously, making his rump move as if he was doing a doggy hula dance. He slobbered all over her hand, then jumped up to lick her face.

"Down, Chester!" Aunt Parisa ordered.

Sophie's English was not so good, but she could understand that.

"Okay!" Sophie said, "Okay!" She made the sign with her right hand.

Aunt Parisa came over and slid her fingers under Chester's collar and pulled him off of her. She put her arms around Sophie. Sophie hugged her back. This was one of the things that she liked about America—the hugs. In Japan, she only ever got hugged by her mother. Not even her Japanese grandparents had embraced her like this, but it felt nice. Snug. Warm. Safe.

Another thing that Sophie loved about being in the U.S. was the invisibility. In Japan, especially in the tiny rural town where they lived, she stood out. Her mom, with her blonde hair and bright clothes, stood out more, of course, but she had grown up fitting in. Probably her twenty-two years as an insider had given her the confidence to venture out into the world. Anytime she got tired of being an outsider, a *gaijin*, she could just come back here and blend into the crowd. Sophie often suspected that her mother enjoyed her special status in Japan. Most of the time, she didn't even try to fit in. At special school ceremonies, for instance, when all of the other mothers wore black suits, she would go with mauve.

Sophie, however, got tired of being different. At the deaf school, everybody was deaf, everybody wore hearing aids, and most of the other students had cochlear implants as well. But Sophie was the only one with a Western mother. Her hair was lighter and wavier than the other girls, who mostly had straight black hair. And her body was curvier.

In America, however, her size was average. She was not super skinny, like the girls that she saw on the beach in Japan, and she was not fat, like some of the women she saw on the beach in South Carolina. Some of them had flesh that oozed out of their bikinis, but they didn't seem to care. Sophie envied them their ease, their comfort with their bodies. Well, she decided, this would be the summer when she stopped caring so much about how she looked. At least while they were in America, she would give it a rest.

*

The next morning, after her banana-mango smoothie, Sophie took off her hearing aid and speech processor, tucked her phone into her shorts pocket, and grabbed the leash. On cue, Chester immediately trotted up next to her and allowed her to clip the leash to his collar. They went out the door.

Sophie didn't wear her hearing aid because she thought she might want to plunge into the water for a swim. Water—even just one drop, she'd been told all her life—could damage the expensive device. And it was too valuable to leave wrapped in a towel on the beach while she went in. She could tell from watching Chester when someone or something made a sound.

They set off down the beach. It was pretty much deserted at this time of day, although there were others like her, out for an invigorating walk or jog. Some people came out early to look for shells.

Chester ambled along, nudging pieces of driftwood with his nose, snuffling at a dead fish, a strand of seaweed. Sophie breathed in the ocean air. Some people thought that deaf people could smell better than others, that the remaining senses accommodated for the lack of sound, but she didn't know if that was true or not. She had been deaf all of her life, so she didn't know any different.

A few yards down the beach, Chester's head jerked to the left as if someone had called his name. Sophie looked to see a young man with cinnamon skin and closely cropped hair sitting on a towel next to a boogie board. He raised his hand. She waved back. His mouth moved, but she couldn't hear what he was saying. He was probably speaking in English, so even if she could hear, she wouldn't have been able to understand him. She cupped her ear in a listening gesture and shrugged her shoulders. Then she waved and looked away, tugging Chester further down the beach.

By the time they came back, his towel had been abandoned. He was in the ocean, riding the waves. For a second, she considered jumping into the water and joining him, but she was too shy for that. Sophie watched him for a while, her hand held up like a visor. She would have waved to him again, but he didn't seem to notice her.

He was there again, the next morning, and the one after that. On the fourth, when they reached that point on the beach, Chester lunged toward the boy and barked. His tail began wagging furiously.

Sophie paused and turned her head. He was waving, and then he was getting up and jogging towards them. He was wearing long shorts with a fuchsia floral print. No shirt. So that's what they mean by a six-pack, Sophie thought, her gaze flickering over his abs. When he had gotten within six feet of her, he gave her a big grin. He had those perfect

American teeth—no gaps, no misalignments. He must have had braces.

"Hi," Sophie said. Then she held up a finger, indicating that he should wait, while she dug into her pocket for her phone and pulled up the app that she always used to communicate with her mother. She entered a message in Japanese. The app translated it into English: "My name is Sophie. I am deaf. I don't speak English." She turned the screen toward the boy and let him read it.

Sophie half-expected him to nod and walk away. Communication would be too much of a challenge, he might think. It was summer and maybe he just wanted everything to be easy, effortless. She would understand.

He looked at her with eyebrows raised, like a question, and reached for her phone. His mouth moved. It looked like he was saying, "Mei ai?"

She nodded, but first she changed the setting so that he could key in a response in English.

He took the phone and tapped the keys for a while. It gave her time to study the whorls of his ears, the little gold hoop piercing the left ear, and his long eyelashes.

When he handed back the phone, she read the words which had been automatically translated into Japanese: "I'm Dante. Good to meet you. Do you live here?"

"I'm here for the summer," she typed back. "I'm staying with my aunt. You?"

Chester snuffled his feet, then began sniffing his legs. Dante didn't seem to mind.

"I live here," he typed. "With my dad."

She gave him an inquiring look. Maybe it was none of her business, but she asked anyway. "What about your mom?"

Dante peered at the text on the screen and reached down and dug his fingers into Chester's fur, then gave him a nice, firm stroke on his back. Sophie noticed that the boy had firm, round biceps. He must lift weights. Chester's tail beat back and forth. He reached for the phone again.

"My parents divorced last year, so they don't live together."

Now, having sniffed everything in his vicinity, Chester seemed ready to get on with the walk. He moved away from Dante, and away from Sophie, tugging at the leash.

Sophie held on tight. She read Dante's text and nodded. "My parents don't really live together either. My dad is in Japan."

His hazel eyes got big. "Are you Japanese?"

"Half," she replied. She drew the side of her free hand down the centre of her face.

He chuckled. "We say, 'biracial.' I'm 'half,' too. My dad is black, but my mom is white."

Sophie nodded and wrapped the leash around her wrist. She typed, "My mom is white, too!"

As she stood waiting for Dante to tap in his response, Chester nudged her hip with his snout. He seemed to be telling her that he was ready to get a move on.

Dante handed back the phone. "Hey, it was nice meeting you, Sophie. I'll text you later, okay? It looks like your dog wants to go for his walk. I would go with you, but I'm meeting a friend."

Sophie nodded and smiled. She wasn't sure if she believed him. Maybe he was just trying to be nice, and now that he'd figured out that she didn't speak English, and that she was deaf, he'd decided she was too much trouble. But it was good to know that she could communicate if she had to. If she wanted to.

She felt like letting Chester off his leash just for a moment. He would go flying off, maybe bound into the water, and it would be an expression of the way she felt right then. But she knew that it was against the rules to let dogs run on the beach untethered. She jogged alongside him for a few yards, her bare feet leaving tracks in the wet sand.

That evening, Sophie put on an apron and helped Aunt Parisa prepare dinner. They were having vegetarian shish kebabs. Sophie threaded marinaded mushrooms and chunks of peppers and onions onto skewers, which were then loaded onto the grill on the deck. Uncle Ted, Sophie remembered, had loved burgers and steaks, but Aunt Parisa seemed to have stopped eating meat. Sophie popped an uncooked mushroom into her mouth. It tasted good—vinegary, with a touch of herbs.

Every now and then she checked her phone. There was a message from one of her friends in Japan. Sophie calculated the time difference in her head. What was Eri-chan doing up at four a.m., anyway? Her dad had sent a heart emoji in response to a selfie she'd sent earlier of her and Chester on the beach.

When the last of the vegetables had been skewered, Sophie washed her hands and took off the apron. Dinner was casual. They loaded up paper plates and sat at the table outside. There was just enough breeze to keep the flies away. Chester lay at her feet, eyeing her hopefully every now and again. She would slip him something at the end of the meal.

Everyone was talking between bites, but Sophie didn't try to keep up. She was happy to look out at the waves, at a few surfers straggling in from the water, at a couple of teenagers playing Frisbee further down the beach. She thought back to that boy she'd met earlier in the day. Dante.

She decided not to check her phone again until bedtime. A watched pot never boils, and all that. After dinner, she helped clean up and then watched TV on the wide screen in the living room with her brother and cousin. They were watching some Indian reality show. Of course, there were no Japanese subtitles, so Sophie could only guess what was going on.

Finally, after she had taken a shower and changed into her pyjamas, she picked up her phone and looked.

There was a new text from Dante, asking to be added as a "friend." She saw that he had figured out how to add the app, and how to activate the translation feature. A smile lit up her face.

"Hello, friend," she texted. "What's up?"

Almost immediately, little dots appeared indicating that he was typing his reply.

"Grilling with my dad. Now we're watching sports. You?"

"Grilling with my aunt. Watching reality TV. Dating in India, I guess." There seemed to have been a matchmaker, and young single people looking at photos.

"Hey, can I ask you something?" he texted.

"What?"

"How old are you?"

Yeah, that was important to know. It was always a little hard to tell how old a person of another race was. If he was twenty-five, or whatever, he was too old for her to hang out with. Or at least that's what her mother would say. If he was a lot younger, well, they could still be friends.

"Eighteen. I am in the third of high school." She knew that school started in August or September in the United States, but in Japan, everything began in April. They were in the midst of the academic year, on summer break. She and her brother would graduate in March. "How old are you?" she texted back.

"Nineteen. Just finished my first year at the College of Charleston. Pre-med."

Wow, he was going to be a doctor. He must be really smart. Sophie suddenly felt intimidated. She didn't know how to respond.

A few seconds later, another text popped up. "What are you doing tomorrow?"

What was she doing? "Taking the dog for a walk. Reading a book."

"Do you want to go body-boarding with me?"

She could do that, couldn't she? They wouldn't have to talk so much. They could just splash around, ride the waves. "Okay. What time shall we meet?"

"How about ten? Same place where we met today."

"Okay!" She added a happy face emoji with sunglasses.

*

When she met Dante the next morning, he waved, and then, with hands open at chest level, fingers pointing down, touched his knuckles together. He turned his fingers up, palms out toward her and pointed.

Sophie realized that he was greeting her in American Sign Language. An American Assistant Language Teacher had sometimes visited her English class in Japan. Instead of trying to teach the students to speak, she'd taught simple ASL signs. Sophie remembered this one: "How are you?"

She held her hand, palm facing her, in front of her face and moved it away from her body. "Good."

He pointed behind him to the two body boards laying on the beach. He'd prepared one for her, too.

"Okay?" He held up his fingers in the "okay" sign.

"Okay," she signed back.

Sophie had brought along a tote bag with a towel and bottled water. She spread the towel on the sand and stripped off her T-shirt and shorts so she was down to her one-piece bathing suit decorated with a Hawaiian floral print. She'd gotten it just for this trip. At school, when they had swimming, they were required to wear plain navy tank suits.

It wasn't good to be too showy. She would probably never wear it in Japan.

Dante's eyes travelled from her head to her toes and back up again. When she caught his eyes, he smiled.

She did a few stretches to limber up. Her dad was an athlete, and he had taught her to prepare for physical activities by touching her toes and swivelling her torso. Dante seemed amused. He just stood there, watching her, and when she was ready, he grabbed his body board and dashed into the surf.

It was colder than she expected, bringing up goosebumps on her arms. She waded out until she could crouch up to her neck and get used to the water. Dante was already on his board, paddling out to the swells. He glanced back from time to time, probably to make sure she hadn't disappeared on him. She had never gone surfing before, or even used a boogie board. She watched Dante to make sure she was doing everything right.

He held the board up in front of his chest, fell into a wave, and let it carry him to shore. She paddled out a bit further and found a wave of her own to ride. When she looked back at Dante, he was up on his knees on the board, and then he was flat on the board again, and spinning around. Oooh, tricky. She'd try that next.

After a few rides, Dante got onto his feet. The first time Sophie attempted that, she fell over. He came over, laughing, and reached out his hand. She gave him hers and he pulled her back up into a standing position. He raised his eyebrows and pointed his thumb toward shore. Sophie nodded. She was ready for a break.

They went to their towels. Sophie dried off and dug her phone out of her bag. "That was fun," she texted.

"First time?" he texted back.

She nodded. She ran a tongue over her lips tasting salt.

*

Sophie couldn't stop thinking about Dante's hands. He'd learned signs, just for her! Hardly anyone ever made the effort to learn sign language. Uncle Ted had tried, but most people preferred writing or texting, or just expected her to be able to read lips or have her mother interpret for her.

Well, if Dante was willing to try to learn a new language, so could she. Sophie decided that she would learn ten new words a day. The next morning, after a bowl of Raisin Bran, she took out a notebook, went out onto the deck, sat down at the table, and made a list:

summer

beach

sand

turtle

dolphin

surfing

hot

fish

ocean

She copied the words in English ten times each, and then she looked up the signs in ASL on YouTube. She was sitting at the table, her tablet propped in her front of her, fingers of one hand fluttering like waves over her other hand, which was in a fist.

She felt the boards vibrating under her feet and looked to see her mom stepping onto the deck with her mug of coffee.

"Good morning," she signed. "You woke up early."

Sophie nodded.

Her mom gestured to the notebook. "What are you doing?"

"I'm learning ASL." She repeated the sign with the fist and the fluttering fingers. "This is 'beach.'"

Her mom set her mug down and tried it out. "Beach," she said, finger waves splashing over the shore. "Good for you."

A warm glow infused Sophie. She knew that her parents expected more of her brother than they did of her. She wasn't under any pressure to get into college or get a good job. Sophie'd had to take an exam at the School for the Deaf in order to progress from junior high school to high school, but it had been more of a formality. Some deaf students who had gone to mainstream elementary and junior high schools came to the School for the Deaf in ninth grade because regular high schools were too difficult. If she had wanted to, she was pretty sure her parents would have allowed her to attend public school with hearing kids, but she was happy at the School for the Deaf. There were only twelve students in the high school, and they'd known each other from toddlerhood, so it was more like a family. They could communicate easily with each other, and they understood one another in ways that their biological family members did not.

It occurred to Sophie that there were deaf people in Charleston and on the Isle of Palms, too. Maybe there was a community centre somewhere where they gathered, or a class in ASL that she could take. She would have to look into that. For now, she practiced her new ten words until she had memorized them, then grabbed the leash and waited for Chester to trot up to her. She had a feeling that he was looking forward to seeing Dante almost as much as she was.

The following day, Sophie's mom left to spend a couple of days in Columbia with her grandparents. Sophie watched from the window as she got into the rental car and drove away. She had made a list of all the things that she would miss if she didn't go back to Japan:

> *Tokushima ramen*
>
> *Awa Odori Festival*
>
> *Manga*
>
> *Monkey sightings*
>
> *Her dad*
>
> *Her friends*

Of course, she could learn how to make Tokushima ramen, or a reasonable approximation. The festival had been cancelled for the second year in a row, and, pandemic aside, it was perpetually in the red, so who knew when it would be held again? Manga, well, she would miss going to the bookstore and buying the thick, pulpy comics on the day that they were published, but there were electronic versions that she could read on her phone. She always loved spotting monkeys by the side of the road or cavorting around the golf course when she tagged along with her dad, but there were other creatures in South Carolina—rabbits, squirrels, deer, dolphins. She would miss her dad, for sure, but he wasn't around that much anyway. They could continue to text each other and she could meet up with him when he played in the States. And her friends? Well, they were all working or going to classes at far away universities, or would be. She would make new friends.

Dante had sent her a text the night before asking when she'd be free.

"I have a surprise planned for you," he texted. "Something that involves wildlife."

Of course, Sophie was up for anything that had to do with animals.

"I can go out with you tomorrow," she texted.

He must have had his phone in his hand, because little dots indicating that he was replying immediately appeared. A few seconds later, Sophie read, "Great! I'll pick you up at nine. Dress casually."

The next morning, Sophie dressed in a pink tank top and denim shorts. She put her hair in a ponytail and pulled a visor over her head. She was going to try to slip out of the house before anyone noticed, but Aunt Parisa was in the kitchen.

"Good morning," she signed. "Where are you going?"

Sophie hesitated. She could make up a lie, but her aunt probably wouldn't mind if she went out with someone her own age. She'd probably be happy to hear that Sophie had made a friend at the beach. She held up a finger, asking her to wait, composed a text on her phone, and showed it to her aunt: I'm going somewhere with Dante.

"Hold up," Aunt Parisa texted back. "Who's Dante?"

"A guy I met while I was walking the dog."

Aunt Parisa grinned, nodding slowly as if everything was becoming clear to her: all those walks on the beach, all those furtive glances at her phone's screen followed by secretive smiles.

"Can I meet him before you go?"

Sophie shrugged, then nodded. Just then, they both heard the rumble of a Jeep. Aunt Parisa parted the curtain and looked out the window. "He's here."

They both watched from the window as Dante jumped out of the Jeep and ran up the stairs. When his knuckles sounded on the door, Aunt Parisa opened the door. "Hi!"

"Hi!" Dante raised his hand in greeting.

Sophie stood by as the two of them greeted each other in English and exchanged a bit of small talk. Aunt Parisa was probably getting his whole life story, which she would then relay to her mother.

Finally, Dante turned to her again. "Ready?"

Sophie nodded.

"Have fun!" Aunt Parisa called out.

Sophie slid her feet into her white Keds and followed Dante down the steps.

"Where are we going?" she signed.

Dante cupped his hands together and pushed them away from his body. Then he flattened his hands, held his thumbs up, and carved parallel arches in the air.

Boat. Dolphins. That sounded perfect. Sophie gave him the thumbs up sign and climbed into the Jeep. She gazed out at the blue sky, decorated with fluffy white clouds, as Dante cruised along streets lined with palm trees. The windows were down, and wind rippled her hair. Gradually, the small businesses thinned out. Dante tapped out a rhythm on the steering wheel with his fingers while he drove. Every now and again, he looked over at her and smiled. Finally, they crossed a little bridge. Sophie peered into the salt marshes, hoping to see dolphins in the shallows. She didn't see any, but she spotted shorebirds wading among the tall grasses, poking for fish and frogs with their long beaks.

They pulled into a parking lot. Sophie saw that there were racks of kayaks in crayon colours—bright yellow, green, orange, and pink.

Dante cut the engine and grabbed his phone. "Ever been kayaking before?" he texted.

Sophie nodded. It had been a while, but back in elementary school, she and her deaf school classmates had spent a few days at a Y.M.C.A. camp. Kayaking had been one of the many activities they'd engaged in. Sophie remembered that all of them had tipped over their kayaks at one point or another. She figured it would be a good idea to take out her hearing aid and speech processor and leave them in the Jeep. She wouldn't be able to hear anything, but she didn't want to risk ruining her equipment. Hearing aids were very expensive.

"Let's go!" She pointed to the kayaks and hopped out of the Jeep.

Dante handled the rental fees, then helped her get into a life vest and choose her kayak. A tall, fortyish woman with short, bleached hair and sculpted arms handed them paddles and gave Dante some last-minute instructions. Sophie studied the map that she held out, paying attention as the woman traced the route that they should take with her finger. They would be going down an estuary teeming with wildlife.

'There are no alligators, because the water is salty," Dante texted her. "But there might be sharks. Stay in your kayak."

Dante hefted his kayak—an orange one—over his head. Sophie lifted her blue one and followed him to the dock, where they set down their paddles and eased their boats into the water. Sophie watched as Dante got into his, feet first, and did the same. They locked eyes, nodded, and began to paddle away.

At first, they were side by side, but Dante paused to take a photo with his phone, and let Sophie get ahead of him. She got into a steady rhythm—right stroke, left stroke, right stroke, left stroke—and moved swiftly through the water. She passed a flock of pelicans bobbing on the water. They seemed utterly uninterested in the two kayakers in their midst. Further on, she paddled past white wooden houses on stilts set on the banks. Some of the docks out front had American flags flapping from poles. Every now and then, Sophie looked back to make sure Dante was still behind her.

They'd been paddling for about half an hour when Sophie saw a ray swim by. She was about to turn around and point it out to Dante when a big wave suddenly crashed into her, knocking the paddle out of her hands, dumping her into the water and flipping the kayak. Water went up her nose, burning her sinuses. As she grabbed onto the side of the boat, she felt something brush past her. There might be sharks. Stay in your kayak! She tried to remember what she had learned at Y.M.C.A. camp about righting her boat and climbing back in.

The life jacket kept her bobbing above water, but the kayak blocked her view of Dante. She tried to work her way around it, straining to see where her paddle had floated off to. Again, she felt something against her legs, but this time it was more like a caress. And then she saw the bottlenose and gentle eyes just to her left. It was a dolphin, checking her out! She knew that it was illegal to swim with wild dolphins so she wasn't about to encourage it, but she felt so lucky to have come this close to one.

She wasn't scared anymore.

She finally caught sight of Dante, who was paddling toward her furiously, his lips pressed together in grim determination. She raised her hand out of the water. When he spotted her, his shoulders relaxed. He paused to wave back.

Together, they righted the craft, and Dante held it steady while she climbed back on. He retrieved her paddle and handed it back to her, then he tapped out a text on his phone and showed it to her. "A big speedboat went past creating a wake. I tried to warn you."

So that's what it was. She hadn't heard the boat, nor his shout. This was one of those situations that her mother always warned her about. Well, everything had turned out okay. Actually, more than okay. She hadn't really been in that much danger. And she would never forget those gentle eyes upon her, or the feeling of that marvellous creature as it brushed past her, like a blessing.

Dante suggested that they go back to their starting point, but Sophie shook her head. She wanted to keep going, so they did, paddling side by side or with Dante in front. They saw plenty of seagulls, more pelicans, and more dolphins swimming playfully in pods, but there were no more up close and personal encounters.

When they finally went back to the dock and returned their kayaks, Dante pulled Sophie to the side of the hut.

"I'm sorry," he signed. By his face, she could tell that he thought the whole outing had been a failure, but there was nothing further from the truth.

"Today I had one of the greatest experiences of my life," Sophie texted. "Thank you."

"Really?"

"Yes!"

He studied her face, as if trying to make out whether she was telling the truth. And then, he leaned forward, and she raised her arms and laced her fingers around his neck, and their lips came together—her first kiss.

VICKY CHONG

Transplanted Love

The plaque on the wall inside Nye's Specialist Surgery Clinic caught Marc Wong's attention as Nurse Kate took his temperature and blood pressure while Dr Nye flipped through his file.

In nothing do men more nearly approach the gods than in giving health to men.

—Cicero (106 B.C.–43 B.C.)

"Your need for a kidney transplant has not changed since I last saw you in December 2007. Time is unfortunately not on your side. Have you found a donor yet?" Dr Nye asked as he recorded Marc's blood pressure.

For the past few months, Marc had considered who amongst his relatives he could approach. He had two younger brothers, but they were not on friendly terms, due to disagreements about the allocation of company shares upon their mother's death two years ago. So bad was the wrath they no longer met up for the annual Chinese New Year reunion dinner. He wasn't desperate enough to approach them. His older sister would probably agree, but at fifty-nine, she was too old, and in as poor of health as Marc, suffering from hypertension and high cholesterol. Asking his wife and children for their kidneys was out of the question.

He thought of his many cousins but crossed them out immediately. As one of the richest men in rich Singapore,

Marc had never needed to beg for anything, and he was not about to start now. The only option was to do his operation in China or India, if he were to trust the doctors who had been recommended to him there.

"No, there is no one I can approach." Marc was unusually calm. "I am looking into doing the transplant in India or China. I heard it's much easier there as kidneys are readily available."

Dr Nye shook his head as he continued to write, but Marc ignored him.

"I contacted a friend in China," Marc began, and Dr Nye stopped his writing to listen.

"He found a doctor in Tianjin who has a ready kidney to offer me. What do you think?"

Dr Nye hesitated before he answered, "As a participant and signatory at the Istanbul Summit on organ trading and trafficking two months ago, I do not condone it."

"Look, Dr Nye, I understand where you are coming from. But it's not as if you can chope a kidney for me in Singapore like how we chope a table at a crowded hawker centre. I can't even get on the waitlist here for a kidney from a cadaver. I could die by year-end, Dr Nye, you said so yourself. A doctor in China already has a kidney for me. I cannot afford to lose this opportunity."

"You are taking an enormous risk by going to China for the operation. I've heard of too many cases of patients returning home with many complications," Dr Nye warned.

"What if I fly you to Tianjin as my consulting doctor? I am sure the Chinese doctor will agree. All they want is money. With you there, I am confident the transplant will be successful. Just name your price."

"It's not that simple…" Dr Nye started.

Marc got up, strutted around the tiny consultation room, and waved both his hands impatiently at whatever Dr Nye was about to say.

Dr Nye could see that Marc was adamant about this China transplant. He signalled for the nurse to leave the room.

They watched her close the door. Dr Nye turned to Marc.

"Mr Wong, calm down. Take a seat. Listen to what I have to say. What I am about to tell you cannot be revealed outside this room." He waited a moment for Marc to nod his head. "If you are serious about paying for a kidney, I know of an organ broker who had arranged that for two of my Indonesian patients. I am only giving you his contact, seeing that you have already made up your mind."

Marc's eyes lit up.

"You must promise that my name shall not be discussed in this transaction at all."

Marc nodded again vigorously.

"I am just your transplant surgeon. I do not condone the act, do you understand?"

Marc nodded. He understood perfectly.

*

Three weeks later, Marc arrived at Dr Nye's clinic. In each of his hands, he carried a canvas bag, which was now very popular with the green movement. Each bag contained a metal box comprising eight pieces of Champagne Truffle mooncake from the famous Raffles Hotel. He had reserved them a few days ago. So popular were these mooncakes that they sold out within a few days. His driver had just collected them and they were still chilled. The Mid-Autumn Festival was just around the corner and he felt like celebrating, something he had been deprived of since being diagnosed with diabetes.

He pushed open the glass door and greeted Lydia, the clinic's receptionist, at the counter. "Good morning, Miss Tan."

Lydia looked up and gave him a stiff smile, the kind of smile he once saw on a female Japanese robotic model in a documentary. "Good morning, Mr Wong. Please take a seat. Dr Nye is still not in yet."

Marc placed the bags on the counter. "Here, I bought some mooncakes, one box each for you, Nurse Kate and Dr Nye."

Lydia looked at the bags, "Oh, thank you!" she exclaimed. Her pleasure seemed genuine despite the earlier cold treatment.

She took the box out and mouthed a silent *wow* at the special mooncakes. An involuntary gasp escaped when she saw the price tag on the brochure accompanying the box. The common lotus-paste mooncakes cost a quarter of this, and he knew even that would be an extravagant expenditure for her.

She licked her lips unconsciously at the unexpected treat. "I can't wait to eat one," she told Marc.

Marc smiled at her childlike delight. "Go ahead, please. I'm sorry I can't join you, since I'm diabetic."

Lydia pouted and chided herself aloud for being so thoughtless. "Sorry, I forgot. I think I'll leave it until tonight. I'll savour it bit by bit at home."

She turned to store them in the refrigerator in the back pantry. He sank into the chair and watched as she returned to the counter.

Marc frowned as he studied her. She must be slightly older than his own daughters, but she appeared more mature. There was a sense of familiarity with Lydia that disturbed Marc. She reminded Marc of someone. He searched his memory, and the image of his first girlfriend, Janet Tan, appeared. Yes, that's right. Lydia had the same eyes and mannerisms as Janet. They looked incredibly alike.

Marc's thoughts floated back to Janet and the happy times they had spent together. Regret washed over him as he recalled how he was forced to break up with her when he left for his university studies in England. His parents had made it plain enough that he was to cease all contact with her. A gold-digger, they had labelled her. He knew Janet and he had no future together. He was the scion to a popular department store family while she, a small town Malaysian, was working as a salesgirl in his store. She couldn't even speak proper English. Yet, he must have loved her, for every girl he subsequently encountered failed to send his heart racing. Even now, an unexplained grief surged through his body as he remembered her.

Marc felt a squeeze on his chest and bent forward. The memory of Janet often brought a pain to his heart.

"Are you feeling okay?"

Marc looked up. Janet was crouching in front, speaking to him, her expression worried, that same look she had given him during their final meeting, oblivious to the fact that Marc was leaving her. They had checked into a five-star hotel on Orchard Road, and she had been excited. There, they had given each other their virginities. After the lovemaking, he had started weeping, and she had the same look of concern.

Marc took a deep breath and Janet's face faded into Lydia's.

"Mr Wong, here, drink some water. You look terrible. Are you all right?" Lydia handed him a cup of warm water.

Marc blinked a few times and let out a deep sigh. "I'm fine. I was just remembering someone..." He took a sip from the cup and placed it on the table.

He stared hard at Lydia.

"You remind me of someone... so much like her... my ex-girlfriend from long ago," Marc said.

Lydia's eyes turned cold, and she stood up from her crouch. Dr Nye entered at that moment. He went up to Marc and shook his hand.

"Hi, Mr Wong. Sorry to keep you waiting. Come, let's go into my room."

Lydia watched the door close, then stepped forward to put her ear against it. Her breathing quickened.

So, Marc Wong has found himself a donor at last. She wondered how much money had been exchanged. What story would they come out with this time to explain the relationship between Marc Wong and this Indonesian donor to the hospital ethics committee before the transplant could proceed?

What was now being discussed in Dr Nye's room was illegal in Singapore. She recalled what Marc had said about her mother. Marc couldn't even recognise Lydia, his own flesh and blood, standing before him. The hatred she felt towards the father who had deserted her surfaced once again. *Why is it that the rich always have it so easy?* Marc Wong should be made to suffer more for what he had done to her mother and her. Well, it looked like his punishment would soon be over. After the transplant, Marc could continue his wonderful life with his wife and children, and probably even live long enough to enjoy some grandparenting, leaving Lydia to her own misery.

Although two such similar transplant cases had been successfully arranged previously by this clinic, Lydia had not been bothered then. The situation was different now. She hated the patient inside the room, and she was determined to not let his transplant proceed. He had to suffer for what he put her through.

She considered the various options. She could tip off the relevant authority secretly about this case, but that might jeopardize her job with Dr Nye. Dr Nye was a kind man and she wouldn't wish any harm on him. On the other hand, she could confront Marc Wong directly about her illegitimate birth, and blackmail him. Think of how much money she could get.

Lydia smiled at the thought of what she could buy, and the first thing that came to her mind was the boxes of Champagne Truffle mooncakes from Raffles Hotel.

*

Lydia was at the Chatterbox Café in the Mandarin Hotel fifteen minutes before the appointed time. The hotel was just across from her office, and she had come immediately after work.

Her heart thumped wildly in her chest as she waited. Whether it was due to the brisk walk or the apprehension of meeting Marc Wong outside the clinic, she was not sure. Her fingers drummed on the table, as her gaze shifted to the entrance every time someone entered.

She recalled Marc's first visit to the clinic six months ago. She had recognised him immediately from the newspaper cuttings her mother had kept in a shoebox. She had been shocked. Last Wednesday, when he brought her a box of mooncakes from Raffles, she had irrationally hoped he would acknowledge her as his daughter and was angry he hadn't. That was seven days ago. There was still one last piece of mooncake left in her refrigerator, meant for tonight. She had telephoned Marc the next day to thank him for it, and requested this meeting at the same time. From his hesitation before replying, he had been surprised at the invitation, and she thought he would refuse, but he had not. Instead, he suggested meeting here in this café. His agreement threw her off guard at first. She had prepared a string of excuses for the meeting, but found she had no need for them in the end.

Over the next few days, she had felt jittery at work, half-expecting Dr Nye to ask her about the meeting, but he had not done so. Marc had kept the arrangement to himself, something she was grateful for.

At the appointed time of half-past five, Marc appeared at the entrance and their eyes met. He waved and, ignoring the waitress who was about to show him to a table, strode towards her, a warm smile on his face.

"Hello, Miss Tan. Been waiting long?" he asked, sitting down across from her. The waitress quickly took the napkin off the table and laid it on his lap.

"No, I've just arrived," Lydia lied.

The maître d' appeared and greeted Marc with easy familiarity. "Mr Wong, good to see you. Everything is well, I trust? Chicken rice as usual?" he asked.

"Raju, I'm very well. Give me a cup of black coffee." He looked over at Lydia's beverage and asked her, "Have you tried their famous chicken rice? Shall we order?"

The Mandarin Hotel chicken rice was rated one of the best in Singapore. At ten times the price one could get at hawker centres, Lydia almost wavered, but she shook her head, and the maître d' retreated.

"The other good place for chicken rice is at Maxwell Market. Have you tried that?" Marc asked.

Lydia shook her head again. "The queue is too long and one can never get seats there. But, I guess you have never faced that problem."

Marc laughed, missing the bitterness in her voice. "I don't carry tissue packets with me, and I can't very well use my name card to chope seats. This is my go-to place for a chicken rice fix."

Lydia stared at Marc awkwardly, wondering how she should begin her conversation. She had never been out alone with a man before, other than Dr Nye. She racked her brain for something to say and was relieved when Marc spoke.

"Miss Tan, I must apologise for shocking you last week at the clinic, telling you that you looked like my girlfriend." He looked away, face flushed. "That's why I decided I should meet you, in case you misunderstood me. That was an awkward moment for us and I thought I'd better clarify myself."

Lydia was reminded of why she had arranged to meet Marc and her hatred for him boosted her courage to get right to the point. "Mr Wong, I was just going to ask you about that. What was your girlfriend's name?"

Marc frowned and appeared to be taken aback by her question. He recovered quickly, though, and answered, "Her name was Janet Tan."

Lydia dug into her handbag, took out a photo, and handed it to him.

Marc's face paled as he stared at the photo of himself and Janet, taken on 17 July 1981, Janet's nineteenth birthday.

"Who are you?" he whispered, his eyes searching Lydia's face for clues, his knuckles white from clutching the photo too tightly.

Lydia straightened her spine and declared in a clear voice, "I'm Janet's daughter."

"And your father…" Marc's hoarse whisper was barely audible.

"I never knew him. He left as soon as he found out that Mom was pregnant." Lydia's voice was cold and hard.

At least Marc had the decency to look ashamed. His face remained flushed and both his hands clasping the coffee cup trembled when he drank. He studied the photograph with a faraway look.

"This was taken at Changi Beach, which was very popular with young people during my time in the eighties." Despite his sad eyes, he smiled at Lydia as he spoke.

Changi Beach was no longer the hip place to go nowadays as far as beaches were concerned, Sentosa being the preferred beach for volleyball and foam parties. Lydia had never been to either. The word *beach* conjured a luxury of time and idleness beyond her lifestyle.

"We were very much in love. I did not want to leave her, but my parents gave me an ultimatum," he stated matter-of-factly. "Janet told me she was pregnant, and we agreed she would get an abortion. I gave her the money for the operation." He put up his hand to stop Lydia from interrupting. "It's not that we didn't want you, but we could not afford to keep you, Lydia. I was about to leave for university. My parents were dead set against the relationship. I was so young…" He looked down, and his shoulders sank, as if the 4R photograph was actually heavy.

"She promised my mother that she would go for an abortion… I don't know why she didn't." He looked up abruptly. "Where is she now? Can I meet her?"

Lydia's voice was icy. "What for? To make amends?"

"You may not believe me, but I loved her very much and had wanted to marry her when I returned. She had promised to wait for me." He paused, took another sip, and continued. "Whenever I returned to Singapore from UK during school breaks, I looked for her, but she had moved away. Father said she told them she was returning to Malaysia for good."

His eyes crinkled as he gave her a quivering smile, an expression which ironically conveyed both sadness and joy. "At first, when we found out that she was pregnant, we were both overjoyed, even giving names to the baby—Lionel, if it was a boy, because she was very sure it was going to be a boy and she wanted our son to be brave like a lion. I chose Lydia, for a girl, just to match the name starting with L. I can't believe she really used the name."

"You had names for the baby, and still intended to kill it?" She waited for his answer, but he remained silent.

A pained look flashed across his face.

"Mom died eight years ago," Lydia said suddenly. The look of shock on his face pleased her. "She had an aggressive form of breast cancer. We only found out when it was too late."

There was pity in his eyes as he reached across to cover Lydia's hand with his. "You must have been very young then."

She pulled her hand away. "I don't need your sympathy, Mr Wong."

"You must have already guessed I am your father. What do you want then by asking for this meeting now?" Marc asked. "To confirm our relationship? And perhaps for me to welcome you into my family?"

She scoffed at his suggestion. "No thanks."

"Then what? Money?" His voice was low.

"That's right. I want money. I'm sick of working while your other children get to study overseas. I want to study in a university too, and I want everything that you have given them. Why should I be deprived of what is rightfully mine? You brought me into this world, but my world, Mom's and mine, was a world of suffering." She broke off, her voice shaking as tears pooled in her eyes.

Lydia waited for his response, but there was none. She took his silence as his denial, and her anger rose. "Mr Wong, I know all about your plans to buy a kidney. May I remind you that this is illegal in Singapore? All I have to do is to make a call to the authority and you will not be able to go through with the transplant operation. Worse, think of your reputation when the news gets out."

"Your mother was right to want her first born to be as feisty as a lion, or in this case, a lioness." He smiled. "She would have been proud of you for fighting for your rights. Janet had always been too considerate, always putting others first. She didn't want me to disobey my parents and wanted to break off our relationship. I had been confident my parents would accept her in the end because she was kind and sweet-tempered."

"You took advantage of her because she was poor—"

"I loved her—"

"Just as you are taking advantage of Mr Sunny now."

Marc stared, unflinching, into Lydia's challenging eyes. "If that's what you really want to do, go ahead. If that's the punishment you think I deserve, I am willing to accept it. If the price I have to pay for all that I've done to both your mother and you is to die, so be it."

Lydia knew Marc to be a shrewd businessman, and for him to throw in the towel with nary a fight left her fazed. He had so much to lose—his business, his children, and even his reputation if he was caught and jailed. So why was he behaving this way? Her anxiety grew and matched in tandem with his nonchalance.

"You don't understand, Mr Wong, this is very serious. You could be jailed if I speak out," she blurted.

Marc nodded without answering, wearing that sad smile of his.

She stood up, and without another word, walked out of the expensive café.

*

Marc's mobile phone rang as he was driving to work. He pushed the button on his Bluetooth.

"Mr Wong, this is Dr Nye. I've just received a call from the hospital's Organ Transplant Ethics Committee. They have approved your transplant. When can you come in to make the necessary arrangements?"

Marc listened with apprehension. So, Lydia had not informed the hospital. He wondered what she was up to. Almost two weeks had passed since their meeting at the Chatterbox Café, and he was certain that the approval would not be given.

"Mr Wong? Are you still there?"

"Dr Nye, I'm very happy to hear that. Shall I come to your office now?" Marc asked.

"Yes, I'm free for the next two hours. I'll wait for you."

Marc hung up. The thought of seeing Lydia again filled him with dread. He remembered the bitterness in her eyes as she stood to leave the café.

Having survived five decades, Marc had lived through many experiences, good and bad. His children were his pride and joy, but now, with Lydia in the picture as one of his offspring, this was no longer true. To say that his wife and children were shocked when he broke the news to them five days ago about having an illegitimate daughter was an understatement. His wife was still not speaking to him, especially since he had proposed changing his will.

Many of Marc's achievements were evident in the crystal trophies that were displayed on the shelves in his office and illuminated by tiny halogen lamps. In addition to the numerous golf trophies he had won in various tournaments, one particularly large one stood out and took centre stage—his successful launch to take his company public had won him The Entrepreneur Award. Since this win was voted by members in the business community, he had been ecstatic about it. Then there were also the many small *In Appreciation* plaques to complement his many philanthropic acts, including the setting up of G W Wong scholarship, named after his grandfather, the founder of the company.

Marc sighed. There were just as many things he had done that he was not so proud of, too. Janet's abortion had filled him with shame for many years. Marc laughed at the thought, ironic that he should be ashamed of something that was never carried out.

Now, he was about to enter a transaction that would leave another mark on his conscience forever. He was about to purchase a kidney to save his own life. This was illegal, an exploitation of the poor. Desperation for survival has driven the Indonesian man, Sunny, to sell his kidney, just as desperation to stay alive had driven Marc to buy it. Why then did this sound like a hollow excuse, even to his ears?

Marc had cooked up a story to explain Sunny's relationship to his family—a distant aunt living in Indonesia. Without her knowledge, he had linked Sunny to his aunt's son-in-law. Sunny was to be a distant cousin-in-law who was supposedly grateful to Marc's aunt, enough to want to help save her favourite nephew's life. Although this sounded incredulous now, the hospital's ethics committee accepted his declaration under oath. Perhaps the oath that he was persuaded to take added to the credibility.

Marc arrived at the clinic half an hour later. To his relief, Nurse Kate was staffing the counter. When he steeled his nerves and enquired about Lydia's whereabouts, the nurse replied that Lydia had gone over to the hospital next door to collect the approval documents for Marc.

Marc hurried into Dr Nye's office. They shook hands, happy their plan was moving along smoothly. Dr Nye repeated to Marc what the chairman of the committee had told him. Just then, Kate entered with the approval letter. They read through it carefully again. With this letter, they could now arrange for an operation date.

Kate brought in the appointment book and they compared dates, Dr Nye with his trusted diary, and Marc with his mobile organizer.

A knock on the door interrupted them. Lydia entered, her eyes worried as she ushered in a group of three men.

"Dr Nye, they are from the Ministry of Health, and they want a word with you immediately," she said.

One officer handed his name card to Dr Nye, politely, then to Marc, snidely. "Sorry to interrupt you, Dr Nye. We were informed that Mr Marc Wong here is involved in the illegal purchase of a kidney from an Indonesian man named Sunny, who is now in custody. We would appreciate your cooperation by giving us all the relevant information regarding this case."

The officer turned to Marc. "Mr Wong, you would need to come with us. You may call your lawyer to meet us at my office."

The other two men swooped in on Dr Nye's table and took away all the documents. Dr Nye and Nurse Kate could only look in helpless silence, stunned.

As the officers led Marc out of the office, his eyes met Lydia's. There was desperation in her eyes as she shook her head, as if she was apologising and pleading for his understanding.

Marc gave her a weary smile as he walked out of the glass door. *Forgive me, too, my lioness.*

NASH COLUNDALUR

We Mourners

I believed everything D'Souza told me. And when he said that he was going to die that day, I knew he would.

To honour him, we writers, mourners, and fans, in our black jackets and ties, sat at our usual table at Desmond's, D'Souza's most beloved restaurant in Bangalore. Here he had regaled and indulged us on numerous occasions. But what was to be a solemn evening of dedication to our departed friend was about to go unbelievably wrong. I really should laugh it off. None of D'Souza's parties were anything close to being sane, but on that day, we were hit by the most extraordinary of impediments.

*

We had stood looking at the still man in the black box, this man who we thought would live forever. He was an atrocious friend, sporadic in the attention he gave us, and never letting us come close to his emotions. But when he loved us, he did so extravagantly.

He had called me. "I feel like dying," he said. "I have written enough."

"But there is plenty more to write about," I replied.

"No," he said.

D'Souza, sounding frighteningly and uncommonly tired and emotional, said that he was revolted by his own life. I had never heard him speak this way before and thought that maybe he was just bored and perhaps slightly ill. In an attempt to alleviate the situation, but with my heart beating faster and alarm rising within me, I asked him, mundanely, if he wanted an aspirin.

There was just silence.

"I'll come over now," I said.

It was too late. I found him slumped at his desk, his hand clutching his heart. The page he was writing on held nothing but scratches. He had scratched every word that he had written, but all of them appeared to be of the same length. Our much-loved writer had run out of words. His fountain pen, its shiny nib crushed, had fallen from the desk, and rolled to the door, as if trying to escape. I picked it up gently and tried to straighten the nib, but my hands were shaking. I didn't know what to do with it. I did not want to place it back on his table. I did not want to place it in my pocket. In the end, after the paramedics arrived and D'Souza was taken away, I put the pen in my bag.

*

We made our solemn journey from the funeral to Desmond's. The sun threw itself onto Bangalore. It hit hard, steaming the city's open sewers. The city's hidden odours of urine-splashed roadside walls, petrol fumes and acrid fried street food all came ferociously alive in the heat to envelop the metropolis in an ominous shroud. I felt that the city had abruptly started to decay, and I was sure D'Souza's passing had something to do with it.

Fat Suresh walking beside me was suffering in the heat. He claimed to have read all of D'Souza's work. I suspected he thought he was a far better writer than D'Souza. Suresh's own work was restricted to lengthy letters written to the editors of local newspapers. He had his own contorted view of everything, and he felt the need to constantly express it.

He pulled a face at the sight of an old beggar, sitting motionless on a dirty cloth on the busy pavement. He looked as though he had been there for years. I walked faster, trailing behind some of the other mourners, allowing them to lead. I looked down at the huge number of shuffling feet of men and women, at sandaled feet and bare limbs.

I stepped away from the noisy hawkers on the pavement edges. Unexpectedly, all had become silent. I could only see their mouths move. All around me, the great chaos of everyday life was now only visible; the staggering noise that accompanied it was gone. D'Souza's death was upsetting me more than I had thought. I felt a big dank hand snatch at my body. Suresh had yanked me towards him and away from a ladder leaning against a shop.

"Never walk under a ladder. Bad luck," he said, leaving me to rub and nurse my bruised arm.

Someone had momentarily switched off the city's soundtrack, but now Bangalore exploded with sound again. We arrived at the restaurant. Two files of mourners, compressed like a black and white accordion, congregated at the entrance, looking confused. We did not know what to do. We had never made decisions here. D'Souza had always done it for us.

"Well, let's start by going inside," I said.

Glad to have some direction, and with the help of familiar waiting staff, who were also dressed in black, we sat at the usual table. This was close to the bar, away from the rest of the diners and facing the courtyard, where we could see the accumulation of drain age pipes from the buildings above. Occasionally the pipes made a whining noise, as if a child had been dropped inside. We were so used to this din that it didn't bother us. An extraordinary number of ceiling fans, placed close together and resembling inverted swirling dervishes, gave the impression that the restaurant was about to take flight. The thick walls and the fans kept the relentless heat outside. The place was not fancy, but we had been here with D'Souza so often that it felt like home to us. Before, I hadn't paid attention to a broken chair that could have been discarded, the slanting picture frames, or the potted plants that had been dead for a while. But now, as I looked around, the place looked unkempt and run down.

The waiters were cautiously courteous and, I thought, somewhat indifferent. I wanted to tell them to behave. D'Souza always paid the bill and tipped generously. I had prepared a small speech, just a few lines, to dedicate the meal to him. Perhaps this was a bad idea.

The mourners around the table were acting odd. No one spoke, and no orders were placed. A few of us were shaking our heads anxiously. I was not sure what the concern was: the gloomy prospect of no new words from D'Souza, the abrupt end to hedonistic parties or the dire worry over who was going to pay for the meal?

*

When we had arrived, some of us had slapped D'Souza's books on the table, as though we were going to chant and bring him back to life. Some of us now began to read from these books. I had every reason to believe that this was the first time that many had even opened them. Only when something ends do we even begin to take the slightest interest in it.

Suresh sat opposite me, facing the restaurant entrance as always. It was bad luck to sit otherwise, he had explained. Despite the ceiling fans, he was sweating profusely and twiddling his thumbs. He was desperate to talk, but needed, like the other mourners, a drink first.

"Whisky for all!" I called to the distant waiters.

With the glasses filled and the first sips taken, we hummed and made small noises. Suresh was ready to talk. "D'Souza," he said, "was addicted to Flaubert. I don't think it was a healthy addiction. His work is a bit too finicky ... for me."

The man had just died, and here was someone who had never written anything sensible already condemning his work. Didn't protocol require us to wait for a while before we started thrashing the dead? It was true that D'Souza's work was influenced by Flaubert; the quest for exactness of wording, the frenetic, thorny foraging for tonality of rhythm, the sweet fruit, the excruciating tearing, word by word, for absoluteness and ...

"Oh! *Le Mot Juste, Le Mot Juste,*" Suresh was crying out, mocking D'Souza's rendering of Flaubert. He raised his near-empty glass and beckoned harshly to an unwilling waiter.

The others laughed and tried their own imitations. Skidding elbows were now rapidly skinning the table of its tablecloth. This was heading towards becoming another boisterous D'Souza party. Except … D'Souza was not there, and he was being derided.

During this clamour I heard a small voice coming from my left. It came from a diminutive man – a poet, I think – who attended all of D'Souza's parties, and somehow, amidst all the rowdiness, he slipped in a severe question.

"How did D'Souza write?" he asked.

I said, "D'Souza would shut his blinds, shut his door, and with the ceiling fan's ancient mechanics throwing hot gusts he had rehearsed putting word beside word." I had caught the attention of the others at the table.

I had asked D'Souza, "How do you do it?"

He replied, "I don't know, it's instinct. I just know when it's right," he said.

"And what is the 'right' result?" I asked.

"Well, the pinpointing of criminality and the purposefulness of the literary form."

I would pat him lightly on the back whenever he said something like that. D'Souza was a dear man, dear to all of us followers. He strutted and sometimes reasoned like an idiot but wrote like a deity, a spirit of words for us lesser writers.

*

They were staring at me. It did not surprise me that they hardly knew D'Souza's work. All they were interested in were the legendary parties that he gave. But at the ramshackle funeral organised by his publisher, for he had no family that we knew of, when accosted by the press, they had bizarrely competed with one another, each claiming to be closer to D'Souza than any other. *Yes, I was the one he used to confide to about his creative process, and his frustrations.* D'Souza did no such thing; the mourners were referring to his unabashed boasts about his sexual conquests, tales that he merrily shared at his parties. D'Souza quoted and misquoted Flaubert several times within the course of the evening meals that he hosted. He fed and watered us with such abandoned generosity and a somewhat skewed view of humanity that we wholly forgave him—partly because half of us had never read Flaubert.

"Madame Bovary, c'est moi," he would say, raising his glass of expensive whisky. Some of those around the dinner table said he should shut his trap about this Frenchman. But then he would come around filling our glasses. Soon afterwards he would read from his new manuscript, and we would all either be taken by it or too drunk to like or dislike.

Then he would come around again, dispensing more drink. At some point during the evening, he would jump and skip over heavy forms on the floor—us scattered there with our steaming booze breath, looking like turds left behind by a large, naughty animal. The restaurant would have been long closed. With whisky glass in one hand, a chicken thigh in the other wrapped in a page torn out of his book, with an expression of doom and the manner of performing an urgent deed, he would leave. He would hit the dark streets, looking for trouble, looking for sex.

On these sojourns of despair, of nightly shamans, of ravenous cabbies, he would randomly fling coins and empty his pockets into begging bowls. He did not have to go far because they would come looking—those pretty boys. A grinning, knowing cabbie, hunched on the wheel, would whisk them away. But in true Flaubertian style he would not limit himself to boys.

*

Suresh now turned his attention to me and began blustering wildly. "What a peculiar man D'Souza was."

Here we go again.

With hands folded and eyes straining he leaned across the table towards me. "His writing was painfully structured, but…" he said.

I knew what was coming next.

"But… tell me." His eyes widened, and his jowls shook. "What was wrong with his everyday life? It was a mess!"

I wished everyone would leave the man's personal life alone. It was an obsession. Yes, D'Souza was no saint. He was constantly seeking pleasure.

"I can't bear myself, dear friend," he had once told me. "I tolerate myself because of the idea that you have of me."

Suresh was determined to provoke. "The death of the lonely!" he announced grandly to the table, in his slow whisky drawl. "They die and leave behind no one to cry for them…"

Everyone looked at him, perhaps thinking of his own miserable death to come.

Suresh shrugged and said, "D'Souza had no family, but he left behind some kind of legacy. Well, you know, we could say that this legacy was his work."

I saw the small poet beside me squirming.

Suresh went on to talk about the beggar he had seen on the way to the restaurant, of whom he clearly disapproved. "He, too, is lonely, perhaps has no family, but what will he leave behind?"

I didn't see the point in this. The man was rambling. I just wanted to read my speech. But I felt like that piece of paper D'Souza had repeatedly scratched—language had left me. I felt sorrow and growing anger.

I tried to shut Suresh up. In a hasty and accusing tone, I said, "Him? The beggar? He will leave that square metre of earth behind. He sleeps and lives there, and when he dies, someone else will take it."

"Pah!" said Suresh.

D'Souza had left behind a great body of work, admired by many. They called his writing cruel and cynical, but in the end, people realised that the books were about them— the insincerity of their lives. His early and seminal work, *Our Forefathers*, predicted that the country and its people, in their great acquisition drive, would ultimately forget what it was that they were working so hard for. This thought was not new, but the message, especially now, when the country was storming ahead, was hard-hitting and very true.

The so-called dedication to D'Souza was now in full swing. I could hear people deliberating on paragraphs from D'Souza's opened books. But I heard nothing good. The poet sitting next to me announced in his small voice to no one in particular that he would write a poem then and there and dedicate it to D'Souza. The timid poet, facing difficulty getting the waiters' attention, suddenly picked himself up, went to a waiter, plucked a pen out of his pocket, and returned to his seat.

It was time for my speech. I was standing up to toast and read when someone gasped loudly—an alarming noise that dramatically silenced our table, the adjoining tables, and the waiters.

It was Suresh. He looked ghastly. "I have just realised," he said, slowly putting his whisky glass down and waving me to sit. Good God, the man was shaking! I felt irritated. This had better be good. I wanted to say my few words and scoot, leave the party and these people forever. Suresh rubbed his blood-red eyes. He looked at us as though he wanted to kill us all.

What is it, man? Spit it out. What have you realised?

He looked around the table, his rotund pillow head nodding slightly, his lips moving. He was saying something to himself as his gaze went from one mourner to another.

Clutching D'Souza's book, he said, "When D'Souza was at this table it was fine, but with him gone, there are…" He was doing this strange thing of gazing at each person again. Then he said, gravely and very slowly, "We are thirteen at the table now."

The courtyard pipes gurgled and let out a scream. The whisky was rushing through me and agitating my blood stream.

"Thirteen? So what?" I cried. I fidgeted angrily, trying to stand up again to read my speech, only to find Suresh's fat hands reaching across the table to firmly push me back into my chair.

"Sit," he said, as though speaking to a dog. "It's bad luck. Of all the days, there cannot be thirteen of us today."

I looked down and put my fist into my mouth, gnawing at my knuckles. I felt trapped. All I wanted was to read my few lines. I didn't care if that miserable lot made nothing of my speech. But I was certain that D'Souza would hear it. It astonished me that I had merrily indulged with these people on so many occasions. I lifted my head to see every one sitting stiffly and looking horrified. They believed in this superstitious nonsense!

The mourners, all twelve of them, were looking at me. The waiters, taking a break from loitering at the bar, were placing food on our table, though no one touched it. I calmed down. I would offer a solution. After the initial shock of Suresh's gasp, the restaurant was humming again. I beckoned one of the waiters.

"Me?" he said, pointing to himself. He appeared at my side, leaned, and indifferently cocked his ear at me.

I should have punched both his ears, but I said, "Would you like to join us?" He said, "What, Sir?"

I tried a little louder and a little slower. Maybe he was deaf. Maybe he was dumb.

"I said, would you like to join us for dinner in dedication of our *dead* friend D'Souza."

"No, sir. I am working."

Working, indeed. Well, what should we do next? If thirteen was a crazy number, surely twelve must be normal. So, I offered to leave the party, despite feeling the real need to be there and finish reading my speech. Maybe I could just read it at home, in private. The mourners ruled it out and said I was an ardent admirer and that they could not do without my presence. I looked around the table, for if they were serious about this, someone else should leave the table. D'Souza was probably laughing at all of this. Maybe Suresh should go. Yes, it should be him, since he started this. He should hoist his bulky self and the twelve hairs on his head (I'm sure about this), and gasp his way out of here, trying to avoid the thirteenth step, the thirteenth day and pull his thirteenth tooth out. But he just sat there, almost looking content that he had started this commotion. Was he just doing this for the drama? That horrified look had vanished from his face and was replaced by the face of a cherub.

"I'm going to find another mourner," I said, exasperated, as I stood up. But no, I was not going to do this myself. I sat back, held D'Souza's book in one hand, and with the other I pointed with authority, the kind that comes naturally with the death of a friend, to another person across the table, delegating him to seek a single man or woman dining in the restaurant and proffer an invite.

The insanely churning ceiling fans were blowing bits of food away. The party was heading towards failure. As expected, the delegated man came back looking jilted. I decided to widen our search. I insisted it was Suresh's turn to head out to the streets and return with a suitable candidate. Reluctantly clutching his whisky glass, he started to mumble and after being asked to leave his drink behind, in a sudden foolish and gallant manner, he made straight for the restaurant's kitchen door. I turned him around and pointed him towards the street entrance. He laughed it off, winked, and promptly fell over. He got up, disappeared, and almost immediately returned with a very young person who seemed more than willing to join us and sat down amongst us. I looked on open-mouthed. This was not good.

I was preparing to make a run for it when his mother came looking for him, threatening to call the police and mouthing obscenities. "Perverts!" she shouted, as she took her twelve-perhaps thirteen-year-old son away.

What next? I stood up and again offered to leave the party. Please, let me go. This time a trio of mourners sprung up, pushed me back into my chair and marched out in unison. They must have been out on a thorough search, for they were gone for a while. Maybe they were looking for crying people, already mourning. I hoped they would not come back once more with a child who had dropped his ice cream. Jesus, I thought, look at these people around the table. The wretched lot looked like they were actually mourning.

Had the poet finished his poem? No, he seemed to be having difficulties. He had written four words: "A Sonnet to D'Souza." He was now shaking heavily and looked as if he was going to die himself. Suresh had his head on the table and was snoring. I wondered what D'Souza would have thought of this. He would have loved it, the bizarreness of it.

I was considering hitting the poet to stop him from shaking when the mourner squad goose-stepped into the restaurant, looking very pleased, holding a man by his arm. Good God, now they had caught a thief—probably running from a crime scene. He was white, long-haired, with a wispy beard. A tourist with a camera. Upon seeing us, he grinned. Amused, he shook hands with all of us, took photographs, accepted a drink and sat at the head of the table, where

D'Souza used to sit. When told that we were keeping that chair empty tonight, he profusely apologised and sat next to Suresh. He turned out to be an English hippie in search of life. Why? Is there no life in England?

Suresh, having woken up, came face to face with what looked like Jesus Christ sitting next to him. He gasped again.

"Do you know D'Souza's work?" I asked our new mourner.

"No. But I know Rushdie's," he said. "Is it anything like that?"

No, it was nothing like that. In fact, it was far from it. We should not even compare the two. Then, without prompting, he went on to say that Rushdie's work was like an onion. "You have to peel it slowly to get to the core of it," he said, miming the act. I took out my folded speech from my pocket and half stood up when our fourteenth mourner announced that he had to leave. I slumped back again into my chair. He had to catch a train—third class, with the common people, the poor, the *real* people, he said, for he had come to see the *real* India and he was going to Goa. He enquired if there was a class lower than third on the trains.

"Yes," I said, "You can travel on top of the train, but that's superior class. It's guaranteed to tell you all about life and the afterlife if you don't duck your head at bridges. Good luck to you, my friend."

I waved at him. "And would you like a copy of D'Souza's work? Ah, yes you would. Here you are. And when you meet these real people and have some real-life experiences, are you going back to your squat in Brixton? Oh, you are."

We had, yet again, lost a mourner, and I was losing my mind. But life had come back to the table. In fact, all appeared to be in full swing. The poet was scribbling feverishly, Suresh was screaming "*Le Mot Juste! Le Mot Juste!*" and books were being thrown at him. The white tourist must have had an effect, or was D'Souza back? I checked his chair, just to be sure.

After all this, I was the one who now felt strongly about having the right number at the table. I was not going to let them, let Suresh, get away with this. Maybe thirteen was unquestionably a cruel number. I had enough whisky and determination in me to fetch someone who would mourn for longer. The poet who was now under the table (what was he doing there?) was the only one who noticed me leaving.

Outside, finding yet another replacement did not take me long. He seemed more than willing to come and mourn for a dear friend, eat a bit and drink a bit. He looked adequately informed and not the kind who would foolishly make literary comparisons. Maybe I was overreacting. I led the new fourteenth mourner inside the restaurant. He looked sceptical.

Of course, my friend, I assure you it is all good. You are indeed the right candidate.

Some at the table looked shocked. Suresh seemed to recognise him. The fourteenth mourner sat down, unsure, as if he had never sat on a chair before. He grinned and said nothing. Sometimes characters in D'Souza's books said nothing. They said a lot by saying nothing. Food was placed in front of him, and the old beggar from the street, wide-eyed, dug straight into it. He quickly got drunk and thanked D'Souza for the meal and wished his soul well. He wiped his mouth with his hand, smiled at me and spotted something on the floor. He bent down to pick it up.

"Is this yours?" he asked me.

It was D'Souza's pen that had fallen from my bag.

"Yes, it is," I said and placed it safely in my shirt pocket. Close to my heart. Now for that speech.

An Impossible Innocence

Blood-red headlines flash across hundreds of screens: *The People's Bank of China Devalues the Chinese Yuan against the US Dollar*. Asian currency, equity, and debt markets go into a tailspin. Hapless telephone receivers bang on sturdy wooden desks. Two dozen men and three women scream "Fuck!" Many more pump fists in the air, yelling "Yes!" Bloomberg chat-rooms and Reuters dealing terminals beep. Multiple lines ring on dealer-boards across the trading floor, one-third the size of a football field. Salespeople, a phone to each ear, shout for prices. Traders, eyes scanning a bank of monitors, one hand typing messages, another holding a phone, bark obscenities and tradable quotes at salespersons and brokers. They sit a metre apart in long rows, backs unguarded, facing uncertain destinies written in unfeeling numbers.

The two-hundred-and-fifty-pound Head of Fixed Income, Currency, and Commodity Trading—Paul—asks a trading assistant: "Reckon we are up seventy million dollars and change?"

He replies, "Give me a couple of minutes. Running the estimates now."

Paul, called Pooh when out of earshot, rolls up the sleeves of his creasing light-blue shirt, unbuttoned to reveal greying chest hair. Trundling to the Head of Currency Trading, he says: "Well done, mate. Can you square my positions if the dollar goes up another percent from here?"

"Sure," he replies, "You should get done. Let me check your position." He gapes at the screen. "Fuck! This is crazy big, man. You will make more than twenty-five million on this trade."

"Thanks," says Paul, poker-faced, bending to peer at the screen through round rimless glasses. "I am buying drinks for your team tonight."

Straightening up, he sees Mark, now Head of Financial Markets, survey the dealing room with the imperiousness he first beheld in a middle-school playground, twenty-six years ago. The principal had feted Paul in the morning assembly that day, for winning the National Junior Mathematical Olympiad. In celebration, three boys pushed him to the ground at lunch. Appreciative onlookers chanted: "Kick the fat nerd." He sobbed, curling up to shield his face, until Mark strode in, declaring: "The new kid is my friend." The bullies stopped kicking, reluctantly slinking away. For good. From then on, Mark borrowed Paul's assignments, sat behind him during examinations, and let him tag along to parties brimming with blondes, beer, booze, cigarettes, and cool dudes. Mark's grades shot up. He gave the salutatory address at their high-school graduation; Paul, the valedictory. Mark convinced a reluctant Paul to join the same bank after college, arguing that it made more sense to make money—lots of it—than roam the corridors of academia as a mathematician till Paul figured out what he wanted from his life.

Their eyes meet. Paul gives a thumbs up. Mark nods from his glass corner office, the only one on the floor, and turns his back. Adjusting a red Hermès silk tie and limited-edition Patek Philippe wrist-watch, he gazes at the boat-shaped SkyPark crowning Marina Bay Sands. The only sight more enrapturing to him than the curved SkyPark is a mirror. Many years ago, a disgruntled ex-trader declared: "I puke when fuck-face gets a hard-on ogling himself." The name stuck.

Paul, smiling wryly, mutters to himself: "Nineteen years, and I'm still here."

*

The cacophony dims. Paul meets the middle-aged pantry lady in the lift lobby.

"Chicken rice for lunch?" she asks.

He replies: "Sorry, dear. Not today. How is your son?"

She breaks into a wide smile, gushing: "He good. You help pay tuition and now he finishing college next year. May God bless you always."

Paul gets into the lift, saying, "All the very best to the young man."

He lights a Marlboro Red at the smoking corner next to Raffles Place subway station. Mildly dizzy from the bitter smoke, he looks for something to lean against, remembering the 2 a.m. broker call early this morning. The US Federal Open Market Committee had unexpectedly raised the Overnight Fed Funds Rate. He sold Asian currencies against the US dollar, booked profits on US interest rate positions, and lay down to sleep, but couldn't. Dressed in office attire at 5 a.m., he tiptoed into his wife Ariadne's bedroom. A red satin gown, caressing her firm round breasts, inched up her silky white thighs. She had told him fifteen months ago, upon the birth of their second child: "You can sleep with me, or with your phone. One or the other, not both." Adjusting his uncomfortably tight underpants, he gently pecked her forehead, kissed their baby daughter, and left for work.

*

Mark chairs a meeting of the Financial Markets Risk and Compliance Committee. He proclaims, "Great risk culture is set at the top, by leaders with impeccable conduct and compliance track records. My secret is simple: I never make any important decision without considering its impact on my family. All my traders know this. They also know that I have zero tolerance for reputational risk." The meeting ends.

Hanging back in the hallways or waiting for the second elevator, the recently hired Chief Risk Officer asks, "What was that about?"

The Head of Market Risk laughs before replying, "The part about family is perhaps true. Mark is half-Asian, you know. And ashamed of it, I think. He worships anything blonde and white, like his wife and her best friend—his overpaid business manager."

Sensing the Head of Sales lurking behind him, Paul swivels: "How are you, Cain?"

"Could be better," is his whining reply. "Just saw last month's bank statement. International School: forty-thousand per child. Credit cards: fifteen-thousand. Mortgage payments: hundred-thousand. I live a simple middle-class life, you know. No yachts, no Ferraris, yet I burn through a million a year."

Paul's deep-set eyes harden.

Cain continues, "Enough about me and my petty sums. You deserve an eight-figure bonus this year."

Paul stays silent, not taking the bait. Still, he cannot hide his disgust watching Cain-the-simple-middle-class-fucking-cobra crawl away. He seethes within: the snake is right. My bonus has been a joke. I'll head to a hedge fund if Mark fucks me again this year.

Clearing emails, Paul spies Ariadne's photo, framed in Royal Selangor pewter, hiding behind a Bloomberg keyboard. He smiles, remembering their first kiss, under a full-moon, next to a stuttering fountain at the entrance to their college library.

Mark calls on Paul's landline, "It's past eleven. Are you joining us?"

"Sorry. It has been a crazy day. I will dial-in from my desk," Paul replies, gesturing to the secretary to patch him into Mark's weekly leadership meeting.

He hears Cain argue: "Paul is a brilliant proprietary trader. If we had done a better job communicating his views to my team and our clients, Sales would also have made a killing today. I am not saying it is Paul's fault. There are only twenty-four hours in a day. I suggest creating a Co-Head of Trading role to free up Paul to focus on making money for the Bank."

Furious at the attempt to lay the underperformance of Sales at his door, Paul snaps, "Your so-called Sales team is a bunch of clueless brokers."

Mark intervenes, "We play as one team. Let's reconvene on a quieter day."

Paul slams the phone on his desk. A bronze Buddha head, a gift from Ariadne, topples over. Picking it up, he reads the inscription, a paraphrased Dalai Lama quote: *Man is so anxious about the future that he does not enjoy the present; the result being that he does not live in the present or the future; he lives as if he is never going to die, and then dies having never really lived.* I will retire in a couple of years, vows Paul. Once this year's bonus is paid out. Spend time with family. Adopt an orphanage. Teach Quantitative Finance. Live a slower, simpler, life, maybe a meaningful one.

An email hits his freshly cleaned Inbox, from the Market Risk Manager–Currency Options, titled: *Extrapolating Volatility Smiles for Far Out-of-the-Money Strikes in Pegged Currencies.* Don't these monkeys have better things to do, he wonders, almost pressing 'delete'? Mark, and the monkey's bosses, are copied. Skimming over the attachment—thirteen pages of formulae, graphs, and theoretical drivel—Paul chuckles, knowing that very little of this will be intelligible to Mark. But his smile soon disappears when he reads that one of his traders, Sam, had sold complex US dollar-Yuan currency options to hedge funds. That the options, though priced correctly to the customer, were significantly undervalued in the bank's systems, generating fake trading profits. And that "The Head of FICC Trading is, therefore, requested to support provisioning twenty million dollars against the potential loss pending the conclusion of an inquiry, and to consider placing the concerned trader, Samuel Cooper, on administrative leave."

Paul rests his forehead on his palm: I'm a fool for letting fuck-face foist Sam on me two years ago. For alarm bells not ringing when Cain hissed homilies about Sam's team spirit. What was Sam thinking, trying to hide losses? He will be fired. For cause. No bank will ever touch him again. He is such a well-read family man. Unlike the hyenas we breed here. First child on the way. Mistakes happen. I have to protect him.

Paul drops a WhatsApp message to Mark: "Need to speak urgently."

Mark replies, "Cigarette in 10."

Paul calls home; Ariadne is out shopping. On their fifth wedding anniversary, over a bottle of 1986 Chateau Lafite Rothschild, he had told her the story of another junior trader, Jay. Mark was then a Director reporting to Nigel— Head of Institutional Sales. Mark's client, a sophisticated hedge fund, called for a price. He looped Nigel in. Together, they approached Jay. "The size is crazy. There is no way I can hedge this deal," protested Jay.

"I understand," began Mark, cut-off by his boss.

"Get out of your fucking petticoat and wear some pants, Jay. We need traders who stand up to pee," screamed Nigel.

The deal got done. Mark made his budget for the year. The Bank lost five times his commission. Appearing before the Financial Markets Leadership Team the next day Mark said: "The Bank has always come first for me; sales commissions a distant second. I have often said no to clients at the slightest suspicion of trader mispricing."

Jay nodded, saying: "I do not expect Mark to understand the pricing of exotic path-dependent options. The misquote was my mistake. I was forced to make a price by gutter-mouth Nigel, despite expressing serious reservations."

Mark did not disagree. The Bank fired Jay, forced Nigel to resign, and promoted Mark to Head of Institutional

Sales, barely six years after he and Paul had joined the bank as Management Trainees fresh out of college.

Waiting for the lift, Paul remembers Ariadne's reaction at the time. "Well deserved," she had said, refilling their glasses. "Mark is a thorough gentleman. Seems to have high ethical standards at work too."

Laughing, he had cupped her face and kissed her. "You are so trusting, my love. Mark knew that Jay had valid reasons to not make a price. And that Nigel's ant-sized brain would never comprehend them. So, he took bullying Nigel along. All he had to do is stay quiet, and offer Jay an innocent shoulder to cry on when the shit hit the fan."

Mirrors on three sides, and reflective metal doors, yet we cannot see ourselves, muses Paul, getting out of the lift. He waits at the smoking corner, encircled by glistening glass and steel towers, watching the subway escalator disgorge a steady stream of people. "Sorry, I am late," says Mark, lighting a cigarette. "I've read the email. Call HR. I want Sam out within the hour."

Paul demurs, "Trading is headed for a record year. I can absorb Sam's loss. He's barely twenty-six. Young family. Big mortgage. Let's dock his bonus this year and move him to Sales. Cain loves him."

Mark sneers, "No wonder they call you Pooh. The size of the loss is irrelevant. Have you given any thought to the implications of this leaking out? The press will have a field day. You know very well the bank has zero tolerance for reputational risk. The inquiry will establish intent. But it is my job to hold people accountable. To demonstrate that bad behaviour has consequences. So: thief, or plain incompetent, Sam goes."

"People have gotten away with far worse," protests Paul, "Sam must have caved in to pressure from Cain. Sales does not give a fuck as to whether we make money as a bank. They think like brokers, only caring about their commissions. We need—"

"I do not agree," interrupts Mark angrily. "You need to find a better way to work with Cain." Taking a deep breath, he softens his tone: "But leave this with me. You and I go back a long way. I will protect you as best as I can."

Paul tries to keep his voice down: "*Protect me?* I must have told you a hundred times to get out of complex products. Or invest in proper systems. We did neither. I should have put my concerns on paper long ago. But didn't. To protect you from looking bad. I am sorry, but I cannot sit on this anymore."

Mark stubs out his cigarette, straightens to his six-feet-two-inches, and smiles. Turning around, he joins the hordes scurrying out of the ground towards glass cages in the sky.

Paul walks to a food court for lunch. Screw the take-away, he mutters; I am not eating at my desk. He drops a packet of pocket tissues on an empty seat, reserving it, 'choping' it, in the time-honoured Singaporean way. Strolling past stalls selling yong tau foo, chicken rice, nasi lemak, and char kway teow, he buys a set of steaming-hot chicken-tikka-masala with fresh-out-of-the-oven naan. Every spicy mouthful is an explosion of flavour, and anger: How dare fuck-face turn his back on me? After all I have done for the ingrate. No half-decent college would have admitted the fucking dimwit if he hadn't copied my examination papers and stolen my application essays. Nor would he be strutting around like a pompous peacock, singing paeans to his so-called leadership, if I hadn't doubled trading revenues. Enough. I will teach the arrogant prick a lesson he will never forget.

Sweat beads roll down Paul's forehead. Dark moons stain the shirt below his armpits. A twenty-something Barbie in high pencil-heels and a figure-hugging navy-blue dress takes the opposite seat, placing a red Chanel clutch on the table. A black Mikimoto pearl necklace highlights her flawless white skin. He stares; she smiles. To herself. He wants to linger, but finishes lunch and ambles to a little patch of green between two white colonial facades. The sun beats down from clear skies in the suffocating humidity. A tall muscular middle-aged Caucasian man, in a dark-grey tailored suit and custom hand-made black leather shoes, pensively types on a Blackberry. His pot-bellied, prematurely aging Chinese subordinate, thinning grey hair betraying bald patches, walks alongside, apprehensively looking up at his face every few seconds.

Paul is assailed by doubt: Why did Mark smile? I shouldn't have threatened him or his precious innocence. He protected me in school then fought for my promotion here at the bank. It's his job to grow revenue. The pit of slithering, cover-your-ass artistes, our Board, will not pay for a new system. The morons will shut the business down instead. I run Trading. Sam fucked-up under my watch. I have to trust Mark.

Drenched in sweat, Paul taps his access card to the lift lobby. The card reader beeps: "Access Denied." He taps again. The plastic gate opens. "Ariadne called," reads a yellow sticky-note on his monitor. The markets are tired and listless; as is he. His secretary comes over, "Should I book Post Bar at The Fullerton for team drinks tonight?"

"I am not sure," he sighs, "what else do I have on my calendar?"

"Routine one-on-one catch-ups with two of your direct-reports," she replies.

Mumbling: "I am going home. Please send my apologies and reschedule all engagements." Paul gets up to leave.

*

Ariadne reads Lama Anagarika Govinda's *The Way of the White Clouds* in the living room. "You look terrible. Is everything okay?" she asks.

"Yes, darling. Be with you soon," Paul replies.

She makes coffee while he showers. They sit at the dining table. He tells her about Sam and the run-in with Mark. "Did you ever share your concerns with Mark on email, or in someone else's presence?" she asks.

"No," he replies uneasily, hastening to reassure her: "But don't worry. Mark is in my corner."

Ariadne looks into his eyes, and smiles. They get up. Brushing against him, she whispers, "It's been too long," and leads him to her bedroom.

Basking in the afterglow, they cuddle. "Let's watch Richard Linklater's *Before Midnight*. The reviews are outstanding," she suggests, slipping into a green cotton frock. He fixes two stiff Lagavulin single malts on the rocks.

"Beautiful," she exclaims, when the protagonist, Jesse, looking at fading wall-paintings in an old Byzantine chapel, tells his wife, Celine: "These paintings here, they make me think of those Japanese monks, you know, with their deal on impermanence. They like to paint with water on rock on a hot day so by the time they're done it's already evaporated."

Paul reaches for Ariadne's hand, not letting go till the credits start rolling.

"It's nice to have you home, Paul," says Ariadne. "The bank was supposed to be a short stop, remember. You wanted to resign after making your first million, to move on to something more meaningful. It seemed so impossible then, but we have many times that now."

Drawing her close, he says, "Like Jesse, I, too, have been to the future. The sex tonight will be the best of our lives."

She laughs, pushing him away, "Unlike Jesse, you got lucky today. Now, off to your room with your phone."

Paul checks his phone for emails. There are none. The bank's email server must have crashed, he thinks, falling asleep.

He wakes up late. Still no emails. The server can't be down this long, he realises, there must be a problem with my phone. He rushes to the office. Taps his card to enter the lift lobby. "Access Denied." He taps again, and again, breaking into a cold sweat. But the gates stay shut. Maybe the access system is down, he wonders, walking to the security counter to be manually let in. The guard scans a screen. "Sorry, sir. It is best you go home. Your bank's HR will contact you. I will keep your access card."

Stunned, he calls Mark but is immediately disconnected. He calls again, reaching Mark's voicemail, but disconnects, without leaving a message.

He joins a taxi queue. Pushing a pram with one hand, a phone held to her ear with the other, a Filipina helper absent-mindedly walks towards him. A baby stares at him with wide-eyed wonder, and breaks into a broad smile.

REGINALD KENT

Babi Pongteh

The boxes wobble and their contents clang as Ze Chian curses under his breath. It doesn't help that Kepayang, an old shophouse painted with garish pastels and gold, sits on an incline. He rings the doorbell with his elbow and hears loud thumps reverberating from the restored staircase. Boon Tat greets him at the door in an apron and an oversized batik shirt. "Ah Boy! Why you take so long to visit ah?" He reaches out to hug him but realizes he can't. He turns and leaves Ze Chian to find a place for his haul.

The night before, Ze Chian had laid out the cluster of cooking implements: mooncake moulds, mortars and pestles and woks of descending diameters; there were so many, they had to be stacked like Jenga.

Then the text from his sister popped up, *Sorry Didi! Still with Qiao En, too much to catch up with, you can manage alone, right?*

Fuck Beatrice. Ze Chian perches the boxes on a table and Boon Tat invites him to sit. The chef instructs his waiter to get two glasses of *bandung*. The interior of the shophouse is thoroughly modern, save the beams and the wooden ceiling that support the second floor. Kepayang is as white and chic as any Michelin star restaurant. No more than ten tables are served at any one time. An unviable business model, but Boon Tat comes from old money. A server, with a smooth round face and a crew cut, serves them two pink milky concoctions. Ze Chian turns to Boon Tat. "I swear this one looks younger than the last one you *chee ko pek*!"

"Say louder lah!" Boon Tat flashes Ze Chian the middle finger. "So he can hear you. So uncultured! He's very good hor, worked at the Raffles before, got ambition, I respect." He leans in. "Not a crime to hire some eye candy also, right?"

"Dirty old man!"

Boon Tat gasps theatrically. "Unfilial, ungrateful boy! You don't forget who gave you that same job when you were looking for pocket money ah!"

The two laugh and catch up, though it has only been a month since they last met at the funeral. Ze Chian offers his mother's hoard to his old boss. Boon Tat beckons the same boy from the Raffles to bring the boxes to him, peers into them, then tells him to bring it all to the kitchen.

"They don't make them this solid anymore. Thank you, Ah Boy. You sure you don't want to take any for yourself?"

Ze Chian shakes his head. "No lah, you use them, give them a good home. A thank-you for helping me cater the wake. Anyway, when was the last time I made *rempah*?"

"Eh, of course, don't mention it. That's the problem with you incorrigible youths. No time for anything, eating that trash like macnoner and playing video games instead of taking the time to make a good rempah."

When he was a child, Ze Chian's mother would come back from her day at the firm and ask him to wait as she made her rempah from scratch, pounding shallots, lemongrass, ginger, galangal, garlic, candlenut and chillies with a mortar and pestle. The backbone, she would say, of Peranakan cuisine. "You see, like this, smooth, no lumps," she'd tell him showing him the thick paste. "When you can't recognize the ingredients, you know it's ready." She would fry and toss the paste with chunks of meat while the rice was steaming. As the dish sizzled in the wok, the air would be suffused with another time. As he ate, his mother would take a shower, and only eat after he and his sister started washing the dishes. He thought, watching her cook, that she would live forever. The women in Ze Chian's family always died before the men. It was as if tradition had decided it was going to spit in the eye of science. Ze Chian thought it was because they never stopped working.

"Before you head off," Boon Tat says, "I have something for you in the kitchen."

Tucked in the industrial freezer is a Tupperware. It contains chunks of meat suspended in a black block. The chef fishes it out and hands it to Ze Chian. "Your mother's *babi pongteh*. I think it's her last batch. Did you find any in her freezer?"

"No. How old is this?"

"About three months, so definitely not as good as when it's fresh but still edible. She traded it for some of my *ayam buah keluak*. Honestly, I forgot about it. You take it, more special if you have it."

*

Ze Chian returns to his mother's old home. Beatrice is in her pyjamas eating a peanut butter sandwich. "How'd it go?"

"Like you care."

"Don't be a prick. What's in the bag?"

"Don't blow off your commitments then. Boon Tat gave me this."

The almost obsidian block thuds as it hits the dining table. Beatrice rises from her sprawling position on the couch and picks it up. Her long nails, painted with glossy red polish, dig into the tight lid. She gives it a sniff, closes it, and then puts it back down. "Babi pongteh. Did he make it?"

"No, Ma made it."

"Thought so, looks and smells like hers. You let her cook when she should have been resting?"

"You think I had a say in what she did? She probably did it when I was at work."

Beatrice ignores the explanation. "Let's eat it tonight, I'll start the rice."

"No."

"What's your deal? You want to keep it in the freezer as a memento? It's food."

"I'll eat it by myself."

Beatrice lets out a snort. "Boon Tat gave it to *us* to eat."

"He gave it to *me* to eat. Go order your Foodpanda. This is mine." Ze Chian grabs it and moves towards the freezer. "Don't you dare touch it."

"Of course, everything of hers is always yours."

"For good reason."

"Oh, and what's that supposed to mean?"

"It means you come back when it suits you," he says. "You treat this family like a business."

Beatrice sighs and places her hands on her hips, covering her pyjamas with breadcrumbs and peanut butter. How did she, this slob, make anything of herself in America? How was she his mother's daughter? It must be easy being successful when someone gives you a leg up. She didn't return a cent of his mother's loan. An entitled brat in besmeared Care Bear sleepwear.

"Didi, come on, we agreed on this. There's no point keeping the house, and it's a good market."

"That's not what I meant. Fuck the house. Where were you when she was dying? Living it up in L.A."

"I told you, I was waiting for my green card. You really think I didn't want to come? Look, I'm sorry. I'm here now."

"Are you? You're in your pyjamas and clearly hungover. When did I become the older brother?"

"Oh, my god, Ze Chian. I'm allowed to have a life outside of this house. You need to figure that out for yourself. Life is not Ma."

What right does she have to his mother's last offering? The freezer begins to beep incessantly, a reminder that it's been left wide open. He places the block in, closes the door and retreats to his old room. Ze Chian regrets taking down and packing up his curtains early. The light from the streetlamps pours in through his bare windows. He shifts in bed, half-dreaming and half-remembering his mother.

He stands at the portico. She's in the kitchen on a Sunday morning and the house is overtaken by an incredible aroma of cloves and cinnamon. "Ah boy," she'd say, "wash for me." He'd uncover the heavy lid of the rice urn the size of his torso glazed with pastel peonies and phoenixes. Always three cups of rice into the pot of the Zojirushi. Ze Chian swirled the grains. As he drained, the chalky water would cloud the sink. He'd rinse and repeat. The moment it ran clear, his mother would tell him without taking her eyes off the stove, "enough." She had started the ritual after Dad had left them. It was her reclamation for the years she had to cook fish and chips or pork chops. *Chao ang mor*, she'd call him after the divorce; he refused to touch anything that was too heavily spiced. Ze Chian turns over and sniffs the air. But this smell, no this is real—cloves and cinnamon wafting into his bedroom. That bitch!

Beatrice is standing in front of the microwave, illuminated by its yellow fluorescent light. She has a bowl of rice with a spoon in it. Ze Chian grabs it from her.

"What the fuck!" she screams.

He opens the microwave and retrieves the Tupperware. When he reaches the hallway leading to the bedrooms, he hears her. "You're deranged! You know that, Didi?!" After he puts his prize on his desk, he locks his door. He pours the steaming contents of the Tupperware into his bowl. His mouth is soon coated with a lingering layer of spices, carried by the pork fat that has melted into the stew. The pork is so tender it disintegrates into the rice. When he's done, he stares into the bowl. He feels his mother's death as dark as dried cloves wash over him, spreading from his mouth to the rest of his body. He begins to cry, that's all she will be now—a dream.

When Ze Chian does dream of his father, they are in Amsterdam. He is always a little boy holding a hand in a black leather glove. They walk by the canals lined with narrow houses. He asks his father what the beams on top of the *grachtenpand* are called. "*Verhuishaak*, moving hooks," his father replies in his thick accent. He asks what they are for, and then he's picked up by the wrist and swung forward, his father shouting, "To lift up little boys like you!"

By his mattress on the floor is a box of abandoned books. Dutch history. After his father left them, Ze Chian read in a mania. He discovered that they liked pancakes, speculated on tulips, and were merchants. During the eighteenth century, it'd take up to two years for a letter to return home from a Dutch East India Company colony like Java, so their sovereigns gave them free rein. Using his phone flashlight, he flips again through some middle inserts, early maps of the Maluku islands in Indonesia— the only place where cloves grew in the world. To create artificial scarcity and spike demand, the fine men from the Netherlands burnt most of the spice groves in Maluku to the ground. They bathed the islands in blood, brutally quashing all resistance. The British who took over weren't much better. They uprooted the trees that remained and scattered them across their colonies for their subjects to tend to. Spice growing was a whole lot of trial and error, with a lot more error than trial. Beatrice carries his father in her, she takes what she wants and leaves with the winds of change, her plunder in her pocket.

"Not the same yet," Boon Tat judges, taking the teaspoon from his mouth, "Not the right mix."

*

It's Ze Chian's fourth attempt. He spends his nights borrowing Kepayang's kitchen after the dinner service. The pork trotters simmer in the black reduction comprising garlic, fermented soybeans, soy sauce, shallots and spices. Boon Tat jokes, "If I tell the team it's babi pongteh for family meal again, I think they're going to kill me. You take this batch home tonight."

Ze Chian takes his own teaspoon, slurps, then slumps on a stool.

His old boss sighs. "Look. Your mother took years to come up with it, cannot expect to figure out so fast one. Why don't you just give this a break, spend more time with your sister instead of this *lao gay*."

"You still think I should patch up with her?"

Boon Tat sets a timer and lowers the heat on the stove. He pulls out another stool. "You're lucky to still have family. You can call me old school, but at the end of the day she's still your sister. Why don't you give her a chance?"

"She keeps asking me how I could have let Ma do this, let her do that. Why I let the doctors treat her that way. Bitch, where the hell was she?"

"You cannot think liddat one. Your *Jie* had to live her life. You know the most, your mother also not the easiest to be around hor. So, she went away, didn't you want too as well?"

"She took everything. Ma had to live so frugally after she asked for those loans. All for a new life in America. Ma was stuck because of her."

"Your mother, or you, Ah Boy?"

Making babi pongteh, Ze Chian realizes, isn't like making rempah. There is no piping hot oil and vigorous frying. It is a slow process—he waits as the stew sits on the stove for hours on a low heat; simmering as the pork turns the broth gelatinous and that fat takes on the flavour of spices. It's a dish reliant on sacrificed time.

He thinks of his father, as good as dead to him. He didn't come to the funeral. Two and even four centuries ago, when Dutch sailors went on a voyage for spices, was it wise for them to think of home? Was it wise to think of the wives and children they left behind—the infants who would not know them when they returned? Was that taste, that morsel, that little bit of flavour, worth it? Were dried flowers on faraway islands worth the pustulating pools of blood?

He would not let Beatrice's decision to leave for America be the nail in his mother's coffin. He would not betray her as his sister and father did. He stayed so his mother wouldn't have to think of dying alone.

Ze Chian counts the streetlamps as he drives home. Lights are just another preservation, a mourning from the day past, a clinging on as it dies. Maybe Boon Tat was right. He did want to leave this country—this sleepy port town, now an illuminated metropolis. It all caught up with his mother in the end. The women in Ze Chian's family always died before the men. He hadn't worked hard enough to keep her from dying.

*

Beatrice hands the property agent the keys. The agent smiles and departs. She sits on the floor, cross-legged in front of the kitchen portico. Ze Chian joins her and says, "Look,

Ma would have wanted us to get along. I know I've been a little shit. Sorry."

"You know I loved her, right?"

"You don't leave the people you love."

"You do when you know you don't work out."

"After you left, she'd have the blankest look when she cooked. She was always somewhere else."

"I'm sorry you took care of her alone. But you of all people should know you can't live for other people."

"What's that supposed to mean."

"You took the first step, you moved out to live with your boyfriend."

"I'm not like you. We've been on a break since Mom got sick. I've been here."

"Didi, I'm not taking that away from you. I never said I was a perfect daughter."

"I'm not asking for perfect, I'm asking for decent."

"I don't know if you were too young to remember. Before you could walk, she used to beat me. It got worse after Dad left. I did everything right for her. Best grades, no boyfriends, all the filial piety nonsense. Yeah, I was angry. Even after you came out, she still loved you the way she loved you. It was fucked up to feel jealous, I know. But your Ma and my Ma are not the same person."

Ze Chian doesn't feel inclined to believe her. His mother was strict, but he had never seen a rattan cane in his life. He had vague memories of her reprimanding Beatrice over grades, but wasn't that every Asian parent? It's not like he didn't experience it too. And what did Beatrice want from Ma after he came out? Did she want her to disown him? It was Beatrice's words against the void left by his mother. For now, this revelation would just have to sit. He gets up and moves toward the kitchen. "Let's eat."

Ze Chian starts setting the table and reheats his last batch in the only pot left in the house, clay, cracked, and charred. Beatrice starts the rice in a new Zojirushi cooker that she'll pack back home. They take out disposable bowls and cutlery.

"I've been trying to make Ma's," he tells her. "It never turns out right. I can't figure out the spices."

She ladles some babi pongteh on her rice and chews. "I honestly think this is better, more authentic."

"What do you mean?"

"You prefer Ma's? Babi pongteh isn't supposed to be black but dark brown. You're supposed to just use dark soy sauce. Ma's is so black and salty because she added Marmite."

"No! That's disgusting."

"I thought so, but I guess you didn't. You were never objective about what Ma made. She made us wait so long for dinner that anything tasted good."

ADELINE TAN

The Inevitability of Falling

Amanda sees what she thinks is a crow from the corner of her eye.

She'd often seen those unruly birds at the opposite housing block, perched at the ends of bamboo poles that stuck out of Singaporean kitchen windowsills like raised arms. The gaudy array of laundry flapped beneath their yellow claws as they cocked their heads to survey the land— bed linen with floral patterns or comic-book characters; boxy school uniforms in white, green and blue; housedresses demure in cut but worn to the point of indecency; striped and checked shirts beside bland-coloured trousers. Then, in a flash, the crows lifted themselves off the pole. Amanda would hold her breath as they surrendered to gravity and *let themselves fall*. In every falling, she had a sensation of being pulled back to her childhood, to an age in which glass cups kept slipping from clumsy hands. Amanda was never sure if she'd actually willed these accidents to happen. Each fall felt inevitable; she was just *there* to tip the glass over. She'd never be able to avert her eyes, from either the glasses or the crows. Even though she knew the glass would smash, splinter and scatter against the tiled floor, causing her father to lift his eyes from his newspaper in irritation, and her mother to gather the shards in grim annoyance. Even though she knew the crows would spread their midnight wings at the last second, she always stayed right where she was, at the kitchen window to witness the birds skim the earth as if over the calm surface of a lake, then land gently on the grass lining the walkway.

Minutes before, she had furiously been running a stainless steel sponge over a badly charred kettle, sweat pooling above her lip. Her mother had frantically called an hour earlier—*Don't ask why I'm in the hospital, the house is going to explode!* Amanda was more puzzled than concerned at her call; Ma always contacted Denise first, or Adrian, if it wasn't a weekday. She had pinched her lips flat when she found the blackened object glowering at her, quietly emitting dry pops and crackles over the blue flame of her mother's stove. When she turned on the tap and immersed the scorched kettle, it sucked hard at its metal body, hissing indignant puffs of steam. Now she was almost ready to give up scrubbing, the kettle still black and bent out of shape, but she didn't dare to entertain the thought of throwing it away. Her mother would say, as always: *Still can use!*

Then that streak out the window. A slash like a zip pulled downward. Fast. Not a black shadow, but a red that gives off its own light. Amanda feels this surge as if it were passing through the length of her body. She knows it isn't a crow—this swooping dive feels heavier, with no wings to break the fall. The sound is blunt and heavy like a giant gavel, a slam that snaps the world to attention. Amanda freezes, then stretches her body across the sink to look past the window grilles, down at the playground where she whiled away her teenage years, at the orange plastic tunnel slide where she hid herself after school, smoking cigarettes. She forces herself to look.

*

The Facebook post by an online news website reveals little—mother and five-year-old son were discovered at the foot of Block 843, Clementi Street 12. No foul play was suspected. *Both were dressed in red, a red string tied to the wrists of both bodies.* Roselyn recognises in the photograph the familiar green and white of the housing block. Uniformed men mill about a blue tent with the word *Police* printed in large block letters. The orange tunnel slide is an unfocused blob in the foreground, as if the photographer took the picture from a guilty distance.

Roselyn shudders, switches off her smartphone, and pulls a rumpled blouse from a pile of laundered clothes. She listlessly runs the iron over the blouse, and dimly remembers the sound. Yesterday, the flat was almost empty like any other weekday, with Sir and Ma'am at work, little Caleb at school and Ah Ma dozing in her room after her stroll at the wet market. Roselyn had just switched off the vacuum stick; the emptiness tickled her ears. Then she heard the sound. It was faint; it felt more like a numbing of the brain than a sound. She ran into the kitchen, unlatched and slid aside the window grille and extended her body as far as she could. She looked to her near left, where a narrow road threaded through the housing estate, and the far right, where the playground marked the ends of the two parallel housing blocks. She could see nothing out of the ordinary.

Nine years of working in Singapore has made Roselyn feel secure—she initially kept her distance from those gaping holes, twelve stories above solid ground. Back in the Philippines, falling out of windows was just one of a thousand things she was warned about, during the two-week training course at a two-storey building in Bulacan. By day, she was taught how to operate electrical appliances, cook Western and Asian dishes for her future employers. She learnt how to bathe their elderly and infants, change their diapers, unfold and collapse their wheelchairs and prams. By night, the girls giggled and nudged each other as their instructor pointed out what not to wear: *No low-cut blouses like this, or shorts like this!* There were groans of dismay when it was emphasised that wearing make-up was out of the question.

Eventually, Roselyn had even learnt to say goodbye to her daughter. Her mother had travelled two hours from their *barangay* by boat to Bulacan, dragging a tired and hungry Charlene. How does a mother tell her five-year-old child—eyes filled with sleep and irritation—that she has to leave her to work in a country far away? What words did Charlene know that allowed her to grasp the situation? In the morning, Roselyn left her curled up on the mattress, hugged her mother and boarded the van for the airport.

Roselyn hangs the last of the ironing in the walk-in wardrobe, slides the door shut and surveys the master bedroom—the spotless 55-inch TV screen on a concrete-laminate feature wall, the ironed bedsheets on the king-size bed, the freshly mopped faux-wood tiled flooring. Sir and Ma'am had hollowed out the flat and renovated it according to their preferences when they decided to move in to take care of Sir's mother. Roselyn straightens her baggy T-shirt and reties her ponytail. She returns to the kitchen to check on the porridge simmering on the stove, watching the plump white rice grains jostle in the pot like tiny magnets, wondering what makes a mother take a child with her in death.

*

"I'm so sorry to hear the news."

"You're back at your mother's? Her cancer's back again?"

"Your dad passed away a few years ago right? Heart attack?"

"Will you hire a helper?"

Over the week that follows, Amanda fields the well-meaning but repetitive questions—via text messages or awkward meetings—with stock answers refined and repeated as appreciatively as she can. Clients say to call whenever she is ready to work again; relatives and neighbours drop by with gentle words and sincere prayers; friends speak of miraculous survival stories of their mums' friends' friends. Amanda knows that they'd all meant to console and encourage, but the weak analgesic effect of their words are like a dentist's candy-pink mouthwash.

From the dining table, Amanda watches her niece and nephew run circles around the sofa till Adrian looks up from some documents and issues them a stern look. They snap to obedience but continue to wage battle, butting shoulders on a sofa that easily accommodates three adults. They ignore the old Jet Li movie playing on the ancient TV with the sound muted. There's no Netflix, no YouTube, no Disney+ in this home. No internet connection. Amanda hears Denise pottering in the kitchen; the easy smell of vegetable soup wafts into the living room. She's grateful for the break. Her feeble attempts at cooking had come up short; the soup was always too salty, the vegetables too bland, the rice too hard, her mother complained. *When's my daughter-in-law dropping by?*

Adrian helps their mother over to the armchair in front of the TV; she's tired after their discussion. Her two grandchildren spring up and ask their *Ah-Ma* if she'd like a massage. She casts a sly glance at them and pulls out two one-dollar coins from her pyjama blouse pocket. They immediately plank her legs on the coffee table and get to work like serious bakers, puckering her dry skin with every knead of their nubby fingers.

Adrian returns and gathers up the documents, taps the bottom edges against the dining table.

"You doing okay?"

"Ask me again next week. It's only been a few days."

"Let me know whenever you need some time off."

"You're already taking care of all the finances," Amanda shrugs. "And I have all the time in the world."

Adrian slips the documents into a folder, jots some to-do items on a Post-It pad, then bends over to retrieve his briefcase from the floor. His small bald patch gleams under the pendant light, and Amanda feels a sudden wave of tenderness for her little brother. She wraps her arms around herself and absent-mindedly rubs her barb-wire tattoo with chipped nails. Not yet forty, Adrian looks the older sibling, with his Rolex watch, stiff white shirt and black pants. She glances at the contents in his briefcase. Everything has its place—folders grouped in their coloured tribes, the identical-twinned notebooks, pens snapped to vertical attention in leather loops. She remembers the unpacked pile of clothes hastily stuffed into her duffel and the boxes containing the rest of her belongings haphazardly stacked in one corner of her old room.

Dwayne and Ashley are now debating how much strength they should apply to ensure optimal comfort for their *Ah Ma*. Amanda's eyes trace the half-curve of her mother's smile as she pretends to squirm with every touch of their tiny hands. She's never seen the full arc of it, has to imagine the other side like a mirrored phantom limb. Dinner's almost ready—three dishes and a soup. Adrian's talking to Denise in the kitchen, his voice calm and low. He helps his wife dole out spades of perfect, fluffy rice into bowls.

How can Amanda blame her mother for how her life has turned out, when Adrian has proved to be the perfect son? They were brought up in exactly the same way, but the pressure of their father's iron fist and their mother's penny-pinching ways broke them differently. Adrian's now a personal banker for wealthy business people, having climbed his way up from hawking financial products to irritated passers-by at roadshows. Amanda barely earns enough as a freelance television director to afford the rent of the too-large apartment she's just given up. Perhaps her brother had the fortune of learning from her; he was witness to her screaming matches with their mother, her stubborn silence towards their father. Rather than being caught in the crossfire, he had the clarity of mind to steer clear of the mayhem, quietly knitting his own destiny.

Tired from the exertion, Dwayne and Ashley pocket their salary and turn their attention to Amanda. She allows them to take over her smartphone; they bicker over what games to download. In the armchair that was once reserved solely for her father, the cracked leather pouches her mother's sleeping body. Her head lolls to one side, exposing her shorn and white-speckled scalp. She suddenly looks vulnerable, her body deflated under her baggy pink pyjamas, an aging child. Amanda pads into the kitchen, opens the garbage chute and empties the dustbin, watching the cut-up credit cards and expired supermarket coupons disappear into the darkness.

*

Roselyn and Farid lie on a grassy slope of the park, the plastic mat crinkling softly under them. As usual, they chose a spot not too far from their friends, behind a row of bushes. Some of the others had coupled up too, while the rest coyly mingle in a group. Farid's lying on his side, emitting soft snores. Roselyn looks at his soft brown face— he looks so much like a child, even though he's only a few years younger. She turns to gaze at the Marina Barrage, a manmade vista of skyscrapers, giant glass greenhouses and the Singapore Flyer, underscored by a ribbon of calm water. She has seen skyscrapers in Hollywood movies—New York, London, Hong Kong—and was awed by them. They loomed over people while clawing at the sky like mirrored fingers. Now they're just blurred images from bus and train windows that she usually ignores. She raises her hand and measures the observation wheel with a pinch of her fingers.

Farid arrived a little more than a year ago; he's still trying to get over his fear of heights. The first time they were alone, shyly sitting apart on a stone bench, they talked about their previous lives in the Philippines and Bangladesh. He spoke of his undergraduate days in Dhaka, where he studied History. *You're so smart*, Roselyn enthused, *I only finished high school, but my Charlene will go to university someday. That's why I have to work hard.* Farid told her about the work he was doing. *Over there*, he pointed to the towers of the

Central Business District. The building project he's assigned
to was twenty stories high when they first met. Soon it'll
be fifty stories tall. In the evenings he sometimes witnessed
the most beautiful views, he said—the sun sinking its yolk
in the purple sky—while he waited for large glass panels to
float down from tower cranes. Late at night, the wind was so
forceful and the ground so far away that he would imagine
himself falling as he stood at the edge where the concrete
gave way to nothing—that feeling of tipping and letting go
was so intense that he had to reach out for his safety harness
to know that he was standing straight up, not bent over like
he had imagined. And that was when Farid slid his hand
over Roselyn's, and she closed her fingers over his.

That was three months ago. They have yet to book a
hotel room and spend an afternoon in private. Whenever
their friends excused themselves from a gathering, Farid
would shyly look at Roselyn, but she always pretended not
to notice. She needs to be sure she will not be cheated again,
and besides, romances like theirs hardly end in marriage.
Roselyn watches Farid stretch lazily and turn to the other
side, and wonders if he conveniently forgot to mention
a wife and child back home, as she did an untraceable
husband?

Her smartphone buzzes in her bag; she frowns at the
screen. There's no Wi-Fi hotspot so the call will eat up a
chunk of her pre-paid plan.

"*Ina*, it's not convenient for me to talk."

"Charlene has run away!" her mother wails.

"What happened? Didn't you say she's doing well in
school?"

"Charlene's a good girl," her mother insists. "She's a smart girl, but she has run away with some boy!"

Roselyn listens to her mother ramble, cutting up and stitching together stories like a patchwork quilt about someone who's now more a distant niece than daughter to her. Charlene will be fifteen soon – Roselyn dimly registers the perils of that age for a girl, but she has chosen to accept her mother's reports on how everything's fine. *Don't worry about us.* She knows her mother does the same to Charlene, painting a rosy picture of a hardworking mother *on her knees scrubbing toilets* in order to build a house for the family— one whose roof won't wash away with the floods—and a better future for her, one in which the journey to school isn't a two-hour trek through the mountains.

How homesick she was during those early years with her first employer, lying on her fold-out bed at night replaying pixelated videos of Charlene saying *I miss you, Ina*, under the persistent encouragement of her grandmother. She'd scroll through the numerous photographs and voice messages sent via Messenger, and whisper back delayed recordings to Charlene, *I miss you too, have you been taking care of your Lola for me?* She wanted to run away and return home, but she clung on despite the difficulties—her smartphone confiscated on weekdays, eating mouldy bread or leftover food laid out for her, the erections she had to ignore while bathing her employers' elderly father. Now, with the Lim family, conditions are better. Every two years, she's allowed to return home for a short vacation. She always took back gifts of clothes and toys, but Charlene clung to her grandmother's trousers and regarded Roselyn first with shyness, then ambivalence, and finally indifference. Her daughter's apathy stung her initially; now it's no more than background noise that Roselyn occasionally registers with a pang of guilt.

"*Ina*, stop," Roselyn says. Her mother's crying uncontrollably now, begging her to find Charlene, *There must be a way*. Roselyn glances at Farid. He's curled up like a baby now, while her friends are calling out to her, *It's time to go*.

The train barrels into the underground tunnel, a sudden switch from light to dark. Roselyn ignores the message from Farid, launches her Facebook app and searches for Charlene's profile. When her picture pops up Roselyn stares into the face of a stranger, a pretend-adult with clumsily applied makeup, as much an avatar as photograph. Roselyn ventures into her daughter's page. In this virtual world, she's twenty-one-years old, in a relationship, born in Manila and currently studying in New York. Roselyn snorts softly. Does Charlene even know how much a plane ticket to America costs? She raises her head and watches her reflection in the train window, superimposed over the grey tunnel wall. She has not spoken directly to Charlene for many months, preferring her mother to send her updates, like passing messages through strings on tin cans. She begins to compose a message, but her fingers hover uncertainly over the screen.

*

A single wail pierces through the high-rise neighbourhood. Amanda's eyes fly open, her body shocked to attention. The air thickens with anticipation, but no one stirs to find out what has happened. After a while the wail becomes a ghost echo, like a dream half-dreamt. She turns over to face the window and brings her knees to her chest, her body already used to the single bed unslept in since her father's funeral.

Was this how she smelt when she was young, layers of stale baby powder sedimented into the still fusty bedsheet? She runs her finger across Wish Bear's stomach, the yellow shooting star almost faded into the background cream. She found the abandoned Bears in the wardrobe—Grumpy and Tenderheart and Love-A-Lot still perched on clouds or swinging from rainbows—and decided to give them a bath. This morning, she laid the sundried sheet over the bed, the Bears looking somewhat happier, and remembered how she once threw her tiny body down on the floor of a department store, screaming bloody murder in the bedding section till her mother dragged her past the averted eyes of a security guard. Months later, on her ninth birthday, Amanda found the Care Bears bedsheet fitted over her mattress. By then, she no longer wanted it.

A moan comes through the baby monitor; Amanda feels the poke of irritation generously spiked with guilt. She gets up and stumbles across the narrow hallway into her mother's bedroom. Light from the attached bath throws a narrow beam across the floor, climbing up the bones of a king-size bed propped against the wall. Her mother's face is a diffused shade of grey, a stone puckering the pillow on the bulky hospital bed. She barely sleeps through the night now, even with increased doses of oxycontin.

"Water," she croaks.

In a state of grogginess, Amanda gropes her way to the kitchen. She has no sure estimation of her body, bumping into her father's altar in the living room, missing the small step that separates the kitchen from the dining area, crashing her fingers against wall cabinets. She curses when she chips a cup against the sink counter, and fumbles for the straw left to dry in the dish rack.

Her mother takes a long time with the drink, sucking in more air than water.

"What else do you want?" Amanda says, her voice rough with fatigue. She doesn't mean to sound uncaring, but that rebellious tone reserved for her mother comes too easily, like a wheel locking into a well-worn groove.

The pain makes her mother oblivious.

I want to die.

The stone, with nothing left to lose, finally casts itself down a deep well. Those words, so incomprehensible to Amanda because they are never uttered—not in that way— to anyone, and especially not to the ones you hate. And she always thought her mother hated her. Hated her refusal to be a *good girl*, whatever her idea of a good girl was, while she blindly strove to become what her mother didn't want her to be. And what exactly was that?

Now, Amanda cannot avert her eyes. The clock pulling in both directions, fast and slow at the same time. They should've been ready for the end, but they were all wrapped up in a flurry of administrative living. Amanda moving out of her too-large apartment, abandoning a life with a man she refused to marry. Her brother avoiding his children's prodding questions while their mother decided on the colour of her casket, what flowers she likes, what she should wear. Their mother tipping over, but no one noticing, not even herself.

Inevitable. Her mother's organs shut down like clockwork within mere weeks—her kidneys, her bowels, her lungs. One morning, she'll whisper to Amanda, *You have to bathe me, I can't do it by myself anymore.* She'll sit on the closed toilet seat like an obedient child as Amanda undresses her mother, soaps whatever hair she has left and lets the suds slide down the purple scar, where her right breast would be. Adrian is summoned to the house in a panic one night, because their mother's thrashing wildly in her bed, threatening to rip the oxygen tube from her nose. Finally, the night-time vigils, with Amanda waking up every other hour to dab her mother's lips with water, watching her quietly snatch air until one night, just before dawn, she wakes up to her mother opening her mouth for the last time, and finds herself pulled back to the moment she witnessed her mother's smile.

I want to die.

Her mother rolls her head back, relieved and exhausted from the confession at the same time. Amanda's taken aback by the tears stealing from her own eyes, clinging stubbornly to her eyelashes. Her mother reaches out to touch her hair.

"Why are you crying? Don't scare me, tough girl." She tries to laugh off the awkwardness and smiles, and her face opens up like the sun.

Amanda slides open her bedroom window and shakily lights a cigarette. *Tough girl.* That's what Ivan loved about her. That's what drove him away. She fiddles with the buttons on her smartphone, unsure about sending a message to him. She remembers the final fight they had.

What do you want from me? she had screamed.

He could only look at her, speechless. *Why do you treat me like I'm the enemy?*

*

"Auntie Rose."

On the roll-up mattress in the living room, Roselyn feels the air-conditioning from Caleb's room.

"Why aren't you asleep? You have school tomorrow." Roselyn pulls her blanket aside, and Caleb burrows in.

"I heard a loud noise. Shouldn't we go investigate?"

"You'll wake up Daddy and Mummy."

Caleb falls silent.

"Daddy will be mad at me. I think I failed my Maths test."

Roselyn puts an arm over Caleb. "Well, you don't know for sure, right?"

He whispers about all the unanswered questions on the test paper, and she counters, *But maybe you got all the other questions right?* Caleb seems suspicious but willing to accept the possibility. He allows her to tuck him back into bed, snuggling under the thick comforter.

In the kitchen, Roselyn dispenses a glass of water for herself. She knows she's one of the lucky ones, even though she doesn't have a room of her own, and on occasion has too many chores that keep her working past ten o'clock. As they like to say in Singapore: *Cannot complain.* She chuckles at the Singlish she's picked up over the years. She was about to renew her contract for the fourth time when she told Sir and Ma'am of her daughter's call, which arrived after weeks of silence. They nodded and wished her well, but Roselyn detected a note of irritation in Ma'am's voice. A new helper will take weeks, if not months, to train.

Caleb will miss her, but he'll adjust. There'll be someone else to know he hates coriander in his soup, to check his bag to make sure he has the right books for classes, to wait for him outside the school gates. To sometimes sneak to the provision shop for a soft drink, or let him spend fifteen minutes at the playground before going home.

Can you send me some money?

Charlene finally picked up when Roselyn tried calling again a few days ago. She was shocked at the sudden click of connection at the other end. Charlene resisted her attempts at conversation, was tight-lipped about where she was, who she was with, what she was doing. Roselyn felt her guilt harden into anger. *Listen to me, I'm your mother. Don't follow in my footsteps*, she wanted to shout at her, but she'd have to admit the paths she'd taken, the wrongs she'd done. She fears the day when she returns. What will she say when she meets her back home? What authority does she have over this daughter she herself has turned into a stranger?

Roselyn slips back into bed and waits for morning to arrive. There'll be no facility to ease her back into her own family. They were trained to be helpers, and when the job ends, they are expected to snap back into the roles they vacated. In that one-storey building all those years ago, the group role-played: Helpers, Sirs, Ma'ams, Children. Some of the girls giggled as they drew moustaches above their lips with mascara. They slipped on shirts and pants. Others wore heavy make-up and high heels. They were taught how to be polite and clean the house in the exact way their Ma'ams instructed, *Do it their way, even if it's slower, or makes no sense*. They were taught how to fend off their Sirs if they hugged them from behind, *Be firm. Say no. Go to the agency for help*. Roselyn was Ma'am in one scenario, and her friends, Helper and Child. *You have to do it for real,* the instructor commanded, *or else the lesson won't be helpful.* The Helper was eating her dinner, and the Child skipped over and insisted on sharing her food. The Helper tried to cover her plate with her body. *That's right,* the instructor encouraged, *Don't let them eat from your plate, and never let them call you Mummy.* Roselyn came over and yanked the Child away. She started to slap at the Helper, and suddenly she burst into tears. Shocked, Roselyn gripped her friend and hugged her tightly, smoothing her hair while rocking her gently.

It's okay, my dear. We're just pretending.

*

Today's the last day of the wake. Amanda was the first to arrive, but all she had to do was open the metal gate that housed her mother's casket. She gazes at her mother through a layer of plexiglass and mouths, *Morning, Ma.*

The funeral parlour took care of everything, and the three-day wake proceeded smoothly under the supervision of bereavement guides. They shepherded the mourners like lambs, knowing that modern families are rarely familiar with the old traditions. Buddhist monks performed the usual rites and the emcees calmly recited what the family members needed to do, saving them the embarrassment of pretending to know. They knelt, bowed, walked around the casket and stuck joss sticks into the urn when directed.

Amanda settles herself at a table facing the road. Adrian told her someone from the neighbourhood would be coming to pay her last respects—an old lady their mother occasionally chatted with at the wet market. Not knowing what to do with her hands, she opens the bento box on the table. She pulls a single strand from the skein of red thread nestled in the middle compartment, as if drawing blood.

Somewhere down the road, just five minutes from the funeral parlour, Roselyn looks out the side window of Sir's car. Ah Ma nags at her son to hurry up; he grunts irritably and searches for a text message on his smartphone. He reads out the name of the funeral parlour, and asks Roselyn to keep a look out. He'll drop his mother off, then take her to the agency to finalise some documents. Roselyn has never been to this part of Singapore, and she finds this mix of car workshops and funeral parlours curious. Behind them, a huge temple looms.

Amanda gazes at the gold, bell-shaped tower piercing the sky, absentmindedly twirling the red thread around her finger. In a few hours, her mother will be cremated in the temple columbarium. An elderly man exits the funeral parlour office, his shirt sleeves rolled up and vest unbuttoned. "These birds stupid or what. Got tree, don't sleep in tree." Amanda looks at where the man is directing his curses. In the blue morning light, a few pigeons roost sleepily on the gravel road, their heads tucked into their necks. The man flails his arms and shouts at them. They lazily flap their wings, lifting themselves off the ground a little only to circle back and settle on the road again. The man sighs. "Later, car come, sure *mati*."

Both Amanda and Roselyn are unprepared.

One witnesses the crush of pigeons under the slow, silent wheels of Sir's car, a red that gives off its own light. The other hears the sickening sound of bone crunching on gravel, so faint it almost feels like a numbing of the brain.

Roselyn looks out the side window and sees Amanda staring at the car in horror. She turns in her seat, twisting her head to peer out of the rear window. A man lifts the birds by their legs—one in his left and two on his right. He tosses them without a second thought into a large rubbish bin by the road. Amanda hears the scrabble of claw against plastic, then silence reigns once again, the emptiness tickling her ears.

Dean and Gina Go to Cold Storage

"Well, shit," Dean says. "I've walked the entire fridge section twice and guess what? No damn eggs. You'd think they sell eggs in *any* supermarket, but I must be wrong—"

He laments this to me all too loudly in his Ontario accent, a grown child sounding nasal. His voice pairs well with his looks: broad face and sun-stung cheeks, messy mop of blond hair, colorful breezy outfit. If we were back in Canada, the land of affable brotherhood, no one would have minded my husband's good-natured volume. Here in Singapore, in the narrow aisles of a westernized supermarket called Cold Storage, he veers sharply out of place.

And though he is never one to quiet down, his booming voice is drowned out by brassy, girlish laughter.

Dean looks past me, and his mouth grows slack. I turn. Two girls—women, probably in their mid-twenties but they look so young—approach us in the cereal and grains aisle. Their giggling is a public display. They flash their eyes and slant their shoulders. Rich, dusky shoulders that emerge from blouses stretched like a sash across their breasts, cloaked by lush jet-black hair gently grazing their asses. Both are wearing red with the confidence of someone born for the spotlight, a colour that turns their skin into liquid gold. My own skin is dark for Chinese complexions but has now faded to sickly beige, like a used Band Aid, after a Canadian winter. Then again, I have never looked so intensely smooth. If they had wrapped themselves in sarongs instead of denim shorts, they would look right at home on a beach in this part of the world. A pair of Thai girls selling sandy trinkets. *Are* they Thai? I wonder. Seeing them, it finally hits me. We aren't home anymore.

Dean is quick to cover his tracks. He reaches for a box of quinoa although he doesn't care for the gritty texture. Somehow, he has acquired a toothpick, which he chews in one corner of his month, a caricature of concentration. He busies himself with math, explaining that prices here are marked up at least twenty percent, but a woman knows. With him distracted, though, I can't help but sneak another glance at the two girls.

Do men know that when women see beautiful women, we don't think something as simple as, "Hey, there's a pretty lady"? We see beauty in precise terms, though not in the conventional way men section us off. We notice sharp eyes, smooth skin, a daring jawline, a careless air of confidence. Then count the ways we don't measure up.

They are not the most striking women I have seen. One is sprouting dark hairs outside the outline of her eyebrows like a toddler took to them with a fat crayon, and the other has a harsh flaring nose. Still, something in the assertive, practiced way they giggle mesmerizes me. Their eyes sidle up to Dean like he is some shiny carnival prize, which makes me want to laugh. Dean is jubilant about Singapore's perma-summer. He has put on his tropical best, wearing a tank top in kaleidoscopic blues, salmon-pink shorts that fit too snugly, and flip-flops. His sunglasses nestle on the brim of his cap, now on backwards. In all our years of dating (a respectable three) and marriage (just over one), he has never suggested a vacation spot outside of the Caribbean, where he can blissfully burn to a crisp and attempt hydration with Coronas. That's just the way with heat-starved Canadians.

When the girls turn their gaze on me, I register a sneer I don't understand. They scan me from head to toe, soaking in information and sizing me up. Their eyes flick back to Dean, still engrossed in the foreign price of grains. They burst into a fresh fit of giggles just as they walk past.

"So. Eggs," I say, when the girls have turned the corner. "I'll try to find them."

"Oh, great call, babe. You'd know better than me where to look." He nods, fixing the quinoa box with a skeptical eye. "I'm just going to stay here and work this out. It's just so expensive, I don't get it."

The way he's fumbling is almost reassuring. After all, he may only be taken aback by the sight of different people. Just like I am. I rub his back. I figure if they were here just now, surely, they wouldn't return to this aisle, those girls with their tight clothes and swaying hair. I can leave Dean here.

My hair is not dissimilar in colour though finer and hangs in a short limp mess around my ears. I am suddenly aware that I had last washed it with Canadian water, at Dean's mom's house the morning of our flight. Dean and I arrived in Singapore in the middle of the night after a multi-stop long-haul. Though the airport with plush floral carpeting was miles more calming and efficient than the barking mess of Pearson, I could not shake off the vivid idea that we were merely on vacation. The equatorial sunlight this morning does little to help. When we walk out in sandals, humidity steams from the concrete onto our bare toes. Palm trees stand incongruous to my season-centric brain. It all feels too unlike real life, too much like a stroll to the breakfast cabana at a beach resort.

Dean thought I would love living in the part of the world he calls "my heritage." He had said so when he first brought up the transfer opportunity his finance company had offered him, back in our glossy condo on Toronto's College Street.

"Dean. You know my family's from Hong Kong," I said, waiting for the coils of our stove to heat up a pot of pasta sauce. I didn't remind him that I was born at a hospital just a few blocks over. Or say that, growing up, my only exposure to Asia came from the rare trips over the Pacific to visit relatives. Hong Kong always unsettled me. It was too crowded, too loud, smarting with its constant thrum.

"I meant 'closer'. Gina, you're missing the point. It's Asia! Of course it'll be dope."

"Yeah, but we don't know anything about Singapore. Is it like a resort? Is it rice paddies? And it's so far away."

"You'll love it. You'll just, I don't know, feel it when you get there."

"Feel what?"

"Feel *it*. Like in your bones you'll feel like you belong."

The idea rattled my brain. I sputtered through an analogy that would apply to him—if we moved to France would Dean, with his Scottish great-grandparents, feel the particles of his body snap back to their factory settings?— but, of course, my argument went nowhere. Scotland was Scotland, France was France. And Dean was Canadian through and through.

Yet, I remembered the easy feeling of anonymity in Hong Kong that I never had in Toronto. Everywhere, a sea of black hair, and I was a drop like any. That night in bed, I said to him, "So, you think you've got good reasons why I'd like it there. And maybe you have a point. I said 'maybe'!" Dean was holding his index fingers up like he had scored a touchdown. I threw a pillow at him. "But how are you so sure you're going to like it?"

Dean tossed his phone onto the bedside table. He turned to me and slipped his arm under my neck, jolting the mattress and snagging my hair, each of his movements heavy, solid, certain. "'Cos, Geenie," he said, nuzzling close, "I love *you*, don't I?"

*

I could always see Dean's blind spots, and they never bothered me. I enjoy living inside Dean's idea of me as some otherworldly being, different and alluring. I can be me, with my nerves and tempers, and he will keep pace. His father, a local councilman, had been cold and austere to him growing up, but Dean is friendly to everyone. He learned to be comforting as well as kind and in just the right ways. I feel safe when I'm with him, like I would be welcomed with open arms anywhere we go.

Though I hadn't thought to include Singapore in "anywhere." This morning, I had walked out of our new apartment into open-air hallways like church cloisters and right into our next-door neighbour. The diminutive figure was taking out the trash. She wore long-sleeved scrubs and a head wrap that revealed a serene, round face the warm colour of honey. My first thought was, how lucky of us to live next to a nurse. Then: Was she not dying of heat, under those layers?

She inched closer to me. Her eyes bored into mine, as if scanning for a connection she should find but couldn't, not quite. I hoped I passed for a decent first impression despite being dressed in an old t-shirt and crumpled shorts, the only hot-weather clothes I bothered to dig out of the suitcases. This could be my first friend here. She would be my guide to all the places I have yet to discover of my new home country: where to get new underwear, local produce, late-night tacos, and other life essentials. Soon, we would pop over unannounced to each other's apartments for a drink, a laugh, or to catch the latest episode of *The Bachelorette*. I smiled brightly. She leaned closer, looked me over with curiosity. A good sign.

"This… yours?" she whispered.

"Yes! We just flew in last night from Canada. So pleased to meet you, my name is Gina. Hi." I held out my hand. She stared at it, then at my face.

A bright voice called out from inside her apartment. My new friend took a quick step away from me. A fair-skinned Chinese woman appeared at their doorway, her words gusting ahead. "Hello! I – Oh. Hmm, hi." Her dark eyes, with that dewy morning look, widened at me. Though older, she wore the starved expression of a has-been supermodel with pride.

"Come in," she said to the woman in the headscarf, "no time to chat with your friend." They vanished without another word. Their door, left ajar, held no hint of invitation.

Dean came out into the hallway then, handing me the keys and his wallet and mumbled something about the shallow pockets of his shorts.

"I just met—." But I stopped. I hadn't met our neighbour.

"These won't stay put." His sunglasses, newly bought at Changi's duty-free when we landed last night, slid back down the sweaty bridge of his nose. "Sorry, you were saying something?"

"Nothing."

*

Cold air spikes suddenly through my sweaty clothes. I've wandered into the refrigerated section, where Dean must have looked already for the eggs. A matronly employee with samples of cheese cubes ignores me, cooing instead at a pair of curly-haired children frolicking by themselves. I give the area a once-over in case he missed anything. My toes curl into the rubber soles of my sandals, making me long for the heat outside. No eggs or lithesome girls in sight.

I make my way back to the cereal aisle, but Dean is gone.

They must be together, Dean and the girls. The frenzied thought grips me. I can't figure out how I am convinced of this, but I know they are. The quinoa box sits so snuggly on the shelf Dean must have placed it back as soon as I left him. Somehow, he and the girls have found a way to meet, to bump casually into each other as if by chance, and I had let it happen. I rush to the next aisle, and the next, past the *Japanese Snacks* and *International Wine & Spirits*. They are over in the next row, behind a display or—

And what would I do if I found them together? If I saw Dean's head lowering to their petite builds or the girls giggling at his jokes? I could stroll right up to them. Put him and the girls into their rightful places or, at least, give their happy time a jolt of reality.

Or I could stay with the problem of the eggs. Racing through the supermarket has been good for one thing: at the farthest corner of the supermarket, behind sacks of rice stacked all the way up to my waist, clear plastic cartons of brown eggs line the metal shelf. I lean on the rice. The staple food of my childhood, lending me strength halfway across the world from home.

"Hey! There you are. I've been looking everywhere for you." Dean appears beside me. "See, I told you you'd find them!"

"You were looking for me?"

"Great work, babe." He puts several cartons into the basket and kisses my forehead and suddenly I am flushed with security again. My Dean wouldn't stray like that.

There is a long line for self-checkout that extends into the aisles. In front of us, a middle-aged Chinese woman taps her bejeweled platform sandal and rakes a manicured hand through her perfect blowout. With other people trying to pass behind, we edge into this woman's space. She whips around quickly, her coral lips pursed, but on seeing Dean, nods and smiles wryly. More people pack into the area. I tell Dean to go wait outside; I'm carrying the only bit of new currency we have and he's only taking up space.

I also send him out because I finally see the girls. They are coming to the cashier area, carrying litre bottles of green tea. They line up behind me, no doubt for the sole purpose of striking up a conversation with Dean. No doubt they are disappointed to see him leave without noticing them, though they don't show it. They chatter to each other with fervent energy and toss their hair just to taunt me, it seems. Each moment we move closer to the front, they find new ways to intimidate me.

To show my indifference to their scare tactics, I study a display stand of toothbrushes. A sign reads: *Mix and Match 2 for 1*. On the sides of the Colgate packaging in all the appropriate reds and blues, the writing is in a small hypnotic scrawl that I pretend to know how to read. They are right there, looming close; I feel them watching. Practically level with me in line. An arm extends to me. I ruffle my shoulders out, swinging my canvas bag to reassert my claim on my space.

It isn't until I hear the woman in front of me yelp that I realize I have stepped on her. On the pain scale, a nipped heel cannot be so great as to merit this reaction. But she turns to me, her face contorting in accusation.

"Oh," I mumble, "oh my gosh, I—" The rest of my apology slithers back down my throat when I see the look of pure poison in her eyes. I imagine what I must look like to her: messy-haired, dressed in a rumpled logo T-shirt, no expensive purse on my arm. Suddenly, I understand. The exaggerated reproach, the ready spite: She thinks I'm a maid. *Is that it?* I want to shout. *But I'm not! I have a degree. A desk job I left to move here. Have you seen my husband? I'm like you!* And, right away, I regret the thought. There is nothing wrong with being a maid.

"You ah," she says, heaving, "you should say sorry." But her eyes dart from me to the two girls, standing next to me now. Back at me again, with a perplexed look. It's as though she suddenly isn't sure which of us to blame.

The girls frown at the woman, who takes their momentary confusion as further afront. She points her talon finger at them. "You must say sorry! Must not be so rude." On and on, she voices her indignation between heavy gulps of breath. The girls seem to understand intuitively how they must act. They bow their heads and say sorry over and over again. People turn and watch.

A kiosk frees up and an attendant waves me to it. I go before anyone can stop me. I keep my focus on the machine, beeping my items through, feeding the bills into the slot, and wondering how I managed to escape the castigation. But I already know the answer. It's my skin, turning red now, but light enough in colour to be granted passage. A manager is with them now. The woman is still scolding. The innocent girls are still sorry. With my head still down, I make for the exit.

Beyond the supermarket's glass doors, I see Dean. His face tilts to the sky, his thin lips rest in a quiet smile. He is leaning against the railing of the ramp that leads down onto pedestrian traffic of obliviously happy people like him. The doors slide open and I welcome the embrace of suffocating heat and the sudden glare blanching everything white.

"Did you see what happened?"

"What?" he asks.

"You didn't hear anything?" I glance back at the automatic glass doors, opening and shutting with the frequency of a gaping mouth. "I stepped on someone."

"You troublemaker." He laughs. "That's it?"

Is it not enough? "You really heard nothing?" I say, but he's already turning away.

"Do you see over there? That car just pulled up. I mean, check it out." He points to a vintage Beetle with the iconic dome shape. But this one, pale pink and heavily coated in golden glitter, winks in the sun. Where am I that someone would drive such a thing?

"Dean." I hurry on my sunglasses. "Dean, I think someone thought I was a maid." He chuckles again, staring at me in bewilderment. "What if it's a problem?" I whisper. "I mean, you don't know what could happen."

He shakes his head. "Babe, hey, it's okay. It's gonna be okay. You keep overthinking things. Yeah?" He says all this slowly, brushing the hair out of my face and smiling his encouragement down at me. In his sunglasses, I see my reflection warped and glinting in the lens. "It's the heat, isn't it? Come on. Let's get you back." He slips my grocery bags onto his arm.

On our walk back, I can't seem to understand how our new neighbourhood looks like a hazy, sultry version of any Main Street in a North American town. Young families dressed in summer clothing push baby strollers, stopping to chat with cookie-cutter versions of themselves; couples buy baguettes from rustic bakeries with large glass windows and wicker lawn furniture lining the front; people dine al fresco—on avocado toast! All is well, no one is paying any mind to what could transpire inside a neighbourhood supermarket—and why would they? It is Sunday; it had not happened to them.

At the intersection before our new home, I position myself in the shadow of the traffic pole as Dean presses the pedestrian button and waits patiently at the curb. It reminds me of his solid up-bringing, how he is as courteous as he is youthful, as gentle as he is oblivious, a potato-fed boy still impressed by New Year fireworks. More people trickle onto the sidewalk around us, lazy and carefree, and overhead the hot breeze rustles palm fronds.

A stout woman stops next to me and shoos a fly from the little pale face of the baby strapped to her chest. She is darker. She is not the mother; I have learned to tell. A man as pale as the baby, with black hair spiking about like shorn grass, and slender thumbs dancing over his phone screen, is next to her. He is the baby's father. The woman beside him stares blankly ahead. When the light turns, she strides onto the road to keep up with his long legs. No one bats an eye at the man, the baby, and the maid, not the couples on their leisure strolls, or the children on their bikes and scooters, or the young, mesmerizing girls in their wispy dresses. And Dean. What does Dean notice?

He doesn't see me glance at him, doesn't hear my breath hitch when his lips tug into a private smirk.

"This place," he nods into the sun, "I think we're going to love it here."

KEN LYE

Man of the House

The screaming drilled right into his skull, though Dinesh was covering both ears with the palms of his large, blocky hands. How could a creature so small make a sound so loud?

In retaliation, he thrusted his unshaven face towards the eighteen-month-old in the playpen at the side of the living room table, and roared a beastly growl of frustration from the pit of his stomach.

In jest. Mostly.

"Hello? Is everything okay?"

Standing at the gate of his flat was the *makcik* from next door, her head wrapped in a black scarf. Dark brown, sandalled feet peeped out from beneath the edge of her orange patterned *baju* butterfly. Dinesh realised that, with his mouth wide open, teeth bared, and nostrils flaring, he probably looked like a fairy-tale ogre about to consume the child whole. He thought of picking his son up to demonstrate that no, he was a good father, that he knew what he was doing, really, he did, but he was not sure if lifting the boy would set him off again. Meanwhile, Prem was standing stock-still in his diapers, his eyes wide open, staring at the old lady a few metres away from him.

"Sorry, Aunty, I was just playing with him."

"*Sayang, sayang*," she said, teasing the toddler from behind the metal bars of the gate.

Prem sniffed back his tears loudly, the chug-a-chug of a drainpipe being unblocked, and then he waddled over to the corner of the playpen closest to the visitor: "Gah! Gah!"

She cooed at him. He gurgled contentedly in response.

"Can I?" the pint-sized woman asked, indicating with her spindly hands the carrying of the child.

He considered the Singapore government's COVID safe distancing requirements that had just kicked in with the start of June: she was only one visitor, and she was wearing a mask.

"Sure, please come in."

He got off his seat at the living room table, unsure which should take priority, grabbing a t-shirt to cover his bare chest, or letting her in. She made the choice for him, kicking her slippers off her feet, and gingerly opening the gate herself. Her eyes were locked on the toddler's as she approached him, as if she were trying to assure a startled animal that she meant no harm. When she reached him, she lifted the boy slowly but firmly, and held him tightly to her chest.

For the first time since his wife had left the flat that morning, Dinesh heard the child laugh.

He pulled his Arsenal sweatshirt over the hard balloon of his beer belly. He barely knew the woman he was allowing into his home. He and Kavitha had moved into the HDB block with their new-born just over a year ago. Their third-storey flat was tucked away in a corner of the apartment building with only one other household next to it, their doors side-by-side. Like most Singaporeans, however, they had only ever smiled and exchanged greetings with their neighbour at the lift landing—and even that was a rarity since they were always rushing somewhere. He did remember Kavitha mentioning something once, though, about the Aunty next door living alone. He hadn't really been paying attention. Just female gossip.

"Your wife not at home?" Aunty asked, bouncing Prem up and down in her arms.

"No," Dinesh replied. "At work."

It was Kavitha's first week back at the hospital. She had quit her job as a nurse when Prem was born. Better for the boy, they had reasoned, to have his mother around all day than to be raised by a helper. Besides, Dinesh had been earning good money as a project engineer. He hated the long hours, but wasn't it his duty as a husband to support his family? Kavitha could stay home and look after the house, just like his late mother had done. Everything had changed, however, with the onset of the pandemic. He was placed first on half-pay, and then on furlough. Three weeks ago, he had been notified that the company he had worked in for seven years had folded. Just like that. He had started looking for a new job, but everyone was suffering, and offers were hard to come by. Except from the health sector. Kavitha's former supervisor and colleagues called regularly about her going back.

It's too risky, you've got a small child at home, he had insisted. But she had looked at him, sad-eyed: "I became a nurse to help people."

What could he possibly say to that without sounding like an asshole? He knew he should be proud of his wife. She was putting her own health on the line. Out there saving lives. A goddamn superhero. Instead, he felt only resentment when she also suggested sleeping in a separate room and minimising unnecessary contact with him and Prem. Just to be safe, she had said, as she watched from some distance away while her husband played with her son, an outcast in her own home. But did she not realise it was hard on him too, not having his wife by his side during this difficult time? He wasn't sure when the economy was going to recover, when he would be able to work again. Meanwhile, their savings continued to dwindle. Diapers weren't cheap.

He also wasn't used to sitting around the flat all day with nothing to do. There were only so many *Transporter* and *Fast & Furious* movies one could watch on Netflix, only so many times he could search online for motorbike parts, his pride and joy left stranded out in the carpark.

How had Kavitha managed to occupy her time with Prem over the last year and a half?

"Your wife is very brave," Aunty said. If she were concerned about her own health, being in the home of a frontline worker, her weathered face did not betray her. Quite the opposite, she seemed to be beside herself with excitement, thrilled to have the opportunity to spend time with the little boy.

"Yes, very brave."

"We owe a lot to all the doctors and nurses. For keeping Singapore safe."

"And how have you been, Aunty?" he said.

"One person on your own, not easy *lah*."

"If you need anything, you can just let me know."

"No, no, you are busy with work."

Her words stung. Out of the corner of an eye, he noticed the laptop screen still displaying the main page of the MyCareersFuture portal. He slid his hand over, and flipped the device shut.

"Actually, if you don't mind," she continued, "can help me change the light? Aunty can't reach. I have the bulb, but scared to climb up in case *jatuh*."

"I can come over right now," he said, putting his face mask on before she could change her mind. He would be able to chalk up one good deed for the day at least.

"Terima kasih!"

He offered to take the boy from her, but she seemed determined to keep her new-found treasure close. She did appear to struggle a little from the weight of the little monster, though, so Dinesh kept an eye on her as he followed the old woman to her flat. Her doorstep was just a few centimetres away from his, but there was a world of difference. The area in front of Dinesh's home was cluttered with a shoe rack, potted plants and his son's navy-blue three-wheeler. A town council's nightmare. His neighbour's was bare, except for a plain grey welcome mat.

"Inside is a mess, don't mind, ah," she said, putting Prem down to fish out the keys from her pocket. The door opened, and Dinesh was immediately overwhelmed by the warm, hearty aroma of fresh bakes, a rich, buttery smell that made him feel hungry and satisfied at the same time.

"Wow, I didn't realise we were living next door to a master chef," he said, admiring the rows of plastic containers on the living room table, each stuffed to its bright red cap with cookies.

"Just my normal. Hari Raya period, business *lagi* best. Good thing government said home baking can resume during COVID, otherwise *mampos*."

He looked at the labels, impressed: *pecan demerara*, Parmesan cheese, and *gula melaka* coconut biscuits. Not the usual run-of-the-mill cornflake cookies with rainbow sprinkles that he was used to. He had actually enjoyed Food and Nutrition in lower secondary, though there was obviously no way he would have dared taken it at O-levels. His older brothers would never have let him live it down.

"Try one piece."

She unscrewed the cover off a tub.

"Thank you!" he said, as he bit down on the crumbly pastry, and the rush of sweetness—but not oversweet—filled his mouth. "Wah, this is good!"

"*Sedap*, right?"

Brushing the crumbs out of his moustache, Dinesh nodded in agreement.

"Aunty's own recipe," she added, two thumbs up in clownish fashion. A proud grin spread across her now-unmasked face, revealing an uneven row of yellowed teeth.

While the adults were preoccupied, Prem was on an adventure around the living room, tottering on his little feet, his diapered behind waggling like a duck's. Luckily, Dinesh managed to catch him by the hand just as he approached a glass cabinet.

"Oi, careful!"

Aunty pointed to the fluorescent lamp over the dining table: "This light here."

The circular bulb was shielded by a half-dome of hard translucent plastic, a band of flowers etched onto the surface.

"I go and get the replacement."

Dinesh surveyed the living room while she vanished into the kitchen. There was only the most basic furniture, as if she had just moved in, though he knew this was not the case. In the cabinet were a few McDonald's souvenir giveaways and some ceramic knick-knacks. He also noticed a collection of what looked like family pictures: Aunty, much younger, clutching a girl and a boy in her arms at Sentosa, at the Botanic Gardens, the zoo. In the picture frames closer to the centre, the boy at his National Service Passing-Out-Parade, the girl in an NUS graduation gown, posing with her mother along the steps of the old Supreme Court.

Suddenly, a stumbling, tumbling sound, things being knocked over. Dinesh darted through the kitchen entrance. There he found Aunty lying flat on her front, moaning in pain, a broken ring of glass tubing beside her.

*

"I've asked her whether she has any family, but she always changes the subject, so I think there's something she doesn't want to talk about," Kavitha said, bringing out the plate of *bhindi masala* that she had just stir-fried, the vegetables still smoking aggressively. There was already a bowl of curry on the table, warmed up from the weekend, but she always made sure there was one dish freshly prepared after she got home from the hospital.

"There's that man that sometimes visits her, though," she continued as she settled into her seat at the other end of the table.

Dinesh trawled through the *masala* gravy with his spoon, and brought a wedge of mutton to his plate: "What man? Her son?"

"No, this man is about her age. He will come and spend a weekend with her. And then I won't see him for a while, and then he'll appear again suddenly. I haven't seen him for a few months now, though. Not since March, before the Circuit Breaker."

"Maybe her brother?"

"No man buys flowers for his sister, okay? Also, you can see from the way they walk with each other, one of his hands on her elbow. Anyway, I'm glad Aunty is all right. Imagine if you hadn't been there."

From their son's bedroom, the familiar squawk of need: attention, food.

"I'm still full from lunch. You eat whatever, just leave a little bit for me," Kavitha said, getting up to check on Prem, though she only allowed herself to be a hovering presence at his door. Dinesh looked at his wife from across the living room, struck by the longing so visible in her eyes to hold her son in her arms—but also the weariness of her body, one side leaning against the wall, shoulders slumped.

It was Kavitha who said she wanted to go back to work, he told himself. He hadn't asked her to. Quite the opposite.

But she knew, didn't she? Even without her husband saying a word. She knew what she had to do for the sake of her family. Earn.

He tried to focus his attention back on his dinner, on the okra so lovingly cooked by his wife. Another thought, however, just as disheartening, forced itself into his head: he had saved Aunty's life today perhaps—but, in all the commotion, he hadn't managed to change her lightbulb.

*

Norlizah and Dinesh spent more time together after the incident, but he found it impossible to call her by her name.

"Cannot, lah. You are around my mother's age."

"You say like that, I also cannot argue," she replied, chortling. She had a hearty laugh for a woman of such a small stature.

Over the next few days, they fell into a routine. Dinesh would bring Prem over to her place in the morning, Norliza looking after the boy while his father took over all her household chores: mopping the floor, scrubbing the toilet, buying the groceries.

"No need, no need," she had protested at first, but he would barge his way in, using his dumpling-cheeked son as a bribe. Her arm was in a sling for two months. How could she manage on her own?

Not that he was any good at housework, at least not initially. He would attack his tasks with gusto and brute strength, but, he quickly realised, without any real skill or thoroughness. This was apparent from the way Norliza's eyes would occasionally drift towards an intransigent dust-ball half-hidden under the sofa, or whenever she surreptitiously scraped at a bit of crust with her fingernail after he had already washed the plates they had used for lunch. She never said anything, though. Did she do everything all over again after he and Prem left at the end of each day? There was no point in offering assistance if he wasn't actually going to be useful. He knew he had to try harder—and so he did, asking her for advice, patiently listening to her answers. The first time he cleaned the windows without leaving any streaks, he felt an odd surge of pride.

Sometimes, as he left her flat, his son seated on the curl of one burly arm, Dinesh would find himself about to say "Thank you" before catching himself.

And then, as the days extended into a week, and then two, there was also the baking.

Once, he received a call from his former colleague Kok Meng while at Norliza's place. Kok Meng, now a food delivery rider, was in his area, calling him out for lunch.

"Already meeting an old classmate," Dinesh replied. "Next time, bro."

"Eh, eh, if you want to meet your friends, it's okay," Aunty said, as he tapped his phone to end the call, a greasy fingerprint left on his screen. "I can postpone the order."

He didn't realise she had overheard the conversation from across the kitchen where she was taking care of Prem. He hoped she wasn't offended by the lie he had told Kok Meng (not that he would call Kok Meng a friend, not really; just someone to complain to over cigarettes about their insufferable boss), but the truth was too complicated to explain over a quick phone call.

"No, I'm happy to help. I want to learn also."

Kok Meng was now part of a former life, after all. A life on hold that, yes, Dinesh would return to eventually— but no rush. After the pandemic. Recently, it wasn't only the household chores that kept him at Norliza's. He had begun helping her with her home bakes as well. Just before taking Kok Meng's call, he had been frying tapioca flour with *pandan* leaves (make sure they are dry, Aunty had warned). This would be stirred into the blend of grated Parmesan cheese and coconut milk powder that Prem had mixed earlier under Aunty's supervision. It was Dinesh's first time making her special *kueh bangkit*—and there were four containers' worth to be collected by a Mrs Chantelle Loh by seven in the evening.

"While the flour is cooling," Aunty instructed, finger stabbing the air to point out all the different ingredients, "put the butter and sugar in the food processor until creamy creamy. *Macam* baby food."

He thought he would be all thumbs, that the finer details would get the better of him. But there was a method to the madness, and what was the food processor but another machine? He was good with machines. And measurements. Aunty had told him to *agak-agak*, just estimate, but while that would have been fine for a veteran like her, he was a novice. Better to Google an official recipe, and then use it as a base from which to modify the quantities. Separating the yolks for the creamed butter, and the whites for the dry mixture proved challenging, but he got the hang of it eventually, though there was the occasional streak of orange-yellow in the translucent gumminess, and—disaster!—a speck of eggshell that would sometimes make its way into the bowl.

"How do you get it out?"

He was already on his fourth attempt, now his fifth, his sixth—but still the pinprick of brown continued to taunt him, slipping past his finger at the very last moment every time he thought he had finally got the better of it. There was only a small fan on the counter-top, whirring valiantly but in vain against the afternoon heat. Dinesh was a big man, used to sweating. He worried now, however, that some of his perspiration was dripping into the bowl. The recipe hadn't called for salt, he was sure of that.

"Use the eggshell."

"What do you mean?" he asked, on the brink of another swear word, stronger this time.

"Use another eggshell to *korek* it out."

"Use another—?"

He didn't know what voodoo, *swami*, *bomoh* magic this was, but it worked, the elusive piece of eggshell floating atop the pool of egg white in his makeshift scoop. A half-stifled chuckle from the old lady as she continued to help Prem fit plastic shapes into the cut-out holes of a wooden block with her one good hand.

There was still a long way to go. Even after the dough had been made, it still needed to be chilled, rolled out, cut and baked—but then, an hour and a half later, the cookies were ready, piping hot, straight out of the oven. Best of all, Aunty's two thumbs up, and her triumphant declaration after tasting a spare biscuit: "*Bagus*! *Pandai*, ah you!"

"I have a good teacher," he said, trying one for himself, and quickly reaching out for another.

"Eh, don't happy happy *makan* all up ah? *Sekali* later not enough."

Ah, yes, this was a business after all. A second batch was still needed, then a third, if Ms Loh's order was to be completed. By the time he had finished with all the baking, and washed up the utensils and crockery, it was nearly six pm. But the apartment smelt of toasted cheese, and there on the countertop, four containers of cookies he had baked with his own two hands, each layer of *bangkit* neatly separated within its vessel by a paper doily.

"What can I say? Looks damn pro, man!" He was glad he hadn't given up.

"You worked so hard, now can enjoy," Aunty said, bringing a plate of *bangkit* to the living room. These were the extras: the mutant biscuit babies, slightly misshapen or disfigured by burnt edges. They hadn't passed her QC. No problem, he thought; I'll get them perfect the next time.

Cikgu and student sat at the dining table, with Prem curled and yawning against the woman's belly. She chomped noisily into one of the *bangkits*, the biscuit breaking apart in her mouth.

"This was my daughter's favourite."

"Is that the girl in the pictures?" he asked, distracted as he stared longingly at the last cookie.

"Yes. And the boy is my son."

"I haven't seen them around," he said, before he realised his mistake. If Kavitha had been there, she would have kicked him.

Norliza was affectionately smoothening Prem's hair down, the boy a small brown cat in her lap: "Our relationship not so good. Few years already, never see each other. My husband left us during their secondary school time. After that, we became very close, because only got three of us, but then—"

She hesitated.

"It's okay," he said. "If you don't want to—"

But she wasn't listening to him, wasn't waiting for his permission.

"They not happy when Adel and I became ... very good friends. His parents live next door to my family in Malaysia, that's how we met. My children said cannot, we are not married. But *sudah* lah, I don't want. Adel also doesn't want. He works offshore, on oil rig. Very different life. When he can come to Singapore, it's good, it's nice. We are happy. The rest of the time, I'm on my own. Also okay lah. But my children don't understand. They say not right. Ask me to choose."

Dinesh scratched the back of his neck. Prem was now fast asleep, Aunty patting his side in a slow, steady rhythm.

"But not just I choose. They also make the choice, right?" she said, her eyes clear, voice dry of sentimentality.

He was a little confused by how plainly she was speaking. How could a mother choose a man over her children? Choose anything over her children? And especially for a man she hardly ever saw, a man she couldn't even see at all now because of the COVID travel restrictions.

And she looked so traditional and conservative.

"Maybe one day. Then can meet my grandson."

Her face remained tight. There were many questions he wanted to ask, but he felt he would be intruding.

"I'd better make a move. You take care, Aunty," he said, fumbling as he reached out to take his son from her.

*

That night, he kept thinking about Norliza, and what she had shared with him. He thought about her story over dinner, and during his late-night run along the nearby park connector (a recent addition to his daily routine)—but most of all, when tucking his son into bed.

"My little man," he said, kissing the boy on the forehead.

*

A few days later, he decided to surprise Kavitha. Even though she was now back at work, she was still the one responsible for keeping their flat in running order.

"I'll just take care of everything on the weekend," she had said, stacking Tupperware containers of food in the freezer—and he hadn't thought to say anything then. But, as the weeks passed, he noticed the strain she was under. And if he was helping Aunty clean her flat, why not his own? He had never seen his own father lift a finger to help his mother, but those were different times.

He would be one of those modern men. She shouldn't have to ask.

And so, he had been secretly learning a few dishes from Aunty that he could wow his wife with: chicken curry, lamb *rendang*, *begedil* potato cutlets. Although he and Aunty never spoke again about her family, they still spent every day together. He was now an unofficial partner of her home-baking enterprise, even making deliveries on his motorbike, which meant she could expand her business to customers unwilling to travel to Mountbatten.

She had accompanied him to the nearby wet market the morning of the surprise, and helped him to choose the ingredients ("Buy chicken, make sure you press first, must spring back. If the flesh too hard, that means not fresh"). He had then spent all afternoon cleaning the flat, and preparing dinner. By evening, the living room floor smelled of ocean breeze, the kitchen of coriander, turmeric and onions.

The look on Kavitha's face as she walked through the front door made all the effort worthwhile.

"Welcome home!"

He figured that while she was aware he had been spending time with Norliza, she would assume that he was helping her with only the simplest of chores, that he was most likely keeping her company just to exploit their neighbour for free childcare. There was no way she would be expecting any of this.

"Oh, Babes! What's going on?"

"It's just to show you—"

"Oh my goodness," she shrieked, dancing on the tips of her toes, "you got a job!"

She ran into his arms, squealing in excitement, and buried her head in his chest: "I told you it was just a matter of time!"

She spun round, studied the dining table: "So where did you order all this food from?"

It took a few moments before Dinesh was able to speak. A few moments where he felt his whole body collapse into itself, like there was a suction pump in the base of his stomach, pulling in on everything.

"No, no one's gotten back to me yet," he replied. He decided there was no need to add that he hadn't sent any applications out in the last week. He had been busy helping Norliza, and looking after Prem. He had started jogging, cutting down on cigarettes. He was even eating more healthily. It was while running along the Kallang River one evening, seeing all the children with their mothers, grandparents and helpers—never the fathers, never—that the realisation had hit him: Why return to a job he didn't like? Having to work through weekends, suck up to his boss? Maybe later, when Prem was older. Maybe never.

Kavitha was visibly crest-fallen, and standing now as awkwardly as Dinesh by the table. She was still in her nurse's uniform, a figure of green. Their hands separated.

He could not tell whether he had released hers, or the other way around.

"What is all this food for then?"

"Just some things I've been learning from Aunty to say thank you to my wife for being so wonderful," he managed to say.

"Oh, Babes."

With the back of her head towards him, he couldn't tell how she felt, but it eventually became clear.

"It's okay, things will be alright," she said halfway through the meal. "Life is so crazy now, everything is upside down, but I'm sure we will all go back to normal soon."

He didn't reply, just pushed a half-eaten *begedil* around on his plate.

*

By the end of July, more restrictions had been lifted. Singapore had even held General Elections in the middle of the pandemic. The economy remained winded, however, and international travel severely limited. Norliza still relied on Dinesh, who was only too happy to continue in the role, with the government grants and his share of their business profits (he had said no, but she had insisted) allowing him to contribute to his family expenses.

At the end of each day, orders fulfilled, household chores done, he and Norliza would take Prem to the playground downstairs together. Sometimes, they would go even further afield to the beach along the East Coast Parkway. Kavitha would join them on the weekends, the adults tucking into

Dinesh's chicken curry while Prem built sandcastles next to their picnic mat. The boy's father kept a watchful eye on him while Norliza told them all stories about growing up in post-war Singapore, and Kavitha provided inside knowledge about the country's progress against this virus.

It was on one such Saturday afternoon that Dinesh's phone buzzed with an incoming message from Kok Meng. Dinesh had just returned with Prem from the edge of the sea, and was towelling salt water off the boy. He disregarded the notification, but his former colleague persisted a few minutes later with a call, the shrill ringtone harder to ignore.

"Bro, so you on?"

"What?" asked Dinesh, the phone clipped between his ear and shoulder as he wrapped a corner of the towel around a finger, and stuck it into his son's right ear.

"The company is back up again."

"Appaa!" Prem whined, stamping his feet with dinosaur toys in hand. "Appaa!"

"The old man is looking for all of us to come and take our old jobs back," Kok Meng continued.

Beside Dinesh, Norliza was ladling *sayur lodeh* into plastic bowls as Kavitha tore chunks off the baguette loaf, both women laughing at a joke one of them must have made.

"Appaa!"

PETER MORGAN

First Draft: David in Singapore, Maureen in Wales

Scene 1: Freedom

Maureen cast her eyes over the view from her slate quadrangle office, attentive to the decay and endurance of the University. The Welsh Sea in the distance churned.

Seniority, perhaps a touch of sympathy for her age and position as Head of Drama, had secured her the windowed sanctuary on the three-hundred-year-old campus. Maureen's career rise, to use a cliché she'd never tolerate in her classes, had been meteoric. Not a Deanship, as she'd once wished. Compelling and thought well of by my students, but not sufficiently political, she'd told herself. Still, it was an enviable career and a decent office with yards of oak bookshelves and a sea view, as consequence.

Her University profile read, in part:

Prof. Maureen J. McTeer was National Producer for the British Broadcasting Corporation's radio performing arts department and is now the Drama Specialist in the Creative Writing Programme in our English Department. Since the success of her first play, 'Landscapes for Lovers' in 1987, Maureen has written numerous award-winning dramatic works for theatre, radio and the visual media.

The accompanying profile photo was, she thought, still a reliable, if younger, representation.

There was a clatter in the quad. With the recent influx of students from Asia, she'd realised the formidable range of plays in her teaching repertoire had been, unsettlingly, a tad Eurocentric. Asia was out of range. Terra incognito, her frumpy, bear of an ex-husband, the cartographic historian, had said.

Since the BAFTA six years ago, it was muttered she was reclining amid her awards and renown. But Maureen hoped for a last Edward Said-ian 'Late Stage' work. Hemingway's *The Old Man and the Sea* had reinvigorated his literary reputation; something not dissimilar would restore confidence in her capabilities and prove her gossipy colleagues wrong, surely? But otherwise, she was content. Especially now the cartographer was fusting about in London or somewhere hopefully equally distant. She hadn't felt a need to set aside space in her heart for another.

What's this? She still hadn't learned to mute her phone's alerts. She would often receive an invitation to speak here or there. Unless it was a Tier One institution, she always politely, regretfully, demurred.

"Dear Prof. McTeer," the email began. And went on at some length—this could be edited for clarity, she thought. But it was a not un-intriguing opportunity. A week's work in Singapore as Artist-in-Residence. The Program Director had made the predictable excuses about not flying her business, and the hotel near the school was quaint, if a bit of a tired colonial, but otherwise, she would be warmly welcomed. And the students—some exceptional, he'd written—would value her perspective. She tried to imagine Singapore and couldn't conjure an image more recent than colonial buildings, swaying palms and trishaws. She thought about googling but then realised an unvarnished view might be to her advantage. She gave herself the weekend to consider and, by Monday, had decided that while there was some risk of the week being fruitless, there was little harm. Live adventurously after the constraints of marriage.

"Dear Dean Chabon," she wrote, "I'm off the week of 3 April. No classes to cover, a wonderful opportunity and perhaps a chance to attract a foreign graduate student or two [agreed code for 'exorbitant international fee paying']. And no financial burden to our College, for which I am sure you'll be grateful. I trust you are supportive..." She hesitated about whether to insert a period or question mark. She wasn't going to beg permission for a decision rightly hers. As a concession, she deleted the catty "for which I am sure you'll be grateful" but ended with a definitive period. Chabon was adult enough to speak up if he had any concerns. What was being in one's early fifties and single, if not a time of liberation?

She did know Singapore was on the equator, and so the weekend before the trip, she tried on her summer clothes, admiring herself in a couple of sundresses that would pass classroom muster. Not bad, she thought, seeing her figure in her bedroom mirror.

Scene 2: Herodotus

Oliver, the Program Director, was unexpectedly charming. The whole week was going to be worthwhile after all. The jovial American had invited a couple of faculty to a welcome Saturday dinner. "I've choped a table in Little India," he said, although she didn't know what that meant. Apart from the slightly odd ordering of Chardonnay with curry, which she'd never known as a suitable pairing, there was an informal warmth compared to her stiff British colleagues.

Monday morning, Oliver reviewed the program. First, a public lecture that evening, about which she had been alerted and had prepared for—regrettably likely poorly attended, he warned. A Tuesday class on a topic of her choice. And then one-on-ones spread over the balance of the week, with the students, who will have complied with my edict to attend, he explained. He handed her a sheaf of papers.

"And of your charges?" she asked. "A bit of background to help me critique more effectively?"

"Well, I'm inclined not to prejudice, but since you ask…"

More opportunity for concision and clarity, she thought, as he went on. Hopefully, the students were not incorporating all of this friendly fellow's habits into their writing. Despite her efforts, the blur of jet lag and the mostly unfamiliar Chinese and Malay names meant she'd have to rely on her wits to match student work to Oliver's comments. Still, she did catch some comments … so and so is really worth your attention, and such and such might be interested in further study, and David, despite the name, a Chinese-Singaporean, really has promise.

"I'm not sure his contemporary gay retelling of Herodotus' travels is the ideal niche. But I allow the brighter ones more latitude," Oliver had said. He added he hoped she might give an encouraging steer to study overseas to one or two of the best, such as the sort-of classicist David.

One is either a classicist, or one is not, she'd resisted saying, continuing to want to edit Oliver.

Over the next few days, Maureen became familiar
with the city-state's Arts College campus—essentially post-
modern expose-the-workings, Pritzker-winning architecture
that meant a jumble of shipping containers stacked five
floors high. An unintentional analogy of the precarious
industrial nature of modern education? She had been seeing
the students — most more promising than Oliver had
intimated — for much of the afternoons. Finally, on Friday,
the last student crossed the cantilevered walkway connected
to her pallet-sized seminar room. David, he'd introduced
himself before she'd had a chance to shuffle the papers to
retrieve his work.

All Singaporeans looked younger than they are, she
thought. She'd expected David to be a short, teenager-
like emo, in glasses, a just-out-of-BA Eng. Lit. type. She
stared for a moment. He was tall and handsome even.
Thirties? No facial hair, caring eyes. He had inexplicable
energy about him. After a week, she began to discern what
Asian male type she might be attracted to. Not done to
be the dreamily gazing older female, though. She tucked
her eyes down to his profile — thirty-two, the cover page
said. A stint as an intern at a local indie bookshop, some
copyrighting at a local press ... by no means especially
worldly.

David, too, was surprised. She had an outgoing and
engaging charm, not the officious gruffness the other
helpful but unengaged writers-in-residence had shown.
He eased into the seat at the tiny industrial seminar table.
He couldn't help but notice the light outline of her figure
beneath the dress.

She'd asked a few preliminary questions. Ambitions?
Interests? Hope for the session with her? He answered

concisely and with a clever sense of the ironic. A thing for an older woman would indeed never occur to him, she thought.

The forty-five-minute session ran over to an hour. Not equals. And there was something naïve, given his un-worldliness, about his focus on historical fiction. But, if he were her student, she'd pry him away from that theme and get him to experiment more with form and genre. Then set him free. Even to return to Herodotus, if that was his sincere desire. With young students, the problem was life experience. Still, those dark eyes and loose limbs. He took detailed notes and asked intelligent questions. She imagined having a smooth, hairless chest in her seminar back in Wales, not just the bears she encountered in class and at the Faculty Club.

*

Maureen returned to Wales. Oliver encouraged David to ask Professor McTeer about a PhD. Of course, delighted, she replied. I'll put you in touch with the Dean. He has a side-line in historical fiction; you'd be a pair! A cautious response was best. They exchanged occasional friendly emails. She learned he still lived with his parents, no word of a girlfriend—or a boyfriend, although one never knew nowadays.

*

David was disappointed to be passed off to the older male writer. He knew he'd lived a sheltered A-level, National University of Singapore undergrad life. The odd girlfriend, a bit of an awkward fascination with the male torso, especially during and after National Service, but nothing done about it. Two trips overseas. Graduation Gap Month to Europe. And the second, a snorkelling trip to the Maldives with a girlfriend, who had abandoned him soon after. But at least I've had had jobs in my field, he thought. He started imagining some *Downton Abbey* existence at a quaint Welsh university. Weekend strolls in the countryside, the company and experience of those loose British women, experimenting with soft drugs and afternoons at the pubs. A tangle of news sites, film and novelistic fantasy, he knew, but perhaps some scenes would come true.

Would she at least be a reference? He wrote, anxious to chope his place in the program.

Delighted, came the fast reply.

The application went in with Oliver's encouragement and Prof McTeer's reference.

The admissions committee, chaired by Dean Chabon, reviewed the paperwork, although the need for international students and their higher fees meant, secretly, a low threshold. Still, there was academic propriety. The Dean summarised David's application, saying he was a viable, if perhaps naive, candidate.

"You've met him, Maureen?" Dean Chabon asked. "Impressions?"

"Malleable and promising," she said. She was surprised to feel herself blush. The two male professors looked at her oddly. Was she that obvious?

"Well then, this … David? David will be a welcome addition," the Dean said.

Scene 3: Cherry Tree Cottage

Each of the three years of his PhD felt like a distinct novel to David. Year One mixed being adrift in the unsupervised post-graduate world of British university life with the opportunity to explore messy liberal London. He'd often take a train to the city for the weekend. At first tentatively, and then once he gained familiarity and traction, more boldly exploring the city. He fell in with a couple of classmates who were originally from London. Ellen took him to places like Smithfield's—that temple of farm-to-table, marrow-loving inhibition — and then on to indiscrete Soho bars. Could they have drunk three bottles of white between them? Sam asked him to a reading, which turned out to be at Kenneth's, the legendary gay bookstore. He ended the year committed to the intellectually stimulating PhD, but feeling somewhat between a tourist and an awkward flaneur in this new strange land. He was shocked at the number and range of casual new acquaintances he had made, once freed of family and lifelong school affiliations. That first summer back in Singapore, he'd started off feeling how provincial his city-state was. But by the end of the summer, he'd readjusted to the coffee-time meetings instead of evenings of drink.

For Maureen, she wondered if the closeness she'd felt when they had first met had been an illusion.

"It's *always* sexual when it involves men and women," a colleague in the Sociology department was fond of repeating. "Always."

She'd thought herself a sharp judge of character, especially male character. This wouldn't be the first time Sociology was wrong.

Oh well. She was busy — a new idea had spawned into a draft of a play. Her own graduate students kept her hard at it, and she had the cottage on the coast. She'd go whenever she could — tucked in behind a farming community. No one disturbed her, and no one knew of her comings and goings. Well, except for the discreet old Welsh farmer, who'd wave, seemingly in welcome and simultaneous dismissal, as she drove past down the lane. Maureen used Cherry Tree Cottage, as she'd named it, as her writer's retreat. During her married years, it had been with relief that she went, alone, for weekends or even weeks at a time. There is a cramped warm kitchen, low-beamed ceilings, gas-fired fridge, and a stone fireplace with a wounded oak mantel. More books and an ample dining table she could write at amidst the breakfast dishes and teapot until noon if she felt like it.

Year Two began quietly enough. David and Maureen would pass in this or that hall, make close eye contact: always sharing generous smiles and friendly conversation. Although the embers, if even that was too strong a word, seemed hidden under their otherwise non-overlapping lives and the solitary demands of both their writing.

But then there had been that Sunday afternoon. Ellen, Sam, David and some other students met regularly at the Pike and Oak, sharing gossip and the occasional bit of their own writing. Maureen had come in with a townie friend. As the group David was with broke up, he passed Maureen. She introduced him to her friend and asked him to join their table.

"I'll catch up," he said to Ellen and Sam.

Soon Maureen's friend begged off, leaving the two of them. He noticed her citrus perfume but found being alone with her at the pub intimidating. She was glad to have a chance to talk alone but worried about being overpowering.

"If you have work to do…" he said.

"You'll want to catch your friends, won't you?" she said, even though they were long gone.

They laughed at the ridiculousness of tripping over each other's excuses. David was sensitive to the flush of his Asian genes in response to the earlier Welsh stout, even though he'd fortified his tolerance over the previous year. Maureen had been drinking a cheerful Merlot with her friend. A nod to the barkeep and another round of beer and wine arrived.

*

"Shall we chat again?" she'd said. She unlocked her Volkswagen Cabriolet.

"I'd like that," David said. He thought her a bit unsteady, but he didn't have a license, and he assumed she lived nearby; everything was close in Swansea.

"A week's time?" she said.

"Same place?" he said.

"See you then, if not sooner."

After a few weekends, meeting for an innocent drink at the Pike and Oak became a habit. They'd discuss his or her work. No improprieties; grad students in the UK drank with their teachers all the time, and technically he wasn't even her student, she told herself.

Sundays became 'their' days. One time Maureen suggested going for a drive before the usual. "You won't have been able to see much of Wales without a car."

The Volkswagen's sunroof was folded down. Once out of the city, they drove along the tall, hedge-lined, narrow roads. David was alarmed at how many times an oncoming car or tractor would approach at speed. Reckless. But then both drivers would slow suddenly, find a pocket amidst the hedges and wave cheerfully as they edged past. They would continue this way, tearing along the windy Welsh countryside roads before emerging on some open heath with an expansive view. She said some of the boundaries between fields have been there since first being settled by humans. Or they'd see a distant, impossibly old castle ruin to explore.

After the Christmas holidays, Maureen thought to invite David to Cherry Tree. He'd take the train, she'd drive. Discretion still advised. They'd meet at the end of the line, and no one would be the wiser. So, one Sunday morning in February, David found himself pulling his overcoat closer, alone on a windy train station platform. Had she forgotten? Had he got the byzantine Welsh spelling wrong? But then the Cabriolet appeared.

"Had to top up the petrol. Sorry," she said warmly.

This first time was only a day trip.

"A brisk ramble, and then I'll show you my secret retreat."

They hiked up a nearby footpath and, at the ridge, had tea from a Thermos. Neither could tell if the bumps into each other in the tight, crowded space of the cottage—a quick tour before we are off, she'd suggested—quickly apologised for, were accidental. Then they raced to the train line, and he just caught the last run back.

This became their Sunday ritual. David begged off the London escapades with Ellen and Sam. He felt Maureen's warmth, and she revelled in the companionship. David made her laugh as she hadn't for years.

One Sunday, they missed the train. They could drive back together or return to the cottage. Maureen claimed she was too tired to drive all the way. The living room sofa could be pulled out as a bed. The farmer was diffident as always upon their quick return.

"No, you mustn't apologise," she said when they again bumped into each other. They played at jostling together and tried to catch each other as they came down onto the leather sofa.

David finally had his *Downton Abbey* moment, at least in a small stone-cottage, Welsh kind-of-way. And Maureen had a chance to run her hand across a non-bear-like chest.

They fell into an uncomplicated pace of weekends at the cottage for the rest of the term, always mindful of maintaining the train and Cabriolet subterfuge. Faculty-student relationships were frowned upon and certainly not permitted if there were a supervisory role. Best to avoid the curiosity of the Dean and his boys-will-be-boys colleagues. Maureen had the decent excuse that she was progressing her play, and the frequent weekends away were in that aid, she'd explain to anyone enquiring. David's weekend dashes to the train station fit the pattern for many students with a distant lover. Some even imagined he'd let loose and was seeing a man in London.

"When do we meet her?" Ellen would ask.

"Or him?" Sam added.

He had never imagined himself drinking tea while a British woman prepared him bacon and eggs for breakfast. They'd talk endlessly about his stories and her plays.

*

"Your voice is changing," Dean Chabon had commented. He had read the latest draft of Maureen's play. "More lively, youthful." Whatever else she thought of her old colleague, he was an exceptionally skilled writer. Instead of being angry at the implications about her previous work, she felt herself, again, blushing.

Even though she wasn't his supervisor, she *had* encouraged David to roam through styles and genres, patiently clarifying and pointing out future directions; it was the education he'd never had. He'd even had some journal and anthology publications.

After the initial flurry of sex, he'd enjoyed the conversations more than the ageing flesh, but he still felt hopelessly in love with the erudite, statuesque woman.

The Dean's summons was nothing unusual, Maureen thought. Sometimes, she wondered if he just liked having her in his office. But she disliked him lording over her — quick work then and back to the play, or perhaps a crafted note to David. But an hour later, they were still at it.

"Students and faculty…"

"But there is no reporting relationship," she'd protested.

"Abundance of probity," he'd said.

"Shifting the cricket wickets?"

He knew full well she was aware of his early days as a reckless new lecturer. Bi-sexual. Weed. A different era. She had him, but both would lose if this continued—mutually assured destruction.

"Well, I can't tell you not to, but Maureen, I do appreciate your contribution, and I'd be incredibly saddened to see you cross some me-too cancel culture hashtag line. I'd defend you to the end, of course…"

By this point, the old friends had reached enough of an accord. They strolled to the Faculty Club and made amends over gin and tonics. But she knew she couldn't trust him. Or anyone else on the faculty.

Who had told him, she wondered? Her ex? A jealous colleague?

Scene 4: Welsh Rambles

"Tied up with some marking," she'd said, cancelling her and David's bi-weekly tryst twice in a row. She wasn't ready to tell him about the medical appointments yet. Chabon's cautions and the news were too much. But then, just when he thought he'd understood the excuses as a polite way of telling him she was no longer interested, she suggested a week-long stay at Cherry Tree. "To celebrate the end of your second year!"

"Bring this," she said, offering him a Chatwin-esque leather rucksack. "A present. To use on our rambles."

New positions. Intensity. And the week meant a less hectic, more domestic routine. The pace allowed the two introverts to explore each other more.

David was to spend the summer teaching courses in Singapore and might reasonably expect, now that he'd had several articles and a novella published, to take on a lecturer's position after graduating the following year.

Maureen was hoping to revisit Singapore that summer and was about to suggest doing so when a wave of the fatigue overcame her.

"Better to say our goodbyes for the summer here," she said. Their overnight bags were by the door, and there was a train to catch. She tugged at his belt. He looked at his watch. She shrugged her shoulders, leaning against him in complicity.

"For you," he said, loosening his pants.

"If this is for me," she said, "then…" She tugged him to the rug in front of the fireplace. By now, their clothes were strewn.

"Let the memory last all summer," they said to each other.

Make up for the time wasted with other men, the bureaucracy, all the accommodations I've made, she thought.

Scene 5: Choped

He returned a week before the third year's start. There was a threat of a delay due to the pandemic, but he arrived between measures. The third in the series of novels had begun, with a prologue at the cottage. He would be less free this term with his tutoring responsibilities.

"Did it last?" he said.

"Delightfully, the whole time, and as a consequence, undistracted by other men and entirely focused on my play."

"May I read it?" he said, finding his adopted beginner's Welsh accent again.

"Afterwards," she said, leading him to the laden dinner table.

In the morning, he'd insisted on reading more scenes from her play. She made eggs, fried mushrooms, tomatoes, and smoked haddock.

At the end of the meal, they discussed his work. Herodotus would be put to rest until his second novella, now an easier sell, found a publisher.

"Just one question," he said. He tried to use as diplomatic a tone as he could in critiquing Maureen's work. "Why does your play end so abruptly?"

"Well, it is not quite finished." She looked off to the ceiling, eyes squeezed shut and then broke down sobbing.

*

The first term of Year Three was spent with Maureen increasingly fatigued. The cancer was progressing undramatically and as predicted. Toward the end of term, she took a leave of absence. David visited the hospital almost every day. And then the hospice. Some days he worried what the other students and faculty thought.

"Just delete everything on my computer at Cherry Tree," she'd asked. "What's for public consumption has already been published." She'd said it as firmly as she could. "Take the last play, if you would like. But only if you'll promise to keep it to yourself." She'd wanted to punctuate the sentence with a strong exclamation mark. But, in her weakened state, it was at best a period.

The Welsh funeral arrangements flummoxed David, who was used to the Chinese cremation ritual. He stood at the back of the cemetery, away from the open black pit, as if only a loyal, saddened student. The last half of the second term was spent adrift. He drank gin in his poorly heated apartment. He missed deadlines. Ellen and Sam, dissuaded already by his endless busyness during the previous year, tried to entice him but had given up. He was alone.

*

Why do they insist on informality? David wondered. Why didn't the Dean just demand he appear at his office to face his dismissal from the program? Why the faux closeness of a pint at the Pike and Oak?

"Dean Chabon, thanks for inviting me," David said. He gave no hint of his frustration.

Two pints of stout in, the Dean straightened himself. Then, finally, the gravitas David was hoping for.

"I've personally seen to it you've been given three extensions. So you'll have to defer — back to Singapore for the summer, and then, perhaps, restart from the beginning of the year."

The Dean put his broad hand on David's shoulder, not unkindly.

"Or …?"

Chabon turned to the barkeep. Another round. "Or, you can pull it together, knock back the assignments and hand in your thesis. I've seen the drafts. Brilliant, really. We'd actually still consider you for the College next year. Perhaps not as an full-time lecturer to start, but certainly tutorials and then all being well, the second semester, once we knew you were on … er … once you were satisfied you really wanted to be part of Wales, part of the College…" Chabon had lost his place in the soliloquy. "Maureen spoke very highly, and warmly, of you. It's none of my business. Your work is solid—an important addition to offset our Eurocentrism. *Empire Writes Back* and all. We'd like you to stay, but you have to want to," the Dean said.

*

That weekend David set off for the hills around Cherry Tree Cottage, as he and Maureen often had. First, he stopped by the cottage and printed her play, putting it in his rucksack. Then, he purged the old computer before bundling it up and giving it to the grateful Welsh farmer.

Faithful to her last wish.

He chose a demanding hike, hoping to exhaust himself. He passed a wild peat moor and then found a high rock formation that provided natural shelter from the wind and drizzle. He had a view of the churning Welsh Sea. He sheltered himself, and once he was comfortable, he read. The play was about an older female lover and her younger man, divided by culture and continent. There were some revisions to the text from the version he'd read, including, most significantly, the play now had a definitive 'The End' on the last page.

"I've seen what matters," was the main character's last line in Maureen's last play.

Contributors' Biographies

Adeline Tan, born and raised in Singapore, is a freelance video editor. She holds a master's degree in Creative Writing from LASALLE College of the Arts. Her writing has been published in Kitaab's *The Best Asian Short Stories 2020*.

Anisha Ralhan is a copywriter who recently completed her master's in Creative Writing from LASALLE College of the Arts, Singapore. Her non-fiction essays have been published in *Quarterly Literary Review Singapore, The Hindu* and *Arre*. She likes to think of herself as a cat whisperer but Mowgli, her cat, disagrees.

Dawn Lo is a Hong-Kong-born Canadian writer with an MA in Creative Writing fromGoldsmiths, University of London. Her work has appeared in *The Malahat Review, Carousel Magazine, The Offing*, a special project by *Cha: An Asian Literary Journal*, and elsewhere. In 2021, her short fiction was nominated for a Pushcart Prize. She teaches Creative Writing to primary school students.

Jinendra Jain is a banker-turned-writer. His creative non-fiction and poetry have appeared in *Meniscus, Rattle, TEXT*, and *The Best Asian Poetry 2021-22*. He is studying for an MA in Creative Writing at LASALLE College of the Arts, Singapore, a degree conferred by Goldsmiths, University of London, and working on his first book, a personal memoir set in Mustang, Nepal.

Joanne Tan began writing after retiring from the luxury beauty industry to become a stay-home parent to her two young daughters. Born and raised in Singapore, and married to an Asian-American expat, Joanne's prose centres around female identity, particularly the conflicts and ambivalence of motherhood arising from cultural and class divides. A recent graduate of Singapore's LASALLE Creative Writing master's programme, Joanne is completing a novel exploring the identities of Singaporean women as wives, daughters and mothers.

Ken Lye completed his master's in Creative Writing in 2019. His short stories have been selected by online literary journals in Singapore, Malaysia, China and Japan, and included in the anthology, *Singapore at Home* (Kitaab, 2021).

Kevin Nicholas Wong, working as a film producer in Singapore and recently completing his MA in Creative Writing, has always been fascinated with storytelling and its power to convey messages through various mediums. His work, aimed at making people feel less alone, deals with identity, the struggle to find one's place in this world, and the interesting connections humans share.

Mia Aureus goes where her love for storytelling takes her. She studied Journalism in Manila, postgraduate Creative Writing in Singapore, and Film Production in Auckland, where she is currently based. Mia hopes to venture further out into the world to collect more stories that she hopes will make people reflect and discover their own truths amid life's contradictions and ambiguities.

Mohamed Shaker is a Singaporean writer based in Singapore. He holds an MA in Creative Writing from LASALLE College of the Arts. A former and hopefully future educator, his writing explores how Singapore and Singaporeans continue to live with and in their past in the present.

Nash Colundalur is a journalist and writer in India; he won the Guardian International Development Journalism Award, was selected for the BBC Writers Room, London Voices program, and is an alumnus of the University of East Anglia writers' workshop in Kolkata, India. He is currently working on various plays, television dramas, and films that are in development, and is completing his first novel.

Peter Morgan is an educator, information technologist, photographer and writer. He has lived and worked in Kyoto (Japan), Sulawesi (Indonesia) and Beijing (China). His photography has been published in *Queen's Quarterly*, an Argentinean math textbook and a German surfing magazine. His poetry has appeared in the *Southeast Asian Review of English*. His writing focuses on universal truths and local realities, as well as how we see and how we remember. He now lives in Singapore.

Prachi Topiwala-Agarwal is from Mumbai but has lived in Singapore since 2011, with her family. After earning an MBA in 2002 and working in banking she took a career break when she had children. In 2019, Prachi earned an MA in Creative Writing from Goldsmiths, University of London. Her writing explores the diversity of India and the uniqueness of Singapore.

Reginald Kent is a mixed man of Peranakan and British heritage. He holds an MA in English Literature from Nanyang Technological University and is currently completing an MFA in Creative Writing at the University of Washington. His creative work focuses on queer forms and the gay experience. He has also been published in the *Quarterly Literary Review Singapore*.

Sahib Nazari was born in Afghanistan and lived in Pakistan before his family migrated to Australia. He studied Creative Writing and Literature at Griffith University, Gold Coast—the city he calls home. He was runner-up for *The Deborah Cass Prize for Writing* in 2020. His short stories have been published in *Bengaluru Review, Joao Roque Literary Journal, Meridian, Mascara Literary Review,* and *TEXT Journal.*

Sarah Soh was born in Singapore and has previously lived in the United Kingdom, Ireland, and the United States. She recently completed an MA in Creative Writing at LASALLE College of the Arts. Her work can be found in the *Quarterly Literary Review Singapore* and *The Best Asian Short Stories 2020*.

Simon Rowe is an Australian writer based in Japan. He is a 2021 International Rubery Book Award nominee, winner of the 2021 Best Indie Book Award, and the 2013 Asian Short Screenplay Contest. His nonfiction has appeared in *The Paris Review, the New York Times, TIME* (Asia), the *South China Morning Post*, and *The Australian.* Website: https://www.mightytales.net/

Suzanne Kamata, an American, has lived in Japan for over thirty years. Her writing has appeared in *The Best Asian Short Stories 2017* and *The Best Asian Travel Writing 2020, The APWT Drunken Boat Anthology of New Writing, Telltale Food: Writings from the Fay Khoo Award 2017-2019* and numerous other anthologies. Her most recent novel is *The Baseball Widow* (Wyatt-Mackenzie Publishing, 2021).

Vicky Chong graduated with a master's in Creative Writing from Goldsmiths College, University of London. She is the author of *Racket and Other Stories*, from Penguin Random House. Her short story *The Uber Driver* won third prize in the 2018 Nick Joaquin Literary Awards Asia-Pacific. Other short stories are found in the anthologies *The Best Asian Short Stories 2021*; *Letter to My Son* and *A View of Stars*.

Editor's Biography

Professor Darryl Whetter (Editor) was the inaugural director of the first Creative Writing master's degree in Singapore, in a degree conferred by Goldsmiths, University of London. He is the author of four books of fiction and two poetry collections, including, most recently, the climate-crisis novel *Our Sands* (2020 from Penguin Random House). His other novels include the bicycle odyssey *The Push & the Pull* and the multi-generational smuggling epic *Keeping Things Whole*. His essays on contemporary literature and Creative Writing pedagogy have been published by Routledge, Oxford University Press, the National Poetry Foundation (USA), *Les Presses Sorbonne Nouvelle*, et cetera. His latest book is the anthology *Teaching Creative Writing in Asia*, from Routledge (2021).

Zafar Anjum (Series Editor) is a Singapore-based writer, publisher and filmmaker. He is the author of *The Resurgence of Satyam, Startup Capitals: Discovering the Global Hotspots of Innovation,* and *Iqbal: The Life of a Poet, Philosopher and Politician*. His short story collections include *The Singapore Decalogue* and *Kafka in Ayodhya and Other Stories*. He is also the founder of Kitaab and Filmwallas.

THE B·E·S·T ASIAN SERIES

THE BEST ASIAN SHORT STORIES 2017

Monideepa Sahu, Guest Editor ● Zafar Anjum, Series Editor

32 writers. 11 countries. One anthology of its kind in Asia.

The stories in this anthology by Asia's best known and well-respected contemporary writers and promising new voices, offer fresh insights into the experience of being Asian. They transcend borders and social and political divisions within which they arise. While drawing us into the lives of people and the places where they come from, they raise uneasy questions and probe ambiguities.

Explore Asia through these tales of the profound, the absurd, the chilling, and of moments of epiphany or catharsis. Women probe their own identities through gaps between social blinkers and shackles. A young Syrian mother flees from war-ravaged Aleppo into a more fearsome hell. The cataclysmic Partition of India and its aftershocks; life and death in a no-man's land between two countries; ethnic groups forced into exile; are all part of the wider Asian experience.

Life flows on in the pauses between cataclysms, bringing hope. Fragile dreams spread rainbow wings through the struggle to succeed socially, earn a living, produce an heir, and try to grasp at fleeting joys and love. These symphonies of style and emotions sweep across Asia – from Jordan and Syria to Pakistan, India, Bangladesh, Singapore, Malaysia, the Philippines, Thailand, Japan and Korea. Crafted with love, they continue to resonate after the last page.

THE BEST ASIAN SHORT STORIES 2018

Debotri Dhar, Guest Editor • Zafar Anjum, Series Editor

This is the second volume in the series which contains well-crafted stories with innovative characters, gripping plots, diverse voices from 24 writers in 13 countries.

While Rakhshanda Jalil is a seasoned writer known to many in South Asia, Aditi Mehrotra is an aspiring Indian writer whose story delightfully juxtaposed textual passages and news clippings on women's empowerment with everyday life vignettes of domesticity from small-town India. Martin Bradley's story highlighted the intersecting themes of travel, historical memory, and communication across differences. Today, when latitudes shift, cultures collide, and we are all travellers in one form or another, in ways perhaps unprecedented, these stories must be told.

THE BEST ASIAN SHORT STORIES 2019

Hisham Bustani, Guest Editor • Zafar Anjum, Series Editor

War, loss, love, compassion, nightmares, dreams, hopes and catastrophes; this is literary Asia at its best. From a wide range of geographies spanning from Palestine to Japan, from Kazakhstan to the Malaysia, mobilizing a wide array of innovative narrative styles and writing techniques, the short stories of this anthology, carefully curated by one of Asia's prominent and daring writers, will take you on a power trip of deep exploration of local (yet global) pains and hopes, a celebration (and contemplation) of humanity and its impact, as explored by 24 writers and 6 translators, many of whom identify with many homes, giving Asia what it truly represents across (and beyond) its vast territory, expansive history, and many traditions and languages. This book is an open celebration of multi-faceted creativity and plurality.

THE BEST ASIAN SHORT STORIES 2020
Tabish Khair, Foreword • Zafar Anjum, Editor

From the mountains of Uttrakhand in India to the Rocky Mountain in Canada, the stories in this volume represent the multitude of Asian voices that capture the wishes, aspirations, dreams and conflicts of people inhabiting a vast region of our planet. While some contributions deal with the themes of migration, pandemics and climate change, others give us a peek into the inner workings of the human heart through the prism of these well-wrought stories. This volume is the expression of a community, "a community of Asian writing that stands on its own two – no, its own million – feet!", as novelist and critic Tabish Khair says in his 'Foreword'.

THE BEST ASIAN SHORT STORIES 2021
Malachi Edwin Vethamani, Guest Editor
• Zafar Anjum, Series Editor

The Best Asian Short Stories 2021 presents the Asian short story as a constantly evolving, innovative and vibrant mode of literary expression. Edited by Malachi Edwin Vethamani, Professor Emeritus, Nottingham University, this collection brings together the works of twenty Asian writers and writers residing in Asia, namely from Canada, India, Malaysia, Japan, Singapore, Philippines, United Kingdom and United States of America. The broad theme for this collection is the new normal, revolving around the Covid-19 pandemic, with the inclusion of other stories set in the Asian region. The stories on the new normal theme explore how this world-wide pandemic has impinged on private lives and the public world.

THE BEST ASIAN SPECULATIVE FICTION 2018

Rajat Chaudhuri, Guest Editor ● Zafar Anjum, Series Editor

Between singing asteroid stations with a secret, and chilling visions of dystopia, between mad sorcerers with an agenda and time-travelling phantoms perplexed by the rules of afterlife, this volume of stories offers a unique sampling of flavours from the infinite breadth of the Asian imagination. If science fiction, horror, and fantasy are the genres you swear by, but miss Asian voices and settings, then this anthology is your oyster. Call these stories speculative, sff, or by any other name, they are really tales well told, and they always take off at a tangent from the big, blustering 'real'. Here the imaginative spirit is aflame, casting a rich lovely light. Tales from sixteen countries of Asia plus the diasporas. Freshly minted, told by seasoned writers and new talent—a smörgåsbord of Asia's finest speculative imagination.

This volume features stories from 34 stories from 16 countries.

THE BEST ASIAN CRIME STORIES 2020

Richard Lord, Guest Editor ● Zafar Anjum, Series Editor

Fittingly for a crime collection, this debut anthology offers thirteen stories, stretching from India to Japan, with key stops along the way in Singapore, Malaysia and the Philippines. Some of the authors whose work is being showcased in this anthology are Priya Sood, Carol Pang, Timothy Yam, Lee Ee Leen, Wendy Jones Nakanishi, Ricardo Albay, and Aaron Ang, among others.

THE BEST ASIAN TRAVEL WRITING 2020

Percy Fernandez, Guest Editor • Zafar Anjum, Series Editor

Stories from the inaugural edition of *The Best Asian Travel Writing* offer you glimpses into the curious, strange and wonderful experiences in Asia through the eyes and words of our writers. They travelled to find the roots in Cherrapunji, discover the wonders of Bamiyan, volunteer in the high Himalaya, looking for Malgudi among others that offer a frisson of excitement and expectation.

For more titles from Kitaab, visit www.kitaabstore.com

Printed in December 2022
by Gauvin Press,
Gatineau, Québec